G000094730

Also by Ray Hobbs and p̲▭▭

A DESERVING CASE

RAY HOBBS

Wingspan Press

Published in the United States and the United Kingdom
by WingSpan Press, Livermore, CA

The WingSpan name, logo and colophon are the trademarks
of WingSpan Publishing.

ISBN 978-1-63683-017-9 (pbk.)
ISBN 978-1-63683-985-1 (ebook)

First edition 2021

Printed in the United States of America

www.wingspanpress.com

1 2 3 4 5 6 7 8 9 10

1

FOLKESTONE, KENT

MAY 1951

Joe left his car in Bouverie Road West and entered the tall Victorian building where he shared the first floor with Guy Wilcox, a solicitor who occasionally used his services. It was a convenient arrangement, and the two were able to work amiably side by side.

Instead of continuing to his own office, however, he called on Guy's secretary, peering round her door and asking, 'Is he alone?'

Maggie gave him a long-suffering smile. 'Yes, he's alone, Joe.' She took a sheet of headed paper and one of bank, sandwiching a sheet of carbon between them, and fed them into her typewriter. 'He has an appointment at two-thirty, so I'd go in now if I were you.'

'I'll call in later for a chat.' He closed her door and tapped on the window that bore Guy's name.

'Come in.'

Joe pushed open the door.

'Oh, it's you, Joe,' said Guy. 'Come in and take a seat.' Inclining his head towards the adjoining office, he said, 'I've upset Maggie. Has she told you?'

'No, but I can read the signs. What have you been up to this time, you monster?' Joe took the nearer of the two chairs opposite Guy.

'I kept her beyond the time she usually has lunch.' He added pathetically, 'I didn't know what time it was, and how was I to know she was going to the shops?'

Joe shook his head sadly. 'It's just as well you chose the junior branch of the profession,' he said. 'If that's the best defence you can muster, you'd never have made a name for yourself in court. At least, not the kind your mother would have been proud of.'

'You're probably right,' agreed Guy.

Whilst the two men were of similar age, Joe being almost thirty, and Guy a little older, they were quite different. Guy was of average height and stocky build, with neat, dark hair. By contrast, Joe was fair-haired, tall and powerfully built, and he might have been considered good-looking but for a scar that created the effect of a lazy right eye and gave him a deceptively stern appearance.

Guy asked, 'Did you go to the Harbour Club?'

'I did, and I was told that Dempster is a member, but that he visits the place only occasionally. It depends on who's playing there at any given time. If it's a turn that appeals to him, he goes along, otherwise he doesn't go near the place for weeks on end. You know how jazz enthusiasts are. At all events, he can hardly be called a regular.'

'Did anyone remember seeing him on the date in question?'

'No, and I'm not surprised. It was so dark in there, I'd have struggled to recognise my grandmother, not that she was at all keen on jazz, as I recall.' He considered the possibility and ruled it out. 'No, on reflection, I suppose Marie Lloyd and Harry Lauder were more to her taste.'

'Quite.' Guy was a serious person, and that was another respect in which he and Joe differed strongly. 'That's good news. Based on your findings, Mr Hamilton should be able to cast doubt on the witness's ability to identify Mr Dempster.'

'That's what I thought.'

'Thank you, Joe.'

'You're welcome.' Joe stood up to leave. 'Call on me anytime.' He left the office, closing the door behind him. That done, he tapped on Maggie's door.

'Come in.'

Joe opened the door and waited for her to speak.

Maggie laughed. 'What are you playing at?'

'I'm being sensitive. It's high time someone was. I gather Guy made you late for lunch.'

'Lunch wasn't important. It was the shopping.'

'Ah.' Everyone except Guy, it seemed, knew the importance of shopping at the right time. Lunchtimes were always busy, and rationed food disappeared from the shops at an alarming rate.

'By the time I got to the butcher's, they'd nothing left worth having.' With a sigh that, he suspected, conveyed less than her full concern, she said, 'Derek will go mad tonight if all I have to give him is canned meat.'

It was a shame. Joe had wondered, sometimes, about the infamous Derek, who seemed to 'go mad' at the least provocation. Also, he liked Maggie. She was fun to know, and a great help, as well as being very attractive, with friendly blue eyes and medium-brown hair, which she wore in a voluminous bob. She was altogether wasted on her ill-natured husband. 'I know,' he said, as a bright idea occurred to him. 'How does he feel about fish?' It was probably a silly question. After eleven years of food rationing, few people turned up their noses at anything.

'If he can have it with chips,' she said, 'he'll eat anything.'

'A gourmet, eh?'

'Hardly. In any case, it's not an option. The fishmonger was also sold out.' It seemed that she was resigned to an evening of aggressive recrimination.

'If I give you a lift home, we can stop at my place on the way. I've got some plaice in the fridge that you can have.'

'Have you?' Suddenly, her blue eyes were opened wide. 'That's marvellous, but what will you have instead?'

'There's enough to go round,' he assured her.

'If you're sure. I'll give you something for it, of course.'

'I wouldn't hear of it. I caught them off Dungeness Beach, so they don't owe me a farthing.'

'But didn't you catch them for yourself?'

'Maggie, I'm a hearty eater, but I can't face four of them in one week. You're more than welcome to a couple.'

'That's really kind of you. Thank you.' With the imminent threat of domestic disagreement now lifted, she was able to think of other things. 'There was a phone call for you this morning,' she said, handing him a note. It was part of the arrangement with Guy that, in addition to her official duties, Maggie typed Joe's letters and took phone calls in his absence. 'He said he'd phone again.' Pointing to the note, she said, 'He sounds like someone else who might have French parentage.'

'Possibly.' The name was Jonathan Allard.

———————

The phone call came a little before five-thirty, and Joe booked the appointment for ten o' clock the next morning.

'What did Mr Allard sound like to you?' Maggie asked the question as she dropped the post into the pillar box outside the office.

'He sounded English, but he pronounced my surname very much as a French person would.'

'I thought so too.'

'Well,' said Joe unlocking the Rover and holding the door for her, 'he may be the product of an *entente cordiale* – I can't be the only one around here – or he may be a Channel Islander.'

'I can hardly wait to find out.'

'I'll let you know,' said Joe.

Maggie sank into the leather-covered upholstery. 'This is lovely,' she said.

Joe took his place in the driving seat. 'It's nice to be able to use this thing now that petrol rationing's no more than a disagreeable memory.'

'How long have you had it?'

'Only since the end of the war, when my father died.' He turned into Bouverie Road West, then into Castle Hill Avenue and eventually Sandgate Road.

'Oh, that must have been awful.'

'Yes, I was in Rome at the time. My sister had to cope with the funeral and everything at home. Mind you, she's very capable. She can cope with anything, really, including her husband.'

'What's wrong with him?'

'He's.... Let's say he lives in a world of numbers, equations, formulae and that kind of thing. He doesn't often visit our planet, and when he does, he needs an interpreter.'

He drove down Sandgate Hill, past the Castle, and took a left turning that led to a clifftop path. 'Here we are,' he announced, pulling up outside a row of cottages.

'How lovely.'

'The estate agent called it a "fisherman's cottage", which, of course, it still is. I'm just a different kind of fisherman from those it's known in the past.'

'We live in a coastguard's cottage in Hythe, but it's not as nice as this.'

'Wait until I take you inside. You'll see then how tiny it is.' He opened the door and invited her in.

'Oh, this is lovely.' She peered around the room.

'Feel free to have a look around, Maggie.' It amused him that women always wanted to inspect the place, as if they were thinking of making an offer for it or recommending it to a friend.

'I'm just interested in where you live,' she said.

'Right, carry on with the survey, and I'll get the fish.'

She followed him into the tiny kitchen dominated by a refrigerator. 'What a useful thing to have,' she said.

'Mm?' He wondered for a moment if she were referring to the pocket-size kitchen, but then he realised she was looking at the refrigerator. 'I bought it when I moved in,' he said, opening the door. 'I couldn't manage without it now.' He took a sheet of greaseproof paper from a drawer and wrapped two plaice in it, finally enclosing the parcel in a sheet of newspaper. 'There,' he said. 'That should keep your husband happy until you can get to the butcher's.'

'Thank you, Joe. This is so kind of you.'

'No, I'm just a push-over for a pretty face.'

'You say the daftest things.' She smiled nevertheless, and then looked at her watch. 'I must go.'

'Let me run you home. It's no trouble.'

'Thank you, but no, I'll get the bus outside.'

'There's really no need.'

'Yes, there is.' She looked embarrassed. 'Derek might be at home already.' She left the rest unspoken, and he respected her wish.

'*À demain*. See you in the morning.'

———————————

Whilst the appointment was in Mr Allard's name, Joe found that he had two visitors. The other was Mrs Marsh, Mr Allard's sister. They were both well-dressed and spoke with easy confidence, initially, at least.

Joe asked, 'What made you come to me?'

'We made enquiries,' Mr Allard told him, and when we turned up your name, we wondered if you might be a native of the Channel Islands.'

'I'm afraid not. My father was French. Were you looking specifically for someone from Jersey or Guernsey?'

Clearly embarrassed, Mrs Marsh said, 'We're looking for someone who will be sympathetic to our predicament.'

'I'm sympathetic in most cases, Mrs Marsh. Would you like to tell me about your problem? You'll have to bear with me while I take an occasional note.'

At first, it seemed that each was waiting for the other to speak. Eventually, Mr Allard said, 'We left Jersey, as many did, shortly before the occupation, but one member of our family, our cousin, insisted on remaining. He was a fisherman, and it was the only life he knew. In any case, he was too old for the forces, being thirty-eight at the outbreak of war, as well as having a club foot and other problems.'

Mrs Marsh explained uncomfortably, 'He wasn't very bright, you understand.'

'He was mentally retarded,' added Mr Allard, the more forthright of the two, 'at least to some extent. He was as capable of handling a boat, fishing nets and lobster pots as any other fisherman. He just didn't fully understand what was happening and why people were leaving for the mainland.'

'I notice you're speaking about him in the past tense,' said Joe.

'We believed for some time that he was dead,' said Mrs Marsh. 'Since the war, we've heard... well, that the Nazis regarded....'

'That they were unsympathetic towards the mentally retarded,' said Mr Allard, 'and when we learned that he'd been arrested by the Germans, we.... Let's say, we feared the worst.'

'Why was he arrested?' As a rule, Joe preferred to let clients tell their story in their own time, but Mr Allard and his sister were becoming increasingly hesitant.

'We returned to Jersey after the war,' said Mr Allard, 'just for a visit. We'd become settled here during the war, and my sister's husband came from Kent. Anyway, we heard that Thomas, our cousin, had learned from someone with an illegal wireless set about the D Day landings. In his naïve way, he believed that the liberation of Jersey was imminent. So, in a state of excitement, he painted a "V" on the wall of the Pomme d' Or Hotel in St Helier. It was being used as the headquarters of the German navy in the Channel Islands.'

'They say the Germans gave him an awful beating,' said Mrs Marsh, 'before sending him to prison in France.' By this time, she was clearly emotional. 'No one saw him again, and we could only imagine that he hadn't survived the experience.'

'An understandable conclusion to draw,' said Joe.

'That was until last month, when we heard something quite extraordinary.'

'What was that, Mrs Marsh?'

'We heard that his cottage had been sold.'

Joe put down his pencil and asked, 'By whom?'

'We were told that Thomas had sold it. It was his property, left to him by our aunt and uncle, so there was no problem there. On the other hand, though, how he managed to sell it is beyond us.'

Joe considered the matter carefully. Both clients were emotional, Mrs Marsh particularly so, and he had no wish to upset them further. He asked, 'Could it be that someone, maybe a lawyer or an estate agent, guided him through the process?'

'It might have been possible,' agreed Mr Allard, 'but we understand that Thomas conducted his own affairs with only the usual assistance from his lawyer, and that he answered certain questions and read the relevant documents before signing them.' He sighed heavily. 'Thomas was illiterate, Mr Pelier. He couldn't read a word or even sign his name.'

'I see.' They wanted an inquiry agent who was sympathetic, and now they had Joe's wholehearted sympathy. He asked, 'What do you want me to do?'

'We want you to find out what happened to Thomas, Mr Pelier. If he's still alive, as some people would have us believe, we need to know where he is, so that, if possible, we can help him.' Almost desperately, he asked, 'Will you accept the case?'

Joe made an immediate decision. 'Yes, I will,' he said, looking up at the wall clock, 'but telling me your cousin's story must have been far from easy, and I'm sure you'd both welcome coffee or tea. I'll arrange that, and then we can address the matter of my fees and expenses.'

2

Joe took Maggie's shopping bag from her and closed the office door. 'Better luck at the butcher's?'

'Yes, thank you.' She smiled as he put the bag down beside her chair. 'I'm not used to this kind of treatment,' she said, and then before he could say anything, she asked, 'How was the meeting with Mr Allard?'

'It was very useful,' he said, helping her out of her wet coat and hanging it on the coat rack.

'Thank you, Joe. You spoil me.'

'Not at all. It's one of life's normal courtesies. Give me your brolly and I'll shake it in the corridor.' He dealt with her umbrella, finally placing it in the stand by the door.

'Thank you. This is the first chance I've had to tell you that the plaice was very well received. Thank you again.'

'You're most welcome.'

'You helped me out of a corner, and I appreciate that.'

'It was no trouble.' He picked up his briefcase and was about to return to his office, when Maggie spoke to him again.

'I've been meaning to ask you what the initials "RTR" on your briefcase stand for.'

' "Royal Tank Regiment". I took this as a keepsake when I was discharged. The army had so many, I knew they'd never miss one.'

'I've kept wondering about the initials. "Captain J. G. Pelier, MC, RTR.," she read. ' "MC" stands for "Military Cross", I imagine?'

'Spot on,' he confirmed. 'It came out of a Christmas cracker.'

'I don't believe you. The thing I've really been wondering about is, having served in the Army during the war, how did you become a detective?'

A Deserving Case

He perched on the edge of her desk, about to give her a characteristically silly answer, but then he hesitated. She deserved better than that. 'I was in Italy with my regiment when the war ended,' he explained, 'and quite relieved we were, too, after all the unpleasantness of the past six years. I'm sure you felt the same. Anyway, just as things had quietened down, a call went up for anyone who spoke German or Italian.' He shrugged modestly. 'Now, I speak both, and I was foolish enough to volunteer my services.'

'What did they want you to do?' It was clear that her original question had been born of more than idle curiosity.

'They wanted me, and others, to investigate the Ardeatine massacre. It was a lengthy process and it soon became a habit, so that when I left the army, it seemed that the obvious course for me was to go on investigating things.'

'I don't remember hearing about.... Where was it?'

'Ardeatine. It's just outside Rome.' He picked up his briefcase again to leave.

'No, don't go for a minute. What happened at Ardeatine?'

'It's not nice,' he warned.

'I'll be brave.'

'Okay. In retaliation for a partisan attack on an SS unit, the Nazis massacred more than three hundred people. It took a lot of investigating, and that's partly why they kept me in the army until three years ago.' He affected a martyred look. 'I mean to say, nine years is a long time, even with the distractions of war. Of course, I'd like to think that the Army's reluctance to let me go owed something to my natural magnetism, not to mention my impressive repertoire of dirty jokes, but I imagine it was more likely to have been a result of the workload the Nazis had created.'

Maggie seemed absorbed by his story. Eventually, she said, 'I was a wireless operator in the WAAF. As a rule, we didn't get to hear about that kind of thing. It's perhaps as well, I suppose.'

'Was that where you met your husband?'

'Yes.' She didn't seem keen to expand on her reply, so he vacated her desk.

'What kind of case is it?'

'Mm?'

'The Allard case.'
'Oh, that. A missing person. Right up my street.'

———◆◀◆———

A few days later, it occurred to Joe that Jersey was recovering rapidly from the occupation. He based that conclusion on his inability to contact either the lawyer who had acted for Thomas Allard or the estate agent who had handled the sale, both men being permanently out and about or otherwise unavailable whenever he tried phoning them. There were also people on the list Mr Allard had provided who were simply not on the phone, and that had nothing to do with economic recovery. It was simply a nuisance and an indication that he had some letter writing to do. He was fortunate in being able to count on Maggie, and not simply for typing. It appeared that he had something to learn about dictation.

' "Dear Sir",' he began.
'Just give me the body of the letter, Joe. I'll take care of topping and tailing.'
'Sorry, Maggie.' He looked at the notes he'd made, and tried again. ' "I am acting for the family of Thomas Allard, late of number four, Clifftop Cottages, Les Creux, St Brelades...." Do want me to spell that?'
'It would be a great help.'
Joe was feeling increasingly embarrassed. 'How would it be,' he said, 'if I were to handwrite these and let you have them?'
'That would probably work better.' She gave him an indulgent smile and said, 'Don't worry about it. Mr Wilcox is no better than you at dictation, and I've had longer to train him.'

———◆◀◆———

With little hope of an early reply, Joe busied himself with other matters, one of which was to investigate a moonlight flit. It wasn't his favourite kind of job, because someone always had to suffer, so it gave him no satisfaction, but it was bread and butter and therefore necessary. He looked forward to the day when, hopefully, he would no longer have to accept debt and matrimonial cases.

His current task occupied almost the whole of Friday afternoon, but he was finally able to report the man's whereabouts to the client.

With that out of the way, the weekend beckoned, and with it, the rod and line. He felt sorry for people who lived in inland towns and cities, because they had no relief from rationing. Living by the sea and within easy reach of the countryside meant that there was always unrationed food of some kind to be found. All that lay in wait for him, but before that, and more importantly, a letter had arrived addressed to him, and it carried a Jersey postmark.

Dear Mr Pelier,

Thank you for your letter enquiring about Thomas Allard. I do not know much but I hope that the little I do know will be of some help to you.

I knew Tom well before the war. We had been to school together, although he was taken out of the class after a while because of his problem. I do not know what they did for him, because he never learned to read and write. He was a simple lad, but he was also honest and good-natured. He was born with a club foot, his left, and he had an operation on it when he was little, but it didn't do much good, because he still walked with a pronounced limp. One of the fishermen took him on as a lad, and Tom took to the job. He had found something he could do and that he enjoyed, and I was pleased for his sake.

When the Boche came, some of Tom's family left for England, but he stayed with the rest of us. I don't know how much you know about the occupation, but it was a bad time for most of us. The Germans were very strict and they made sure we got away with nothing. The kids used to draw "V" signs for "Victory" in the sand, just at the water's edge, and the sea would come in and wash them away. It was just kids being kids, but Tom, who was in his forties by then, was as bad as any of them. I mention this because, on the morning of D Day, word got around very quickly, spread by people with secret wireless sets, and there was a lot of excitement, as you can imagine. Tom was as excited as any of us, but the poor chap had no sense to call his own, and he got carried away, literally. He took a pot of paint from the harbour and painted a huge letter "V" on the wall of the Hotel Pomme d'Or. The place was full of Germans, who were using it as their headquarters at the time, and they caught him in the act. Well, they gave the poor chap a thorough beating and then they hauled him off to prison in St Malo. We never saw him again after that, and we could only imagine he'd been killed.

Tom's cottage was empty until just recently, when it was bought by another fisherman, a youngish chap called Bernard Herver. They say it was Tom who sold it to him, but Bernard said he never got to meet him. It was all done through an agent. Also, one of my cousins works in the Royal Court in St Helier, and he told me there was no sign of Tom when the contract was presented. He was represented instead by his lawyer Maurice La Barre, who has a practice in St Helier. Otherwise, it is a total mystery.

I wish I could tell you more, and if anything else comes to mind, I will certainly write to you again.

Yours sincerely,
Frederick Maçon.

Mr Maçon's letter told Joe little more than Thomas's cousins had, but their two stories tallied, and that was important. Also, he had to find out more about the business at the Royal Court. He didn't understand that at all, and imagined it must have been some legal requirement peculiar to Jersey. That and other questions clearly called for a visit to what Guy always referred to as the *locus in quo*, in this case, Jersey.

3

After a somewhat lengthy journey to Portsmouth via London, Joe was faced with an overnight sea voyage in less than ideal conditions. In the circumstances, he elected to travel on deck in the open air, but even then, he was hemmed in by passengers affected by seasickness. All told, it was a most unpleasant night, and he was relieved when a deckhand pointed out St Helier in the distance.

'On 'oliday, are you?'

'No, business.'

'Ah well, it's a nice enough place to visit, whatever you're there for.' He grinned as he hoisted the company flag. 'It's even better now the Jerries 'ave buggered off.'

'Were you there during the occupation?'

'Yes, I'm a Jerseyman born and bred.'

It was an outside chance, but nevertheless worth a try. He asked, 'Did you know a fisherman called Thomas Allard? He had a cottage in St Brelades.'

The seaman shook his head. 'It's a small island, right enough, but I don't know everybody.'

'Thanks. I just wondered.'

Eventually, the ferry docked, and Joe was able to set foot on dry land. He couldn't face breakfast after the crossing, so he spent an hour walking the streets of St Helier. He found Royal Square easily enough, and with it, the States Chamber and the Royal Court. Their whereabouts were academic, as he had no need to visit either, but it helped him to gain a general impression of the place that was central to his investigation.

As the shops began to open, he found a café for breakfast, a meal that turned out to be better than any he'd had since leaving the army. Like the mainland, the Channel Islands were subject to rationing, but they seemed to manage their resources more effectively.

Fortified, and with welcome directions, he set out to find the D' Arnaud Estate Agency. In a town the size of St Helier, nothing could remain hidden for long, and he located the firm without difficulty. In a town affected by the ravages of occupation, it had what seemed to be one of the more recently-renovated shopfronts in King Street, and its interior was equally fresh and inviting.

Offering his card to the receptionist, he asked, 'Is it at all possible for me to speak to the manager?'

'If you'll give me a moment, sir, I'll ask his secretary.' She disappeared briefly, returning with a severely-dressed woman, possibly in her fifties, who told him, 'Mr Lebrun has appointments this morning. I could arrange for you to see him this afternoon, but first I must ask you what your business is with the agency.'

Joe showed her his card. 'I'm trying to trace a missing person,' he said. 'His name is Thomas Allard, and this agency recently arranged the sale of his cottage in St Brelades.'

'I see.' She returned Joe's card to him and said, 'If you can come back at two o' clock this afternoon, Mr Lebrun will see you, but I can't promise that he'll be able to help you.'

'Thank you. I'll do that. I'm much obliged to you.' Joe took his leave of her and set out on his next call, the legal practice of Maurice La Barre in Broad Street.

The premises were of a bygone age, almost Dickensian, with a mahogany-panelled reception desk and frosted glass screens, presumably to afford privacy. The receptionist, however, was a young woman, no more than about twenty-five years old.

'Good morning, sir. How can we help you?'

'Good morning.' Joe handed her his card. 'I'm trying to trace a missing person, Thomas Allard, who is, or was, a client of Mr La Barre. Is it possible, please, for me to see Mr La Barre, or maybe to make an appointment to see him? I'm in Jersey for the next couple of days.'

'One moment, please.' The young woman left her seat and tapped discreetly on the door of a private office. Presumably at the occupant's invitation, she opened the door and spoke briefly to him. Finally, she emerged. 'If you would like to speak to Mr La Barre now,' she said, 'he has a little time before his next appointment.'

'Thank you. I'm most grateful.'

'Not at all, sir. Would you care to come this way?' She held the door open for him.

Like his receptionist, Mr La Barre was surprisingly young, about Joe's age, in fact. He rose to his feet and offered his hand. 'How can I help you, Mr Pelier?'

'I've been asked to trace Thomas Allard, who has disappeared. I believe you had dealings with him recently.'

'Who are you acting for?'

'Members of the Allard family. Cousins, in fact.'

'I see. I did act recently for Mr Allard, but I should warn you that I'm not in a position to discuss a client's business with a third party.'

'Of course you're not. That's understood, but my enquiries are of a more general nature.'

'Oh?'

'Yes, you see, I'm a stranger to Jersey law, and I confess to being a little hazy about the protocol governing the way property is bought and sold here.'

Assured that he was not being asked to breach client confidentiality, La Barre relaxed. 'If I can help you with that, I shall,' he said.

'I understand that a contract must be presented to the Royal Court. Is that correct?'

'Yes, it must be presented by a Jersey-qualified lawyer, and the buyer and seller must attend the 'Passing', as it's called. That's the formal process that makes the contract legal.'

'Did Thomas Allard attend the Passing of the contract when he sold his cottage?'

La Barre look wary, and then said, 'I believe he was unable to attend. Please excuse me for a minute.' He opened the door and spoke to the receptionist, who turned out to be his secretary as well, because, after a short time, she handed him a folder containing documents.

'Thank you, Miss Rossignol.' He sat down again and leafed through the documents until he came to a neat, handwritten letter. 'Yes,' he said, 'Mr Allard wrote to me a week before the Passing was due to take place

16

and told me he would be on the mainland on that date. He realised, of course, that he must give me power of attorney to attend in his place, and we arranged that.'

'Are you saying that he actually asked you to assume power of attorney, Mr La Barre?'

'Yes, I thought I'd made that clear.'

'Were they his exact words?'

'It was near enough what it says here. What are you driving at?'

Joe wrote briefly in his notebook. 'It's just that the impression I've gained so far about Mr Allard is that he was unlikely to have understood the process.'

La Barre shrugged and said, 'I can assure you he had no difficulty in understanding either the terms of the contract or the court procedure.'

'Thank you.'

'Is that all, Mr Pelier? I don't want to rush you, but I have an appointment in five minutes' time.'

'Just one little matter, if you don't mind.'

La Barre looked up at the clock. 'Go on then.'

'How did Thomas Allard seem in himself?'

'He seemed healthy enough, if that's what you mean.'

'No difficulty in walking, for example?'

'None, as far as I was aware.'

'Did you know that he suffered from clubfoot?'

La Barre looked puzzled. 'Did he?'

'As I understand it, he did. Thank you, Mr La Barre. You've been most helpful.' They shook hands, and Joe left his office.

La Barre had quite rightly refused to breach client confidentiality, but he'd been more helpful than perhaps he realised. For one thing, he was unlikely to be familiar with the fact that most inquiry agents were adept at reading upside-down writing. It wasn't difficult with the practice born of necessity.

———— ◆►◄ ————

By contrast with La Barre, Mr Lebrun, Proprietor of D'Arnaud's Estate Agency was possibly fifty or a little older, with a bald crown surrounded by greying hair, and he exuded friendliness. He welcomed Joe into his office and offered him a seat.

'I note from your business card, Mr Pelier, that you're based in Kent, but your surname suggests a different story. Are you a Jerseyman, by any chance?'

'No, my father was a Frenchman from Sedan. My mother was English.'

'I see. Well, you're no less welcome for that, so perhaps you'd like to tell me how I can help you.'

'I'm trying, on behalf of family members, to trace the whereabouts of Thomas Allard. I believe your agency recently arranged the sale of his cottage.'

'That's right. I remember the transaction.' Something about the memory made him smile. 'He was a difficult man to pin down,' he said.

'In what way?'

'More often than not, he was unavailable, and when he did appear, he could spare only a short time before he had to return to his place of work.'

'Did he say anything about his employment?'

'Not a thing. He told me very little about himself.'

Joe referred to the note he'd made in La Barre's office. 'Where was he living when he contacted you?'

'Oh, on the mainland. I believe he made one trip to Jersey, and he expected to finalise everything in that one visit.'

'Did he give you an Essex phone number and address?'

'I can check on the phone number, but the only mainland address he gave me was a Post Office Box number. It seemed quite odd at the time.'

Joe was beginning to form a picture, but he needed to know more. 'You did actually meet him, then?'

'Yes, once.'

'How would you describe him?'

'Do you mean physically?'

'Yes, and in manner.'

'In manner, I'm afraid I found him demanding and impatient. He spoke of the cottage as if it were a nuisance or an embarrassment. It seemed he couldn't sell it quickly enough.'

Joe nodded. 'And physically?'

Mr Lebrun thought. 'I'd describe him as dapper. He was white-haired with a moustache, of average height, but otherwise unremarkable.'

'Did you notice anything about the way he walked?'

'Yes.' The question prompted a confident reaction from Mr Lebrun. 'The best way I can describe his walk is that he seemed to strut.'

'So he didn't limp at all?'

'Not that I noticed.'

Joe made another note and said, 'Mr Lebrun, did he give you the impression that he understood completely the ramifications of buying and selling property?'

'Oh, yes.'

'Did he sign anything in your presence?'

'Yes, we ask all our clients to sign a form agreeing with the details we have on file.'

The picture was becoming clearer all the time. 'Do you think I might be allowed to see that signature, Mr Lebrun?'

'I suppose so. Please bear with me a moment.' He left the office, returning after a few minutes with a manila folder. 'It should be here,' he said, leafing through the contents. 'Ah, here it is.' He took out a sheet of paper and handed it to Joe.

It appeared to be a description and valuation, none of which interested Joe particularly, because his attention was drawn to one detail, namely the confident and well-formed signature of a man reputed to be incapable of reading, writing and signing his name.

After his revealing meeting with Mr Lebrun, Joe ate at the Hotel Pomme d' Or, where he was staying, and then, as arranged, he took a taxi to the home of Frederick Maçon.

When he introduced himself, his host said, 'Everybody calls me "Fred". I don't know why I signed that letter "Frederick".'

'I expect you were being formal, Fred.'

'That's right, Joe. Make the most of it, because it doesn't happen often.'

'You can say that again,' said his wife. 'Fred doesn't usually stand on ceremony for anybody.'

'Why should he?' Joe had warmed to the couple already.

'I expect you'll join us in a cup of tea,' said his wife, whom Fred had introduced as Charlotte.

'That would be very nice. Thank you.'

Fred asked, 'What have you learned today, Joe?'

'Rather a lot. Would you believe that Thomas Allard was capable of reading, understanding and signing the contract of sale, not to mention other documents, of which I've seen one... no, two.' He remembered the handwritten letter in the lawyer's file.

'No, I wouldn't. Tom couldn't read his own name, let alone sign it.'

'The estate agent described his walk as "strutting", and his lawyer saw nothing unusual about the way he moved. It came as a surprise to him that Thomas suffered from clubfoot.'

'He needs to wear stronger glasses, then,' said Charlotte, bringing in the tea things. 'Tom was painful to watch, he was so lame.'

'I've seen a letter that was supposed to have been handwritten by him, asking his lawyer to arrange power of attorney, because he couldn't attend the Royal Court for the Passing of the contract.'

Fred shook his head sadly. 'Even if he'd got someone else to write the letter, Tom wouldn't have understood a word of what you've just said.'

'Would either of you describe him as "demanding and impatient"?'

'Not poor Tom,' said Charlotte.

Fred agreed silently.

'It seems I have to look further afield.'

'Well,' said Fred, 'any help we can give is yours for the asking. I hardly need tell you that.'

'Thank you. I'm going to need help, because I don't know who sold that cottage in St Brelades, but I do know that it wasn't Thomas Allard.'

4

Joe took a greaseproof pack from his briefcase. 'Put that somewhere cool,' he said.

'What is it?'

'Jersey butter.' Reaching into his briefcase again, he took out a brown-paper bag of tomatoes and put them beside the butter on Maggie's desk.

'Joe, you're amazing.'

'That's not all.' He took out another bag. 'New potatoes,' he announced.

'Thank you, Joe. I mean, *thank you*. How did you come by these things?'

'Two generous people I visited in Jersey gave me them.'

'I hope you kept some for yourself.'

'Of course I did. I'm not a fully-qualified saint. Not yet, anyway.' He fastened his briefcase and asked, 'Did you bring a packed lunch today?'

'No, I was too busy, and it was all too difficult. Derek was in one of his vile moods. He has an awful temper.'

'What's the cause of his temper? Do you know?'

'He blames the war, but I think that's just an excuse.' She grimaced and said, 'It's also the excuse he uses for his drinking.'

'Drinking's a poor remedy for anything. I've known too many troubled souls seek refuge in the bottle, only to find that it's a false friend. I'll tell you what's good for the state of mind, though.'

'What?'

'A convivial lunch. What are you doing today?'

'Nothing.' Suddenly she looked alarmed. 'What have you in mind? I mustn't be seen out with anyone.'

'You won't be. I'll provide something, and we can have lunch here together and pretend we're at Fortnum's.'

Relieved, she smiled and said, 'All right, but you can't pay for all of it.'

'I'll sulk all day if you don't let me.'

'You're impossible.' She sat down at her desk. 'Now, before I kick you out so that I can open the post in peace, what did you find out in Jersey?'

'It's more than likely that someone has taken Thomas Allard's identity, sold his cottage, and is now masquerading as him. As for Thomas himself, I'm afraid it doesn't look all that good. No one's seen him since he was arrested in nineteen forty-four.'

'Good grief. What happens now?'

'I'll report back to Mr Allard and Mrs Marsh, and find out what they want me to do.'

—▶◀—

The morning was uneventful. Joe was unable to track down either Mr Allard or his sister, so he tried the two phone numbers he'd found in La Barre's office. The first rang at some length, and he imagined it must be the home number. He tried the other several times and got the engaged tone each time. He imagined business must be good for someone. He decided to leave it for a while and try again later. Meanwhile, he settled for preparing the invoice for the debt case that he'd completed before the Jersey trip. He also reckoned up his Jersey expenses. At twelve-thirty, Maggie came to his office.

'You said you were going out to do some shopping.'

'Shopping?'

'For lunch,' she prompted.

'No, I brought it all in this morning.' He pointed to a brown-paper carrier bag beside his desk. 'Are you ready to eat?'

She glanced at her watch. 'I could take my lunch-hour now.'

'Your place or mine?'

'Shall we have it here for a change?'

'Anything your heart desires.' He lifted the carrier bag on to his desk and took out napkins, plates, knives, butter, bread, cheese, crackers and tomatoes. 'Apparently, Jersey milk doesn't make good cheese,' he said, 'so I cheated and got some from another source. It's not Government Cheddar,' he assured her.

'This is a feast.' She took in the array of food and asked, 'What other source was that?'

'I never disclose my sources. Dig in.'

'I still can't believe this.'

'The only problem was that I couldn't lay my hands on any pickles or chutney.'

'You're the opposite of my husband, Joe. He has ketchup with everything, at least when I can get it. He sulks when I can't.'

'I usually have access to better sauces than ketchup.'

'I should hope so. What are they?'

'I just told you, I never reveal my sauces.'

She smiled, shaking her head. 'You're a treat in yourself,' she said. 'Why has no one snapped you up before now?'

'I did once know a girl in Rome,' he said, dropping a tomato on to his plate.

'What happened?'

'She was hit by a speeding police car. *Fine*. I retired from romance after that.'

'Oh, Joe.' She reached across the desk for his hand. 'I'm sorry.'

'Yes, we can't have everything in this life, as you know.'

'Sorry,' she said, realising she was still holding his hand. She released it.

'Don't be sorry. You're allowed to hold my hand whenever and for as long as you like.'

'I only wondered, because you're so kind and sensitive. I didn't know about the girl in Rome.' She finished buttering a cream cracker and cut off a piece of cheese. 'I was engaged to someone once, early in the war. He was a navigator and he was shot down and killed over Germany.'

This time, Joe wanted to touch her hand, and not because it looked smooth and soft, or that it would be the first time in several years that he'd felt a woman's hand. Much more important than that was the realisation that he felt extremely sorry for her.

'I suppose I married Derek on the rebound. It wasn't just that, though. You don't know Derek, so it's hard to explain.'

'Try,' he suggested, 'and I'll try to make sense of it.'

'Okay. If he wants something, he just demands it, and he never gives up.' She looked at him out of the corner of her eye. 'That's the bit that sounds silly.'

'I don't think so. Some people are like determined salesmen. They're almost impossible to shake off, and I think you must have been aware of his good points as well. I imagine he has some hidden away somewhere.' He thought a little more about it. 'People do strange things on the rebound, don't they?'

'I certainly did.'

'It's probably wrong of me to ask you this, but do you feel anything at all for him?'

She looked straight at him and shook her head. 'I think I know you well enough to tell you that I don't,' she said, 'he's trampled too many times on any feelings I ever had for him.'

'I have another impertinent question.' He hesitated. 'No, I shouldn't. Only a cad would ask a lady's age.'

'You're quite right. You are a cad, and I'm twenty-nine.'

'You deserve a better life.'

'What about you?'

'I'll be thirty next month.'

'I meant, don't you deserve a better life?'

'Probably, but yours has priority. Somewhere above the clouds, I imagine, there has to be a guardian angel with your name on his job sheet. I think it's high time he got to work.'

Joe remembered the two telephone numbers in Romford, Essex.

He dialled the first again, but without success. When he tried the other, he got through immediately.

'Good afternoon. Henry Taylor, International Transport.' The switchboard operator had a strong Essex accent.

'I'm so sorry. I seem to have dialled a wrong number.'

'Don't worry. It's easily done. 'Bye.'

'Goodbye.' He now had the name of, presumably, the spurious Thomas Allard's employer. It was a step further, and something else to report to the Allard family. Meanwhile, he was waiting to hear from Fred Maçon about his French contact. That might be interesting.

He sat for a while, thinking about the real Thomas, or 'Tom', as his friends called him. What a hopeless hand the poor chap had been dealt, born as he was with a retarded intellect and a club foot, treated brutally and most likely killed by the Nazis, and it didn't even end there. He'd become a posthumous victim, robbed of his identity by the ruthless bastard who'd stolen his cottage.

<hr/>

Later in the week, he was able to contact Jonathan Allard, who agreed to come to his office. Mrs Marsh was unavailable, but Mr Allard assured him that he was empowered to make decisions for them both. He turned up promptly at four o' clock that Friday.

'I'm afraid I have no good news as yet, Mr Allard.'

'You didn't sound too positive on the phone.'

'Just let me tell you what I was able to discover.' Joe ran through the list he'd made after his visit to Jersey. As he did so, Mr Allard's expression changed from growing scepticism to complete disbelief. 'This person they described,' he said, 'sounds to me like a total stranger.'

'Yes, I can only deduce that someone stole your cousin's identity, and with it, his home. However, I'm still no nearer to uncovering his fate or, for that matter, the real identity of the person masquerading as him.'

'You've done quite a lot, Mr Pelier.' Mr Allard paused for a moment, possibly gathering his thoughts. 'You used your time well in St Helier and St Brelades, but we still want to know what happened to Thomas. That is our first consideration. After that, this impostor, whoever he is, must be brought to justice.'

'With regard to Thomas, Mr Allard, I'm waiting to hear from Fred Maçon, who knows people in St Malo. One of them may be able to help us.'

'Let's hope so.'

'As far as the impostor is concerned, I've spoken to Jersey Police, but they say they need more evidence before they can start an investigation.'

'I can see that.' He leaned forward as if remembering something. 'Did you say you had phone numbers for this person?'

'Yes, I've had no luck with the home number, but the business number turned out to be that of an international transport firm called Henry Taylor. They're based in Romford, Essex. Unfortunately, I don't know what our man's place is in the organisation.'

'I can probably find out.'

'How?' Joe could think of no obvious way.

'I also have contacts,' said Mr Allard. 'I'll be in touch.'

5

Fishing was a relatively new interest for Joe; he'd only taken up the sport when he was based in Rome, but he'd found it absorbing and therefore relaxing, and particularly so when he could enjoy the company of a fellow angler. His companion that wet Sunday night was Arthur Newcombe.

To an outsider, it would seem a strange friendship. Arthur was several years older than Joe, and the two men were from very different backgrounds. Unlike Joe, Arthur had been obliged to remain in his job throughout the war, and it was that profession that constituted the main difference between them. Where Joe represented the mercenary side of investigation, Arthur was a Detective Inspector with the local CID.

For the main part, it was a procedural difference, however, and the two men had long since reached the understanding that Joe would not interfere in criminal investigations unless retained by a defending solicitor, and that Arthur would resist the unlikely urge to interest himself in absent beneficiaries, matrimonial disputes and missing pets. On this occasion, however, Joe had a favour to ask.

'Go on.' Arthur eyed him suspiciously.

'Let me tell you the story first.'

'All right.'

Joe gave a dry and factual account of his investigation so far, and Arthur listened patiently.

'It sems to me,' he said, 'that it's a job for Jersey Police.'

'I couldn't agree more, Arthur, and I'd be happy to leave it to them, but they need more evidence before they'll mount an investigation.'

Arthur nodded. 'So what's this favour you're after?' His tone was less than accommodating.

'I have a Romford phone number and a name. Of course, that's assuming that he's living under the name he used when he sold the cottage.'

'It's not a wild assumption.'

'No, but I need an address, Arthur. I know where he works, but I've no way of divining his home address from this number.'

For a while, Arthur was silent, simply peering through the insistent drizzle. Eventually, he said, 'You're asking me to use a police facility for your benefit.'

'Not mine, Arthur. It's for the people who've engaged me to investigate their cousin's disappearance and the misappropriation of his property. As soon as I have enough evidence to interest Jersey Police, I'll hand it over to them, but I need that address.'

Again, Arthur considered Joe's request. 'If I do it,' he said, 'there must be no further reference to it. In any case, I'd deny all knowledge of it. Also, you'll be on your own after that. There'll be no more "favours, as you call them".'

'Agreed.'

'All right. Give me the phone number, and then we can get on with some fishing.'

—▸◂—

'When is your birthday, Joe?'

'Friday.'

'This Friday?' Maggie sounded surprised.

'Yes, the first of June.'

'When you said you'd be thirty next month, I thought it would be some time away.'

'Well, Friday is next month.' He looked through Maggie's office window and said, 'I hope we can look forward to some better weather. I was soaked to the skin last night.'

'What did you get up to last night?'

'Fishing. Do you fancy some Dover sole?'

'What a question. I'd love some Dover sole.' She added hurriedly, 'Only if you can spare it.'

28

'If I couldn't spare it, I wouldn't have offered it to you. You can pick it up on the way home. Our usual assignation.'

'You're unbelievable, Joe. That's why I asked about your birthday.'

'Because I'm unbelievable?'

She frowned with good-natured impatience. 'You know what I mean. You've been so generous, I'm going to bake you a cake. Is there anything I should know about? Any allergies or violent dislikes?'

Joe thought. 'I can't stand stuffed marrow, horse radish sauce or suet dumplings,' he said.

'I don't usually put them into a cake.'

'In that case I can look forward to it. It's very kind of you to take the trouble.'

'Not at all. You're the one who's gone to a lot of trouble.'

' "Trouble", he told her, 'is my middle name.' He picked up his briefcase and was about to leave, when something else occurred to him. 'Maggie,' he asked, 'were you christened "Maggie", or are you a "Margaret" on Sundays and bank holidays?'

'Not even then. I was christened "Margherita", which is why I'm happy to be called "Maggie".'

Joe considered the name. ' "Margherita" is quite a mouthful,' he agreed, 'but it has an ethnic flavour that I find familiar and downright appealing.'

'My mother was in an amateur production of Gounod's opera *Faust* when she fell pregnant with me. If I'd been a boy, she would have called me Valentine.'

'That wouldn't have been so bad.'

'All right,' she said, 'it's my turn. According to your briefcase, your middle name begins with "G". What is it?'

'Georges, spelt the French way. "Joseph" is spelt the same in both languages and can be pronounced either way. I can mingle undetected in France, right up to the moment of forgetfulness when I surrender my knife and fork after the *entrée*.'

She looked at him in confusion. 'What's wrong with that?'

'The French use the same cutlery for every course. It's one of their peculiar foibles.'

'How awf... unusual.'

'Yes, my father maintained that it was a practical expedient to save washing up. It was a point of disagreement between him and my mother for some years, but she conceded the argument in the end. My father was very persuasive.'

'If you're anything to go by, I imagine he was.'

He said in a low voice, 'The French also serve the cheese before the pud.' His tone suggested that the practice exceeded the bounds of decency. 'It makes me relieved to be half-English.'

———————

He received a phone call that afternoon. It was from Jonathan Allard.

'I can now tell you,' he said, 'that the so-called Thomas Allard, who sold my cousin's house, is employed by Taylor's as an operations manager, and I can also tell you that the real Thomas would hardly know a five-ton Bedford from a parcel lorry.'

'Thank you, Mr Allard. I don't know how you did it, but it's another piece of the jigsaw now in place.'

'If you can keep a secret, I'll tell you. My company is a member of the National Confederation of Freight Forwarders and Hauliers, and it took just one phone call to elicit the information.'

'Your secret is safe with me, Mr Allard. For my part, I'm waiting for two more pieces of information before I can take the next step.'

There was a hint of impatience in Allard's tone as he asked, 'And what is the next step?'

'To hand over the fraud investigation to Jersey Police.'

'Don't forget that your priority is to discover what happened to Thomas.' There was a new hint of asperity in Allard's tone that Joe took as a warning.

'I haven't forgotten, Mr Allard.'

———————

'How did you come to be so accomplished at languages, Joe? Presumably, you learned French from your father, but how did you pick up the others?'

Traffic was heavier than usual, and Joe was waiting in the queue to join Sandgate Road. 'My father resented the British attitude towards foreign languages, namely, that we make little effort to learn them, but expect every other nation to speak English. He was determined that I should be an exception, and he brought me up to be bi-lingual. Not surprisingly, I was a very confused child, hardly knowing from one day to the next whether I was on my head or my feet, or even *ma tête ou mes pieds*. He also insisted that I learned German at school, because he suspected, quite astutely as it turned out, that the blighters would have another go. Then, when Mussolini looked all set to tread the same path, he persuaded my headmaster to let me forsake Geography and take Italian instead. Consequently, I became proficient in three modern languages, whilst having only the vaguest idea of where two of them were spoken.'

'You do put yourself down, Joe.'

'I suppose I do.' He eventually arrived at the head of the queue and turned into the main road. 'The Americans I met in Rome couldn't cope with it at all. I heard one of them say, "That poor guy has absolutely nothing going for him, and they expect him to interrogate high profile Nazis. What do the British think they're doing?'

She smiled at the picture. 'I don't suppose they go in for self-deprecation.'

'Not as a general rule,' he confirmed. He drove past the Castle and took the left turning that led to the coastal path.

'I'm really taken with your house,' said Maggie as she emerged from the car.

'A humble abode, but my own.'

'You're lucky. We rent ours, and I can't see the situation changing in a hurry, at least, not while Derek's spending all our money on best bitter and anything else he can lay his hands on.'

He let her in and closed the door behind her. 'Is he actually an alcoholic?'

'Apparently not. I had a friend of mine, who works with Alcoholics Anonymous, spend some time with him. They spent a whole evening together, and his conclusion was that Derek wasn't an alcoholic. To use his terminology, he's "just a hopeless drunk".'

'I believe you said he uses the war as an excuse for his drinking. Where did he get to?'

'The Normandy landings. He was invalided out before he could get further than France.'

Joe rested his hand on the kettle. 'Cup of tea?'

'No, thank you. I have to get back.'

'Of course. Was he wounded?'

'Not in action. He fell from an armoured car and hurt his back. He was probably drunk at the time.' She gave an apologetic look and asked, 'Does that sound awful?'

'Given what you're experiencing, no, it doesn't. D Day can't have been easy, but if, as you say, he's using it as an excuse, I've no sympathy for him.' He took out the greaseproof paper. 'Does he talk much about Normandy?'

'When he's not out for the count, yes. It's as if it was the only thing that ever happened to him, and he's very scathing about those he calls "D Day dodgers", whoever they are.'

'He's talking about anyone who wasn't there, and that includes me. D Day veterans can be very scornful about the Eighth Army, even though Italy was a similar kind of bloodbath. I asked you that because, generally speaking, men who are – the word they use nowadays is "traumatised" – tend not to talk about their experiences, but to bottle them up.' He reached into the refrigerator for two Dover sole, which he held up for her approval.

'They look magnificent, Joe. Yes, I think it's no more than an excuse. Mind you, he keeps talking about asking the doctor for something to help him sleep.'

'Maybe he's convinced himself that he's suffering from battle fatigue or some such malady.' He wrapped up the sole in greaseproof and newspaper as before, and handed them to her.

'Thank you again, Joe.' As an afterthought, she added, 'For the sympathy as well as the fish.'

'You're welcome to both,' he told her, kissing her cheek. His hands cupped her waist, and they stood together. She rested her forehead against his chest, and then, with no warning, she broke away. 'I must go,' she said.

He nodded. 'Absolutely, but my original offer's still open. I'll gladly give you a lift home.'

'Thank you, but I'd better get the bus.'

'All right. *À demain.*'

———•◄•———

The short journey from Sandgate Hill to Hythe gave Maggie a chance to reflect on the blink of an eyelid during which Joe had held her. It was the first time in years that she'd known anything like that brief act of innocence. That was all it was; he hadn't tried to kiss her, at least not properly, and there'd been no intimacy. It was likely that his purpose had been nothing more culpable than wanting to give her comfort, but she'd had to stop it, simply because she was afraid of where her own feelings might take her.

She was so occupied with her thoughts that she'd not noticed the conductor taking fares, and the request, 'Fares, please' came as a rude shock.

'Oh, the light railway, please.'

'Threepence, please.'

Maggie dug three pennies out of her purse and dropped them into the conductor's waiting hand. 'There you are.'

Joe's action had been a reminder, if she needed such a thing, of what might have been. His gesture was the antithesis of what she could expect at home, where sympathy was a stranger, and tenderness was a rite celebrated only in novels and on the cinema screen.

She hoped Joe hadn't misunderstood her reaction. By sharing intimate details of their lives, they had become friends rather than simply colleagues, and the last thing she wanted was to damage that friendship. She had to speak to him about it, and she had until the next morning to decide what she was going to say.

———•◄•———

The Dover sole won Derek's approval. He didn't seem to wonder, even in passing, where she'd acquired it. It was one of those matters, he maintained, best left to Maggie, and on this occasion, dinner was as civilised as she could reasonably expect, although conversation was laboured.

She asked, 'Did you have a good day?'

He shrugged. 'Much the same as usual.' He was manager of a nursery, and his grasp and knowledge of horticulture were such that he was respected by all those who dealt with him. It was a reputation that should have given him satisfaction but for his habitually negative outlook.

'I did.'

'Did what?'

'I had a good day, just in case you were wondering.'

'Oh.' He looked at her across the table, his thoughts no doubt far away. Eventually, he said, 'I think I'll look in at the Black Swan tonight, and see who's there.'

'Why not?'

'Will you be all right on your own?' He always asked her that, although she doubted that he cared. It was more a formality than a question that warranted an answer.

'Yes, I'll be fine. I've got a new library book, so I'll read for a while, and then I think I'll have an early night.' Hopefully, she would be asleep when he returned, and that would lessen the likelihood of her having to submit to his drunken attentions.

'Right, I'll see you later.'

———▶◀———

She had fallen asleep, and might have remained so, had Derek not collided with the bedroom doorframe, although it was his shout of anger and the outpouring of expletives, rather than the impact itself, that roused her.

Having vented his feelings, he sat down heavily on the bed to remove his shoes and socks. Beneath the covers, Maggie gritted her teeth at the associated grunts and sighs. It was a familiar and tiresome ritual.

Eventually, he climbed in beside her, creating a sudden, plunging dip in the mattress that forced her to shift her position so as not to be thrown against him, and made it impossible for her to feign sleep any longer.

With her back to him, she asked, 'Did you have a good night?'

'So-so.'

'Good. It was worthwhile, then.'

His reply was a grunt.

It was never going to become a conversation and, in any case, she wouldn't have welcomed one at that time. Instead, she braced herself for his first move, which was to shuffle up to her. Then, his hand moved to her arm, which he stroked heavily and squeezed from time to time. After what he possibly saw as a decent interval, he seized her right breast, proceeding to squeeze it like a baker kneading dough. She couldn't imagine what pleasure he could possibly derive from it. Certainly, it gave her none; the process was far from gentle, and she found it quite painful. Instead of lingering there, however, his hand descended to her thigh and gathered up the hem of her nightdress.

When he turned her on to her back, he did so without subtlety or affection, neither of which she had come to expect, but she positioned herself appropriately while he reached into the bedside drawer for a contraceptive. It was an act of optimism or maybe just a habit, but he always included it in the ritual before crouching over her, breathing stale beer fumes in her face and attempting to coax himself into the state of readiness that usually eluded him.

After a while, she heard the familiar grunt of disappointment followed by a muttered, 'Not tonight.' It was the one mercy alcohol afforded, although his impotence occasionally gave way to anger, which he directed unfairly at her. On this occasion, however, it seemed she was to be spared the brunt of his frustration.

Relieved and thereby relaxed, at least for the moment, she moved back on to her side and waited for sleep to overtake her.

6

When Joe arrived at the office, he stopped outside Guy's door and listened. Except in the line of work, he would never think of eavesdropping on a private conversation, but this one made him smile, reminding him as it did of his abortive attempt to dictate a letter to Maggie. It seemed that Guy was faring little better.

He heard Maggie say, 'You've already said that, Mr Wilcox.' Interestingly, she still addressed Guy formally, and he seemed content for the practice to continue.

'Sorry, Maggie. "In accordance with your instructions…." Should there be a comma there?'

'You can leave punctuation to me, Mr Wilcox.'

' "In accordance with your instructions, I have prepared the appropriate affidavits…." That's with two "f's", Maggie.'

'I know.'

'I'm sorry. "In accord…." I'm sorry. You already have that.'

' "…the appropriate affidavits", Mr Wilcox.'

'Yes, quite.'

Joe continued on his way, thankful that he wasn't the only dictating dunce on the floor.

About ten minutes later, Maggie knocked on his door.

'There's a Mrs Danby to see you, Joe. She says she has an appointment for ten o' clock.'

'And so she has. Thank you, Maggie. I'll come through.'

'Do you think I could have a word with you later, when you have a moment?'

'By all means.' He thought she looked like someone about to make a confession. 'Are you all right?'

'Yes… yes, thank you. I'll explain later.'

'Okay.' He went to the outer office and found Mrs Danby, a woman maybe in her late forties or possibly a little older. 'Mrs Danby? I'm Joseph Pelier.' He shook her hand. 'Would you like to come through to my office?' He led her along the passage, opened the door for her and invited her to take a seat. 'Now,' he said, 'would you like to tell me what's troubling you?'

'Is it so obvious that I have a problem?' Her speech suggested a fairly ordinary but educated background, probably at a grammar school.

'Not blatantly so, but I can tell that you have something on your mind.'

'I'm afraid I have.' She had removed her gloves and was compulsively teasing out the fingers. Eventually, she said, 'It's my husband.'

'Tell me about him.'

'He keeps going out without saying where he's going, and it's always at the same time, on the same day, every week.'

'Have you any idea what he's doing on those occasions?'

Her lips tightened, and she said, 'I'm afraid he might be seeing someone else.' Her neatly-dressed hair and carefully-chosen clothes marked her out as unexceptional, although it was possibly unfair of him to think of her in that way. It was just possible that her husband was amusing himself elsewhere, but Joe had to persuade her to keep an open mind.

'There are numerous possibilities,' he told her. 'It's not bound to be that.'

'Well, what else can it be?'

'Men do all kinds of things that they don't want anyone to know about. There are the Freemasons and the Buffaloes, for example. They have their secrets, at least as far as I know, although I have to confess, I speak as an outsider.'

'But they don't keep their membership from their wives.'

'No, they don't, at least, not usually.' He tried another approach. 'What interests does he have?'

That had her stumped. 'Until all this began,' she said, 'I'd have said he had very few. There's the evening paper, the crossword and listening to the wireless, I suppose.'

'Does he have friends that he goes about with?'

'Not really. We've always lived very quietly.'

Mr Danby was beginning to sound like a man who needed some excitement in his life, and it was possible that Mrs Danby did in hers, too. 'Which night of the week does he go out, Mrs Danby?'

'Thursdays. He'll be out this Thursday, at six forty-five on the dot.'

'How does he travel?'

'Oh, by car, now that petrol rationing's been lifted.'

'Okay, I'd better make a note of your address, his car registration, colour, make and model, and a description of him, just in case I have to observe him on foot.' He made extensive notes, trying not to smile when she described the long lock of hair that he arranged carefully, like a subtle disguise, over his bald patch. 'Now, is there anything else you can tell me?'

She thought for a moment. 'I don't think so.' Suddenly, she remembered something. 'He takes a case with him.'

'What kind of case?' It was sounding increasingly as if Mr Danby had become a member of an exclusive brotherhood.

'It's more of a valise, really.' Somewhat shamefaced, she said, 'I opened it when he was at work.' She shook her head at the memory. 'You'll never guess what I found.' Without waiting for a response, she said, 'It was an RAF officer's uniform. Quite a high-ranking officer, judging by the rings on the sleeves.' She said apologetically, 'I don't know if that gives you much of a lead.'

'You're absolutely right, Mrs Danby. I'd never have guessed in a thousand years.'

'Are you going to put a tail on him?'

'I'll keep an eye on him, yes.' He wondered if Mrs Danby amused herself on Thursday evenings by reading Raymond Chandler mysteries. 'I'll make a start on Thursday evening, Mrs Danby, and I'll let you know what I find out.'

'Thank you, Mr Pelier. You can't imagine how worried I've been. I've read that some people wear fancy dress when they're... you know, in the bedroom. It's to make it more exciting, I suppose, but I never thought my husband would go in for that sort of thing. Anyway, I'll leave it to you to see if you can come up with the goods.'

'Leave it with me, Mrs Danby.' He got up and escorted her to the exit.

When he returned, he found Maggie at his office door, clearly with something on her mind. 'Come in and take a seat, Maggie. I've just learned that I have to put a tail on a guy and come up with the goods. My client speaks fluent Raymond Chandler,' he explained. 'Her husband goes out secretly every Thursday night with an RAF officer's uniform in a valise, and she's worried that he's conducting an affair in fancy dress. I must say, I'd find it an awful distraction, but each to his own, I suppose.' He waved the matter aside. 'What can I do for you?' It was clear that, during his disclosure, her mind had been elsewhere.

'Last evening,' she said a little tentatively, 'I left you very abruptly.'

'I didn't notice.' Correcting himself, he said, 'I mean, I knew you'd gone, but I didn't think your departure was all that abrupt.'

'After you'd given me the sole,' she prompted.

'Oh, that.' He could tell it was still troubling her.

'I was very rude,' she insisted. 'You were being sympathetic, and I treated you as if I felt threatened.'

'No, no, no,' he protested, 'let me tell you, I've been here before. I'll sound like an awful cad when I tell you this, but I honestly believe that it's the Frenchman in me that makes me want to call women *"cherie"* and kiss them on both cheeks. I certainly didn't mean to offend you. I was just offering sympathy and support.'

'I realise that, and you didn't offend me.' She managed a half-smile. 'I don't think you're capable of causing offence.'

'You're too kind. What are we arguing about, then?

'I didn't want to encourage you… along certain lines, by being too intimate, and then I realised that it was all very innocent.'

'Good.' He considered his response and said, 'One day, I may just shove your husband over East Cliff, or any cliff that's handy, and claim you for my own. Other than that, I have no set plan, and I realise you're in a difficult situation, so your best course is to regard me as harmless.'

'I shall,' she said, getting up, 'and I'll try to be harmless too.'

'Good. I'll see you later.' He threw her a kiss, which she returned with an embarrassed smile.

—•†•—

A Deserving Case

Joe was parked not far from his office. It was convenient of Mr and Mrs Danby to have their family home in such a handy location. He could see their house quite clearly, and his dashboard clock told him that he had maybe a minute to wait.

It seemed that Mr Danby was a man of precise habits, because almost dead on a quarter to seven, he left the house, valise in hand, and got into his Series 'E' Morris. Joe started up the Rover and, as the Morris pulled away, he did the same. Following someone by car was about the hardest way to do it, so he was being particularly careful not to lose sight of his man. They turned briefly into Castle Hill Avenue and then into Sandgate Road, with Joe maintaining an interval of about fifty yards.

It turned out to be a short journey, because Mr Danby took a left turn before Sandgate Hill. Joe followed and saw him stop outside a large house with mature trees and a wide drive. He pulled up short, thankful for the cover of the trees. From his vantage point, he watched Mr Danby walk up to the front door. After a short time, the door opened and a man welcomed him in, of all things, the uniform of a group captain in the RAF.

Another car arrived, carrying a man and a woman, also carrying hand luggage. He sat in his car and waited as two more cars arrived. By this time, their drivers were obliged to park at the roadside, and carry their luggage in. If the participants had in mind sex in fancy dress, it was going to be no end of a party.

At almost seven o' clock, Joe was almost certain that everyone had arrived, and his judgement was immediately rewarded when he saw, through the window, at least three men in RAF uniform. Also, on that warm summer night, with windows open, he had no difficulty in identifying the theme of a popular radio comedy programme. It was not broadcast on Thursday evenings, so he could only deduce that the party inside the house were listening to a recording device.

———◆◄◆———

At ten o' clock the next morning, he rang the bell on Mrs Danby's door and waited. When she saw him, she gave an exclamation of surprise.

'Mr Pelier, I wasn't expecting you.'

'No, Mrs Danby. As you're not on the phone, I had to take pot luck.'

'Oh, well, come inside.' She led him through the hall and into a well-furnished sitting room, where she directed him to a seat and asked, 'Would you like coffee?'

'Thank you, but I won't. I have quite a lot to do this morning. I just wanted to set your mind at rest about your husband's activities.'

'Oh, what have you found out?'

'Tell me, Mrs Danby, does he listen to *Much-Binding-in-the-Marsh*?'

'I should say so. It's his favourite programme. He even makes notes while it's on. What are you saying?'

'Last night, he and several others went to an address off Sandgate Road, where they dressed in costume, and where I suspect they indulged in the fun and atmosphere associated with the programme, possibly re-enacting some of the episodes they'd heard. The theme song came very clearly from inside as they played it, presumably, on a wire or tape recorder. Strange and quaint his pastime may seem to us, but I have to reassure you that your husband is as innocent as a cherub.'

Mrs Danby sat, open-mouthed, as he delivered the news. When he'd finished, she shook her head in amazement. Eventually, she said, 'The silly old fool.'

———◆◆———

'I've heard of it happening,' said Maggie. 'They become so involved with the programme that they want to be a part of it, and that's the only way they can do it.'

'And all that time, his wife thought he was indulging in a different kind of fantasy.'

'Well done, Joe. You solved the mystery in three days flat.' Maggie looked at her watch. 'Mr Wilcox is coming to join us in a minute for coffee.'

'Why?'

'You'll see.'

After a minute or so, the door opened and Guy walked in. 'Happy birthday, Joe,' he said, offering his hand.

'Happy birthday, Joe,' said Maggie, lifting a cake tin out of her bag.

'I don't believe it. It's my birthday, and I'd forgotten.' Joe watched as she lifted the lid and took out a cake. It might not have been as rich as fruit cakes had been prior to 1940, but it looked rich enough. 'Maggie,' he said, 'where did you find the fruit?' Dried fruit was no longer rationed, but it was far from easy to find.

'I have my sources,' she said, 'but I never reveal them.'

When he'd sampled the cake and been suitably sociable, Guy returned to his office to prepare for an appointment.

Joe said, 'It's a big cake. Are you going to take some home to please Derek?'

'Certainly not. It's your cake, and he's getting none of it.'

'I don't think anyone's ever made me a cake until today. I'm quite speechless.'

'Then don't say anything.' She stood in front of him with her arms outstretched. 'I promise I shan't run away this time,' she said.

'Good. In that case, I can thank you properly.' He gathered her up in an innocent birthday hug.

7

Just when Joe began to wonder if Arthur Newcombe had forgotten about his request, or possibly had second thoughts about granting it, he received a phone call from him.

He leaned forward to turn down the volume of the BBC Symphony Orchestra and picked up the receiver. 'Joseph Pelier.'

'Good evening, Joe. It's Arthur. I called at the King's Head last night, thinking I might find you there, but I missed you.'

'Yes, I've been quite busy lately.'

'Oh well, that's good news, and I've got more for you.'

Joe picked up a pencil and opened his message pad. 'Go ahead.'

'The phone number you gave me was for a Thomas Allard. Don't they make expensive sports cars?'

'Yes, but I don't think this chap's connected with them. It's an old Jersey family name going back probably to Norman times.'

'Oh well, his name's Thomas Allard and his address is Fourteen, Alma Street, Romford, Essex. Have you got that?'

'Yes, I have. Thanks, Arthur.'

'Well, bear in mind, that's the last time.'

'That's understood, Arthur, and I'm obliged to you.' He was also delighted to have the address.

'Are you going fishing on Sunday?'

'Actually, I thought of going up to Ramsgate on Saturday night.'

'Sea bass, eh? I wouldn't mind a crack at some of that, myself.'

'I'll pick you up, then. About nine o' clock?'

'I'll be ready.'

In the circumstances, Joe was happy to provide transport.

———➤◆———

'How did you find that out?'

'Like you and your dried fruit, Maggie. I never reveal my sources.'

'What will you do with his address?' Maggie was opening the post, but she was no less interested in what Joe had to tell her.

'I'll go there,' he told her. 'If I hang around long enough, I should be able to take a reasonable photograph of him. Then, I'll show it to Mr Allard and probably Mrs Marsh, and they should be able to tell me for certain that Thomas Allard of Fourteen, Alma Street is an impostor.'

'I've been wondering,' said Maggie, slitting open an envelope, 'when you're likely to use your darkroom. It seems to have fallen into disuse.'

'You just want to have a look inside, don't you, just out of feminine curiosity?'

'There is that,' she admitted, 'and the whole thing is a mystery. I know nothing at all about photography.'

'In that case,' he said grandly, 'when I develop the film, you can come inside with me and see how it's done, and that will kill two birds with one stone.'

'Thank you.' She put the re-usable envelopes on one side and made a neat pile of their contents. 'Have you got lots of expensive equipment? I'm told men like that kind of thing.'

'Not all men are the same, as you well know, and no, I have one camera and two lenses, although I have to say they would have been expensive if I'd had to buy them.'

'In that case, how did you come by them?' One of Maggie's endearing characteristics was that she made no attempt to disguise her curiosity.

'It's not nice,' he warned her.

'I'll be brave.'

'All right. They belonged to a German officer, who died and left them to me.'

'How did he manage that?'

'He lay in the sand, and I helped myself.'

'Oh.' It seemed that his story wasn't so appealing after all.

'It seems harsh, I know, but, to be fair, he'd tried to shoot me, so I think pinching his camera sort of evened things up.'

She thought briefly about it and gave the transaction her approval. 'Yes,' she said, 'it probably did.' Returning to an earlier topic, she asked, 'Why do you have a darkroom here and not at home?'

'You've seen my cottage. There isn't room for one, and I can't use the bathroom, as some people do.'

'Why not?'

'There's no room in there either. It's too small even for a bathtub. I have to manage without one.'

Peering at him closely, she said, 'It doesn't show, at least, not to the naked eye.'

'When they made the bathroom, I had a shower put in.'

'A touch of luxury.' She looked impressed.

'I suppose so, and you're welcome to use it at any time.'

'I've had some strange offers,' she said, picking up the opened letters, 'but that one deserves a place in the scrapbook.'

———— ▸◂ ————

Joe screwed the nine centimetre lens on to the Leica, focused it on the door of number fourteen and waited. It was a little after six o' clock on a bright, June morning and the conditions were perfect for the photograph he needed. He'd parked on the other side of the street, about fifty yards away, and facing the front of the Morris Oxford that was parked outside the address. That way, he was more likely to get a full-face shot as his man left the house and got into his car. He didn't expect any movement much before seven, but he'd left ample time for the journey from Sandgate, and had arrived in Romford earlier than he'd anticipated.

Not surprisingly, the milkman had made his deliveries, as each doorstep bore witness, and doors began to open, here and there, with people picking up their milk for early morning tea or breakfast. So far, however, there had been no movement at number fourteen.

The next event was the arrival of a paperboy, who was evidently well-practised, judging by the ease with which he pushed his newspapers through each letterbox without leaving his bicycle saddle.

A Deserving Case

As he reached number fourteen, Joe's pulse quickened, because the door opened, and a man clad in a vest and trousers, and with shaving soap on his face appeared briefly to take the newspaper and to pick up his single bottle of milk. Joe fired the shutter, but the man's face was obscured by the boy's head, and then the door closed again, leaving Joe to continue his vigil with the vague memory of a man with white or very light-grey hair.

The next arrival was the postman, whose deliveries caused no external activity, but who gave Joe an anxious moment when he stood outside number fourteen, searching for something in his bag, and impeding Joe's view of the doorway as he did so.

It was eight o' clock before the mysterious inhabitant of number fourteen reappeared, and it was a very brief sighting, but Joe managed to take half-a-dozen shots before he was obliged to hide his camera. As the Morris Oxford drew level with the Rover, Joe saw a face with a firm jawline, a chevron moustache and a full head of white hair cut and trimmed neatly. A pair of glasses with tortoise-shell frames completed the ensemble. He glanced at Joe as he went, having apparently suspected nothing.

———◆◄———

He arrived at the office in time for coffee, which he took in Maggie's office. Seeing shadows beneath her eyes, he asked, 'Is everything okay at home?' It was no more than an expression of concern, as there was no way he could help, if help were needed.

'Not too awful,' she said, adding, 'you're looking tired, yourself.'

'I left very early to go to Romford.'

'Oh. Any luck?' By this time, Maggie was taking more than a passing interest in the Allard case.

'I'll know soon enough,' he said, gesturing towards the darkroom. 'I have five or six shots of him and I saw him at close quarters as well.'

'What did he look like?'

'You'll soon see the pictures, but I'd say he was about fifty, white-haired and stern-looking. Having said that, we can all look stern, and very few men, in my opinion, can look at all genial behind a chevron moustache. Did you know that, during the Great War, soldiers were ordered to grow them? It was to make them look fierce.'

'I didn't know that.'

He shrugged dismissively. 'I don't think the Germans were impressed. In the end, it was kilts and bagpipes that really put the wind up them.'

'I supposed they would scare the uninitiated.'

'They scared me in the last war, and we were on the same side.'

Returning to the subject of pictures, she asked, 'When are you going to develop the film?'

'This afternoon, if you have time to spare. I'll show you how to prepare the developer, stop bath and fixer, but then I'll have to load the film into the developing tank in total darkness. After that, I'll invite you in.'

'How kind.'

'When we've developed the film, we'll leave it to dry overnight and print the pictures tomorrow, hopefully when we've both had a proper night's sleep.

——◆◄◆——

Maggie was at the office when Joe arrived the next morning.

'You're an early bird today,' he remarked.

'I like to be here in good time if I can manage it.' She'd left early that morning simply because she wanted to leave the house as soon as she could, but she couldn't tell him that. She didn't want to make him think she was forever moaning.

'I'll just have another look at those negatives,' he said, closing the door behind him.

Maggie got on with sorting the post. If she could have moved into the office and made it her home, she would have grasped the opportunity just to escape from the place she had to call her home, but which felt more like Rapunzel's tower.

The door opened and Joe came in. 'There's some promising stuff there,' he said. 'The pictures look clear enough.'

'Can you be sure of that just by looking at the negatives?'

'Positive.' He winced. 'I'm sorry. It's an old music hall joke, but I can never resist it.'

'Tell me a proper one. You said you knew lots of them.'

'Are you feeling broad-minded?'

'Yes.' After the previous night, she was ready for anything.

'Okay.' He thought for a moment and then cleared his throat, as if to make an announcement. 'A young woman was driving through darkest Dorset, when she became hopelessly lost, and the more she looked for road signs and landmarks, the worse it became. Before long, her engine coughed, spluttered and finally stopped. She was clean out of petrol. The only thing to do was to look for help, so she set off on foot in search of civilisation.' He stopped to ask, 'Are you still with me?'

'Yes, I'm hanging on.'

'Good. Well, before long, she came upon a farmhouse, so she knocked on the door, and when the farmer's wife answered the door, the young woman told her what had happened and asked if they had any petrol to spare. The farmer's wife said, "Petrol? We ain't got none o' that. We uses 'orses on this 'ere farm." "Oh dear," said the young woman. "What can I do?" "Tell you what," said the farmer's wife. You can stay here the night if you want to." The young woman said, "Oh, may I?" "Arr," said the farmer's wife.'

'I'm sure they don't really say that, Joe.'

'But can you be sure? Listen, and you may change your mind.'

'Sorry.'

'Okay. "The only thing is," said the farmer's wife, "we've only got two bedrooms, and that means you'll have to share with my son. 'E's not very bright, so 'e won't bother you." So, to cut a long story fairly short, the young woman stripped down to her petticoat and climbed into bed beside the farmer's son. After a while, she thought what a shame it was, that here was a fine, strapping lad going to waste, so she snuggled up to him. Oddly enough, instead of responding, he moved away from her, so she snuggled up again until he was right on the edge of the bed. At that stage, he got out, walked round to the other side and climbed in again. Funny, she thought, snuggling up to him again. Three times it happened, with him getting out of bed and climbing back in on the other side. Eventually, he said, "Oi knows what you're after." She said in her sexiest tone, "Do you?" "Arr," he said, "you want the whole bed to yourself!" '

'Oh dear,' said Maggie, dabbing her eyes with a handkerchief. 'That was a terrible joke, but it made me feel better.'

'You must feel better,' said Joe. 'It's obvious from your tears. What's the matter?'

'Nothing. I've told you, I feel so much better.' And she did.

———◆◆———

That afternoon, they printed the photographs.

'We use a safe light at this stage,' Joe explained. 'The emulsion's sensitive to all except red light, and that's why it looks like Christmas in here.'

'Oh, don't. I'd rather not think about Christmas.'

'Okay, from now on, we'll call it, "Humbug Time."'

He showed her how to determine the exposure, and they prepared the developer, stop bath and fixer.

'It's almost like cooking,' she said.

'I find it easier than cooking,' he confided.

'Most men would.'

They slotted the film into the negative carrier and focused the first exposure, and then clamped a sheet of photo paper on to the enlarger.

When it had been exposed for the required time, they put it into the developer bath until the picture came up clear and sharp.

'That,' said Joe, dropping the print into the stop bath, 'is the man we're dealing with.'

8

Jonathan Allard looked through the photographs, handing each one to his sister. Finally, he said, 'That's not Thomas.'

'It's not,' agreed Mrs Marsh. 'Even allowing for the glasses and the moustache, this man doesn't look at all like Thomas.'

'Would a dark-haired man go as white as this?' Mr Allard tapped the nearest photograph. 'Grey, maybe, but not white. Thomas was dark-haired, like me, but with a heavier beard.'

'He had a blue chin,' added Mrs Marsh. 'It was quite striking.' She added, 'Memorable, too.'

'Have you any photographs of Thomas? I'm thinking of evidence.'

'When we left Jersey,' said Mr Allard, 'the Germans were on their way, so we packed in a hurry. Believe me, photographs were very low on our list of essentials.'

Joe made a note to that effect. 'If you're both agreed, then,' he said, 'I'll contact Jersey Police and put the facts before them.'

'With our blessing,' said Mr Allard, passing the photographs back to him. 'I don't know how this man came by Thomas's identity, but we want him brought to justice.'

'Yes,' said Mrs Marsh. 'You might learn more about that when you find out what happened to Thomas.'

'I'm working on it, Mrs Marsh.' They were expecting a great deal from him. He just hoped they weren't going to be disappointed.

—◆◆—

'They evidently set great store by you,' said Maggie, 'and quite rightly, it seems to me.'

'You're a staunch ally, Maggie. You even make me feel confident, and such loyalty should be rewarded.'

'What do you have in mind?'

'You enjoyed the sea bass, didn't you?'

'I should say so.' The memory of it was clearly fresh in her mind.

'I'm going after another on Saturday.'

'That would be lovely, but you really do spoil me to death.'

'Not at all. I just like to put a smile on your face.'

'Am I really such a misery?' Her expression told him that the question wasn't entirely a frivolous one.

'No, you're not. In fact, you're probably the most cheerful darkroom assistant I've ever had.'

'How many have you had?'

'Including you?'

'Including me.'

He began counting on his fingers. When he reached nine, he stopped. 'Lots,' he concluded, 'and you're still the most cheerful of them all.'

'Give me your cup and saucer,' she said, 'and be about your business, you flattering popinjay.'

'I'll take that as a compliment,' he said, heading for his office.

————◆◀————

Ten minutes later, he put the phone down, assured that, far from being interested in the Allard case, Jersey Police would probably have preferred him not to have wasted their time. Their objections were that a succession of officials had examined Thomas Allard's credentials and been satisfied by them, and that eleven years was a long time to remember even a family member's physical appearance with any certainty. Memory being as fallible as it was, it was extremely likely, they said, that the Allard family had retained an imprecise, and possibly erroneous, mental picture of their cousin. They also suggested that a club foot could be repaired, and that many a youth considered dull-witted had gone on to confound his detractors. It was too frustrating and disappointing for words.

———◆◄———

'All of that,' said Arthur Newcombe as they drove towards Ramsgate, 'suggests one thing, which is that Jersey Police are reluctant to stick their necks out on the basis of flimsy evidence.'

'I wouldn't call it flimsy,' said Joe. 'Not by a long chalk.'

'You wouldn't,' agreed Arthur, 'but a defence counsel could tear it to shreds, and that's what Jersey Police have to bear in mind.'

'Bugger.'

'As you say, Joe, it's a bugger, but I've lived with the problem throughout my career.'

Joe brooded about it for a while, and then said, 'I still have to find out what happened to Thomas Allard.'

'Unless you tread on official toes, they can't stop you doing that. How far have you got with it?'

'Not very far. I'm waiting to hear from a contact in Jersey who has a friend in St Malo, where Thomas was locked up for graffiti. The friend in question was a member of the French Resistance. They have long memories, I'm told.'

Arthur considered the information. 'If you're thinking in terms of criminal charges in connection with this, the same applies. 'They may have long memories, but when a case is being considered, one man's word against another's, isn't worth a gossip's breath.'

'You're a great comfort to me, Arthur.'

'I'd be no use at all if I misled you.'

'True. Let's just settle for a spot of night fishing.'

———◆◄———

On Monday afternoon, Joe read the particulars given to him by the family's solicitor. The young woman was last known to be living in Hastings, but had moved since that time to an unknown address. A disagreement had led to their estrangement, and she'd not been in communication with the family for at least ten years. She was nevertheless a beneficiary under her grandmother's will, and the solicitor, acting as executor, wanted her to be found. For Joe, it was bread-and-butter work, and he welcomed it.

He started by telephoning the South-Eastern Gas Board and speaking to their Consumer Records Department. After some searching, he was told that Miss Dunn, the lady in question, had moved from her address in Hastings to another in St Leonard's-on-Sea, returning to Hastings within the past two years, and was still listed as the consumer at that address.

Such an immediate result was never going to make Joe's fortune, but it would do his reputation no end of good. He picked up the phone and asked, 'Maggie, will you get me Jamieson's Solicitors, please? I think you have their number.'

'Just one moment, Joe.'

He waited a short time and was rewarded when a woman's voice said, 'Jamieson's.'

'Good afternoon. This is Joseph Pelier, the inquiry agent. May I speak with Mr Jamieson, please?'

'I'm afraid Mr Jamieson is with a client. Can I take a message?'

'Yes, please, if you will. It's in connection with the estate of the Late Mrs Constance Davies.'

'Yes, Mr Pelier?'

'I was asked to locate the missing beneficiary. That's a Miss Edith Dunn, and I can tell you that she's now residing at twelve, Foxgrove Drive, Hastings.'

'Oh, that's excellent news. Mr Jamieson will be pleased. Thank you very much, Mr Pelier.'

'Not at all.' He put the phone down, pleased that he'd been able to give satisfaction. Looking at his watch, he saw that it was after five-twenty, so he joined Maggie in her office. She was getting the post together.

'Another satisfied client,' he announced.

'Yet another?'

'It was but the work of a moment.' Correcting himself modestly, he said, 'Well, a five-minute phone call to the South-Eastern Gas Board.'

'I'm no less impressed, Joe.' Even so, she seemed preoccupied.

'Am I giving you a lift as far as my cottage?'

'I don't know. If you are, that's very kind of you.'

'There's a pound of sea bass in my fridge, prepared for cooking and just waiting to be collected.'

For a moment, she seemed taken aback. 'Oh, lovely,' she said. 'I'd forgotten all about it.'

'You've seemed a bit far away, today.'

'Have I? I'm sorry.'

'Don't give it a second thought.' He glanced at the wall clock. 'It's close enough to half-past five,' he said. 'Shall we tear ourselves away and abandon ourselves to selfish pleasure?'

'I don't know so much about that, but I'm certainly looking forward to the sea bass. Just let me drop off the mail and I'll join you.'

'You're a study in organisation.' He opened the door for her and waited while she locked it.

As they walked out to the car, she asked casually, 'You're not thinking of moving away, are you?'

'Not in the next fifty years or so. Ask me again nearer the time, and I may be more helpful.'

'Good, because you're the only friend I have in this place.'

'Folkestone?' He wasn't sure what she meant, so he opened the passenger door for her and waited to be enlightened.

'And surrounding area. Do you realise that, basically because of the situation at home, I have no female friends.'

'I hadn't thought about it, but I see what you mean, and a woman should have female friends, because a man can't even begin to understand a woman's thought processes.' He started the car and pulled out.

'You don't do too badly, Joe.'

'What, at understanding women? Not me. It strikes me that it would take a life's work, and I have much to do with mine.'

'You do, though. You notice things and react accordingly.'

He waited patiently for an elderly couple to cross the road. 'Ah, but that's reacting,' he said, 'not understanding. If you stroke a cat, it'll react by purring and rubbing itself against you, but it hasn't a clue what you're thinking. You might be considering the teachings of Rousseau or Socrates, but the cat doesn't know that. All that's going through its mind is, "Nice stroke. Rub chin against nice person," and occasionally, "Why do I make that funny rumbling noise inside whenever someone strokes me?" '

'I still think you understand more than you admit.'

'You've just got to put me on a pedestal, Maggie, haven't you? Well, go ahead. I don't mind being admired for a while.' He slowed down behind a Morris Minor because there was no room to overtake. 'I learned some curious things about thought processes in Rome,' he said.

'Do you mean when you were interrogating people?'

'That's right. You see, the Germans didn't want us to know anything, and the Italians wanted us to know everything, all at once. We had to switch between slow, calculating and devious on the one hand, and excited, well-intentioned and disorganised on the other. The Italians also speak at an alarming speed.' On reflection, he said, 'But they know how to enjoy themselves, they like to eat, and they know how to cook.'

'What was the name of the girl you knew in Rome?'

'Alessa.'

'That's a nice name.'

'It means "helper or defender".'

'I'm sorry. It must hurt to be reminded of her.'

He pulled into the coastal path and parked in front of the cottage. 'It gets easier,' he said, opening her door.

'Thank you.'

'Not at all. Do you know that in Soviet Russia, a man will never open a door for a lady?'

'How awful.'

'It would be seen as denying her the equality the revolution gave her. *Tovariyshch*, or "comrade", is a masculine noun, but women are also given the title.'

'They're welcome to it.' As she followed him into the cottage, she asked, 'Do you speak Russian as well as your other languages?'

'Not to anything like the same standard. Have you time for a cup of tea today?'

She looked at her watch. 'Yes, go on. It didn't take us as long to get here as it usually does.'

'Take a seat and make yourself comfortable.' He left her in the sitting room while he made tea.

When he brought it into the sitting room, he found her with her head back and her eyes closed. She opened them when she heard him put the tray on the table.

'I thought you'd fallen asleep,' he said.

'No, I was just enjoying the peace in your house.'

'I stirred the tea to speed up the brewing process,' he confessed. 'A purist would be horrified, but that's the nature of the enthusiast, I'm afraid.'

'I'm sure it'll taste just as good.'

He handed hers to her. 'Unfortunately, I've eaten all the cake, so I can't offer you any.'

'I'm glad you enjoyed it. I'll bake you something else.' She finished stirring her tea, but seemed to find something fascinating in it, because she continued to stare.

'Is anything wrong?'

She shook her head and stood up to put her cup and saucer back on the table. She had her back to him, but he could see something was amiss.

'What is it?' He stood beside her and saw that her cheeks were wet.

Slowly, she turned to him and let her head droop on to his chest.

He said, 'It's the difference, isn't it? The difference between your home and this place.'

She nodded. 'How did you know?'

'I don't know. It just occurred to me.'

'I must look an awful sight.'

'You're welcome to use the bathroom to tidy up. There's a pile of clean towels outside the door.'

'Thank you.' As if to no one in particular, she said, 'I'm going to be late.'

'I'll run you down to Hythe and drop you somewhere out of sight. Don't worry. The bathroom's up there,' he said, pointing to the staircase. 'You can't miss it, because the only other room is the bedroom.'

She went upstairs, and he sat down again, drinking tea and wishing all the torments of hell on the bastard who'd blighted Maggie's life. After a moment, he remembered the sea bass and wrapped it in greaseproof paper for her. It weighed easily a good pound. With any luck, Derek might choke on it.

She came downstairs, looking washed out but with her equilibrium restored.

'You're as good as new,' he told her, handing her the fish. 'Get your stuff together, and I'll run you to Hythe.'

'I'm so sorry for making a fuss.'

'There's no need to apologise. A man should respect a woman's tears. The chap who told me that had lived through a few tragic experiences, so he knew what he was talking about.'

'Was that in Rome?'

'Yes. His actual words were, "*Un uomo dovrebbe rispettare le lacrime di una donna.*" There, you've heard it in two languages, so it must be true.'

9

Joe spent the following Wednesday, Thursday and Friday on a missing person case that took him to Newcastle-upon-Tyne, where he was starkly reminded of the ravages of war. As if that were not enough, and in spite of the benefits of the new Welfare State, the people of the city were still experiencing the kind of poverty he'd never known. Now the war was over, the demand for warships was gone and, with the shipyards idle, the demand for coal was also depleted.

By Friday afternoon, he was ready to return home. The population's plight had sickened him to the extent that he felt almost ashamed of his comfortable upbringing and post-war good fortune. Also, he had succeeded in locating the missing son. The result was going to give little cheer to his parents, however, as he had refused to return to them. At twenty-two, it was his legal right.

After such a week, Joe was cheered when he called at the office on Saturday morning and found among his mail a letter from Jersey. Not surprisingly, it was from Fred Maçon.

Dear Joe,

I finally got a reply from my friend Claude d'Albert. He, also, was imprisoned in St Malo, and he remembers Tom's arrival there. He remembers, particularly, the crippled foot and the fact that the poor chap barely understood what was happening. He tells me he took Tom under his wing for a while, but it was only for a while, because Claude was taken, along with several others, for forced labour. He heard nothing of Tom after that, and feared, as others did, that he was eventually put to death for his misfortunes. Claude's experiences in the labour camp brought him to that conclusion. He is, quite naturally, an embittered man.

Knowing that you were seeking hard evidence, I asked him if he knew of anyone else who might remember Tom, hopefully after Claude was moved, and he remembered a girl from Paramé. He is trying to trace her.

You must understand that recalling those times is very painful for some, and I have to ask you to be patient. Some will be unwilling to talk. Others may just take a little longer.

Yours with all good wishes,

Fred.

Progress, if it could be called that, was slow, and Joe could only take Fred's advice and exercise monumental patience.

He drove home, hoping that Fred's friend Claude might find someone who knew of Thomas's fate.

He'd not been at home long when the phone rang, and he wondered if it might be Arthur wanting to know if he was going fishing the next day. When he picked it up, however, he was surprised to hear Maggie's voice.

'Maggie,' he said, 'how did you know my number?'

'I did a bit of detective work and found it on your business card.'

'Of course.'

'I'm just phoning to find out if you're going to be at home this afternoon.'

'Yes, I'm not going anywhere.'

'Good.' She sounded pleased. 'I have something for you. Will it be all right if I bring it up this afternoon, at about two o' clock?'

'By all means.'

'In that case, I'll see you then.'

Having put down the receiver, Joe could only imagine that the 'something' was a cake, or baking of some kind. At all events, both Maggie and the results of her industry were welcome, and he set about tidying the cottage and making it fit to receive a visitor.

She arrived at a little after two, wearing a coat and gloves against the unseasonal cold. She had a cake tin in her shopping bag.

'You shouldn't do this,' he told her, helping her off with her coat and taking her hat and gloves. 'It'll run away with your rations.'

'If baking is the only thing I can do for you, then I'll do it,' she said, opening the tin to release the rich aroma of gingerbread. 'Anyway, syrup's off the ration now, so that's not a problem.'

'I was thinking of the sugar.'

She sank down on the sofa with the tin of gingerbread on her lap. 'It only takes a cupful, and neither of us takes sugar in tea or coffee nowadays. I prefer those things without, and Derek doesn't know yet that he's given it up. It's surprising what alcohol can do to the taste buds,' she said, adding almost to herself, 'and other parts of the body.'

'Right, I'll stop complaining. Thank you, Maggie. I'm most grateful.' He joined her on the sofa.

'I knew you would be. That's what makes it so worthwhile.'

He imagined she would find appreciation hard to come by at home. The thought prompted him to ask, 'What's Derek doing this afternoon?'

'Sleeping off the lunchtime session. He'll wake up in time to eat and then go to the pub again. At closing time, he'll come home and treat himself to a nightcap. That's his latest thing.'

'I'm sorry,' he said, taking her hand. 'I shouldn't have mentioned him.'

'Did you think I might have forgotten about him?'

'Not really.'

With her free hand, she put the cake tin on the floor. 'Talking to you about it makes it bearable.'

'I'd like to say I'm glad, but it would be much better if you didn't have the problem in the first place.'

She nodded in silent agreement. 'I've thought of leaving him,' she confided after a while. 'I've considered it many times.'

'You're afraid of him, aren't you?'

'Yes, I am,' she admitted, 'but there's also the fact that I work for Mr Wilcox, and that kind of scandal would do a solicitor no good at all.'

'I take your point.' A lock of her hair had come adrift and was hanging over her right eye, so he moved it back to where he thought it belonged. 'I suppose I'll just have to fall back on my original plan and push him over East Cliff.'

'He doesn't go there very often.'

'I'll kidnap him and drive him there. You don't have to be there when I do it. I'll perform the deed very discreetly and then come back to you and whisper something cryptic, such as, "The coast is clear", or "the deed is done".'

'And make me yours? That's what you said earlier.'

'Absolutely, and especially if you're going to continue to make cakes and gingerbread.' The lock of hair had escaped again. He restored it again to its former position. 'Stay,' he told it sternly.

'That's not what's meant by training hair, Joe. Actually, you're a better detective than you are a hairdresser.'

'What's the big secret? I could learn hairdressing. It can't be all that difficult.'

'You're struggling with a few hairs. How would you cope with a whole *coif*, not to mention a salon of impatient clients?'

He took the lock firmly and repositioned it. Then, on mature reflection, he said, 'No, I stick to the business I know.'

'You're probably wise to do that.'

'Maggie,' he asked, changing the subject to a more sensible one, 'you're naturally welcome, but what made you come here today instead of waiting until Monday? I'm just curious.'

She was obviously thinking about her reply. Eventually, she said, 'It's as you said the last time I called here on the way home. It's the difference, the contrast. I hate where I live, but as soon as I come here, I feel liberated, if only for a short time.'

'I can see that,' he said. 'It makes perfect sense, just as long as things don't become too liberated, I suppose.'

10

AUGUST

Several weeks passed with no word from Fred Maçon, and Joe wasn't surprised to hear Jonathan Allard voice his dissatisfaction over the telephone.

'You can't imagine how frustrating it is for us, waiting to hear about your progress and learning that you've made none.'

'I'm completely at the mercy of Fred Maçon and his contacts in St Malo, Mr Allard.'

'Be that as it may, my sister and I have discussed the matter, and we would be grateful if you would send us your invoice for your services and expenses to date, Mr Pelier. 'I regret to have to tell you that those services are no longer required. I am placing the investigation in the, hopefully, more capable hands of Nicholas Rainsley.'

Joe raised his eyebrows at the mention of Rainsley, but made no comment. Instead, he said, 'I'm sorry you don't want me to continue with the case, but it's naturally your decision.'

'Exactly. Now, I have what information you have passed on to me, and I assume that you will be prepared to co-operate, should Mr Rainsley contact you for further amplification or clarification?'

'That will depend entirely on how he goes about it, Mr Allard. If he approaches me in a reasonable manner, I've no doubt he'll find me both amenable and co-operative.'

——◆◆——

'What's the latest on the Allard case?' It was lunchtime, and the first opportunity for Maggie to catch up after putting the call through to Joe.

'I'm off the case,' he told her.

'Surely not. What happened?'

'Nothing, which is why they've given it to Nicholas Rainsley. They weren't happy with my lack of progress.' He lifted his bag on to the desk and took out bread, butter and a dish covered with greaseproof paper.

Maggie was naturally curious about the Allard business, but also about the contents of the dish. She asked, 'What have you got there?'

'Smoked mackerel pâté. I didn't catch them. I bought them from a smokehouse on the Marsh.'

'But who made the pâté?'

'I did.'

There was a hiatus of maybe two seconds before Maggie said, 'I didn't know you could cook.'

'I learned lots of things in Italy.'

'But pâté is French.'

'And Italian, in fact, since Roman times. Italian pâté is coarser than the French kind, and the mackerel that's found in the Mediterranean is somewhat different from ours, but here you have, more or less, pâté *alla Italia*.'

'What's the Italian word for pâté?'

'Pâté.'

'You're a fund of surprising information, Joe.'

'Try some.' He pushed the dish towards her.

She took some of the pâté and said, 'I think it's awful that they've taken the Allard case from you.'

'That's the kind of person Mr Allard is. He says to one, "Go", and he goeth. He wanted me to get a quick result, and I couldn't, so Nicholas Rainsley is now charged with doing the impossible.'

'This pâté is lovely, Joe.'

'I'm glad you like it.'

Returning to the Allard case, she asked, 'Does this Mr Rainsley come recommended?'

'By himself, yes, wholeheartedly. He believes that the world and its inhabitants exist to applaud and even glorify him, he's presumptuous, high-handed and arrogant, and he seems incapable of learning from his countless mistakes.' He buttered a piece of bread and smeared it with pâté. 'That, however, is now the problem of the Allard siblings.'

'What is this Rainsley man's background?'

'The Military Police.' He corrected himself. 'I should say The *Royal* Military Police, as they are now. You can tell by the way he issues orders wherever he goes.'

'How awful. What rank did he hold?'

'Lieutenant. That's why he behaves himself, more or less, when he's around me. After brief reflection, he said, 'I imagine Mr Allard would see him as dynamic. He'll learn.'

—————

Maggie was typing a letter for her employer when her door opened and a voice demanded, 'Is Joseph Pelier about?'

She looked up and said coldly, 'I'm sorry. I didn't hear you knock.'

'I asked you if Joseph Pelier was here.' He was smartly dressed, with immaculate shoes, but that made him no more welcome in Maggie's eyes.

'Yes, I heard what you said. My hearing's very sharp, even though I didn't hear you knock. Mr Pelier is expected back quite soon. Perhaps you'd care to wait outside in the waiting area.'

'How long is he likely to be. I'm a busy man.'

Maggie looked him up and down. 'Are you really? I imagine you're Mr Rainsley.'

'How do you know?'

'Your reputation precedes you.'

He looked at her squarely. 'It usually does. Anyway, how long will he be?'

Maggie declined to answer, because, at that moment, there was a knock on the door. 'Come in.'

The door opened, and Joe came in.

Rainsley turned and said, 'Ah, Pelier.'

'*Mr* Pelier, if you don't mind. I imagine you've come to see me.'

'Yes, I don't know if they've told you yet, but I've taken over the Allard case.'

'Yes, I know. Go into my office. I'll be with you shortly.'

Maggie said, 'This time, Mr Rainsley, you won't need to knock, because there's no one in there.'

Rainsley ignored her and left the office.

'He came straight in without knocking,' she told Joe. 'I mentioned it twice, but I don't think he heard me.' Lowering her voice, she said, 'I didn't believe you when you told me how awful he was, but I do now.'

'His attitude almost defies description, doesn't it?'

———◦⊶◦———

On entering his office, Joe found Rainsley studying a document that he must have picked up from the desk.

'This side of the desk, Rainsley,' he prompted, pointing to the visitor's chair, and do try to mind your own business.' He took the letter from him. 'Now, what can I do for you?'

'I want to know about this chap in Jersey,' said Rainsley.

'Do you mean Frederick Maçon?'

'I believe so. Don't you find it amusing that these people have kept their French names, despite the fact that the Channel Islands have been a British dependency for....' He searched his memory for the exact length of time, and ended lamely, 'For so long.'

'You'll find, Rainsley, that anyone with a family worth mentioning will be keen to perpetuate its name. Now, what do you want to know about Frederick Maçon?'

'Where does he come into the picture?'

Joe wondered what kind of briefing Allard had given Rainsley. 'He's an old friend of Thomas Allard,' he told him, 'and he has contacts in St Malo, Dinard and Paramé, who just may be able to shed some light on the way he met his end.'

'Right.' Rainsley appeared to be assimilating the information. 'These places you mention are in France, aren't they?'

'The last time I looked, they were. They're in Brittany.'

'I've no doubt I'll find them on a map.'

Joe contained himself. 'Where did you serve during the war, Rainsley?'

'Mainly Aldershot, but Plymouth as well.'

Joe nodded. 'There wouldn't be much call for foreign languages in those places, I imagine.'

'Of course not.'

'On the other hand, in pursuing this case, you may have to visit Brittany, where they speak a dialect form of French not unrelated to Welsh and Old Cornish.'

Rainsley looked uneasy. 'Languages are not really my thing,' he admitted.

'In that case, you'll be up the sweet-smelling creek *sans pagaie*.'

'What?'

'Without a paddle,' he translated.

'Listen, Pelier, just remember, I got this case because you fell down on the job.'

'*Mr* Pelier. How many times must I tell you?'

'We're not in the army now.'

'Fortunately for you,' said Joe, rising to his feet, 'and on the subject of manners, if you come here again and you want to speak to Mrs Earnshaw, be sure to knock on her door and wait until she invites you in. Do you understand?'

'I don't need a lesson in manners from you.'

'You certainly need one from someone, and as I'm the only one here, you'll have to take it from me, that if you ever barge in there the way you did this afternoon, I will personally throw you out! Good day to you, Rainsley, and good luck with the case, or maybe I should say, *Bonne chance*.'

Rainsley made no reply. Instead, he gave Joe a haughty look and left the office.

With Rainsley off the premises, Joe looked in on Maggie. 'He'll knock next time,' he assured her.

'I heard you telling him. It's the first time I've known you be angry.'

'He has that effect on people.'

Maggie was shaking her head in disbelief. 'How does he make a living as a detective?'

'He usually gets the bread-and-butter cases that call for a lot of leg work and persistent enquiry. I really don't know what Allard was thinking of when he hired him, but he's in for a rude awakening.' He looked at his watch. 'Anyway, I'll leave you to get on. I have a missing beneficiary to find, but I'll see you later. *À bientôt*.'

He opened the cottage door and stood aside for her.

'This is becoming a habit,' said Maggie.

'It's a good habit. Take a seat and I'll put the kettle on.'

When he returned from filling the kettle, he found Maggie waiting for him with a question.

'What kind of people usually become private detectives, Joe?'

'Apart from misfits such as Rainsley and me? Many of them are retired policemen. They go into it because it's what they're used to, some because they're ex-CID, and some because the job calls for methodical and routine enquiries, alertness and keen observation, all things that they're noted for. Also, having served in the police force, they know the law and how far they can go without overstepping the mark, and they also know certain avenues of inquiry that are not always apparent to the rest of us.'

'It was meeting Nicholas Rainsley that made me ask.'

He laughed. 'You won't find many like him,' he assured her.

He made tea, brought it in from the kitchen and sat down again. 'I wonder how far Rainsley will get with the case,' he said, 'before Allard has to sack him and find yet another sleuth. I suspect it won't be very long.'

' "Sleuth" is a funny word,' said Maggie. 'It sounds as if it doesn't know whether to sound high falutin' or derogatory.'

'Yes, I don't think Sherlock Holmes ever called himself a sleuth. He always insisted on "consulting detective". I believe it was to set himself apart from the inquiry agents of the day, who were a crude, unsophisticated collection. In any case, he saw himself as Scotland Yard's first call when they were stumped, so he was, in effect, a consultant, at least in his own eyes.'

'Not a modest man, then.'

'Not even his mother would call him that, although I suspect that Holmes never actually had a mother. Confidentially, I think he was the result of a laboratory experiment.'

'You're not exactly a shrinking violet, Joe, but you're better than Sherlock Holmes in my estimation.'

'You've got me back on that pedestal, Maggie.'

11

Maggie seemed preoccupied at lunchtime, the following Monday.

Joe asked, 'Problems at home again?'

She shrugged hopelessly. 'They're a fact of life.'

'I suppose they are. It was a silly question.'

'Not really.' She attempted a smile and asked, 'Will you tell me one of your jokes? I need cheering up.'

'The situation must be dire for you to want that, but here goes.' He adopted his usual storytelling posture. 'A missionary wanted to improve his relations with the local populace, so he asked the chieftain, "Will you accept me as a member of your tribe?" The chieftain looked doubtful, and said, "You'll be required to pass the initiation test." '

'Did he really speak like that?'

'I should explain that he was an educated chieftain, who spoke standard English. Anyway, the missionary said, "Very well. That being the case, what must I do?" ' Joe paused to add another word of explanation. 'It's just possible,' he said, 'that the missionary and the chieftain had attended the same university, but don't quote me on that.'

'Let's assume they did,' said Maggie, who was clearly keen to hear more.

' "Think carefully about this," said the chieftain, "because it's no small step." "My mind is made up," said the missionary. "Very well," said the chieftain, "First you must drink a pint of our home-brewed beer, of which forty percent is alcohol." "All right," said the missionary. I'm actually a total abstainer, but I'll try to oblige." "Good," said the chieftain. "Next, you must shoot a leopard with a bow and arrow. Finally – and you may find this at odds with your Christian scruples, but I can make no exception in your case – you must deflower one of our native maidens." The missionary was so keen to be accepted that he agreed. He drank a pint of their best native bitter and then staggered off into the jungle. He was gone for three days and three nights, and the chieftain had given him up for lost, when, to everyone's astonishment, he crawled out of the jungle, lacerated, bleeding from head to foot and in the final stages of exhaustion. "Right," he said, rising to his feet, but swaying alarmingly, "Wheresh thish maiden I have t' shoot with a bow'n'arrow?".'

Maggie smiled. 'That was a silly story,' she said, 'but I enjoyed it.'

'You never laugh at my jokes.'

'No, but they make me feel better.' She took a packet of sandwiches from her shopping bag. 'Cheese,' she said without enthusiasm.

'Snap,' he said, putting his on the desk.

'What's new? I noticed a letter from Jersey this morning.'

'It was Fred Maçon commiserating with me that I'm off the case, and telling me he's heard from Rainsley.' He added with a grin, 'Fred's not impressed with Rainsley.'

'I'd be surprised if anyone is.'

'At all events, Rainsley has the Allard case, and I have another matrimonial.'

She frowned in sympathy. 'Bad luck. I know you don't like them.'

'They're bread and butter, Maggie, and I have to be thankful for that. Also, this one's different, and you know what they say about a change being as good as a fortnight on the French Riviera.'

'I can't say I've ever heard that, but how is it different?'

'Most of my suspicious spouses are wives. This one is the husband.'

Maggie considered the anomaly and said, 'I suppose men are more likely than women to stray.'

'It's the nature of the beast,' he agreed with little conviction. 'Man must reproduce, and woman must nurture.'

'Chance would be a fine thing.'

Realising that the subject was a sensitive one for her, Joe declined to comment. Even so, Maggie went on to say, 'If things were different, I'd love to have children. As they stand, it would be irresponsible of me.'

Joe nodded sympathetically.

'Not that there's any danger of it happening.'

Once more, Joe made no comment, although her last remark had left him wondering.

'Am I allowed to ask what the circumstances are in your new case?'

'Before I say anything, I have to ask if you know, or have ever known, Mr H or Mrs H?'

Maggie shook her head. 'I've never heard of either of them.'

'In that case, you are allowed to ask, and I shall tell you in guarded terms that Mr H fears that Mrs H has taken a lover and is visiting him on a regular basis. He's concerned that she is, in fact, dropping more than her H's.'

She tried not to smile, but said instead, 'Poor man.'

'Don't squander your sympathy, Maggie. In my opinion, he doesn't deserve it.'

'Why not?'

'If you met him, you'd know what a disagreeable person he is. Frankly, I don't blame his wife if she's grazing in pastures new. He's bad-tempered and overbearing, and you wouldn't believe how clumsy he is. It's little wonder his wife shows no enthusiasm for marital goings-on.' Noticing a shift in her eyes, he said, 'I'm sorry. Have I offended you?'

'No,' she said quickly, 'I'm not at all prudish.'

'Mr H is. He refers to it as "bedroom business".'

She appeared thoughtful. 'On the one hand,' she said, 'I hope she's enjoying herself.'

'And on the other?'

'I hate to think what he might do to her if she really is playing away.'

'Depending on the circumstances, it might just prompt her to do something about the situation she's in.'

Once again, Maggie looked pensive. 'I think men and women stray for different reasons,' she said.

'That's certainly been true in my experience.'

'I think women must look for the fulfilment they can't find in their marriage, whereas men....'

'I have to admit that in many cases it's purely physical. They're looking for something they don't get at home. Some men, though, are serially unfaithful, and the lure is often little more than the thrill of the chase.'

Maggie looked at him enquiringly. 'You've really studied the subject, haven't you?'

'I wouldn't say I've studied it,' he said, 'but in my business, I see these things happening all the time, and it's true to say, especially of the male of the species that, "civilisation, whatever its kind or degree is a direct result of the repression of the sex drive in mankind".'

'Was that an original thought?'

'No, Sigmund Freud trotted that one out.'

'So you have studied it.' Her expression suggested that she'd known it all along.

'Only indirectly. When I was called for my army medical, I had two long waits, and someone had left a copy of *Civilisation and its Discontents* lying around, so I read it.'

'All of it?'

'I'm a quick reader,' he explained.

'Why did they make you wait twice?'

'The first time,' he told her, 'We had to wait for the doctor to arrive. It was December 1939, it was very cold, and there was lots of snow.'

'What about the second time?'

If Maggie wanted detail, he decided, she would have it. 'As you know, at a service medical, it's necessary to produce a urine specimen. Now, I hadn't had much to drink that day, and I was struggling to oblige, so they made me wait until I could.'

'Did it take long?'

'It seemed to take forever. I tried thinking of liquid matters, such as fountains and streams and dripping taps, and I tried thinking of all the jokes I knew, as well, but that didn't work. However, one of the chaps in the waiting room was a milkman, and his horse had a problem with its prostate gland. He had to encourage it to relieve itself every morning before work, and he wondered if it might work with me.'

'How did he encourage it?'

'By whistling. Everyone in the waiting room whistled like mad for me, and then someone brought me a glass of water. I was just finishing it, when there was a gushing noise outside the surgery, and it made me suddenly desperate to go.'

'What had happened?'

'The milkman had left his horse and milk cart outside the surgery, and the whistling had proved too much for it.'

'Another silly story,' she said, 'but I feel better for it.'

———

Two weeks later, he had a meeting in his office with Mr Hollingberry.

'It's good news,' he said. 'Your wife has made five visits during the past fortnight, and each of them to the home of a lady, who appears to be a friend. Other ladies also attended.'

'Why does she do that?' Mr Hollingberry had a way of sounding permanently indignant.

'I imagine that, like most women, you wife values the company of other women. They talk about things that wouldn't interest you and me, but that are vitally important to them. They need that outlet.' As he spoke, he thought of Maggie, trapped in a world that excluded friends of her own sex.

'Are you married, Mr Pelier?' Mr Hollingberry's untidy moustache quivered.

'No.'

'In that case, how do know what women want?'

'You don't have to be married to learn these things. On the other hand, there must be many married men who never learn them. It's a matter of keeping an open mind.'

Mr Hollingberry snorted. 'I've never heard such nonsense in all my life. If she wants to talk to someone, she can talk to me.'

Joe opened his drawer and took out an envelope. 'I wonder,' he said.

'You wonder what?'

'If she can talk to you.' He handed the envelope to his client. 'That's my bill, by the way, and aren't you glad that your suspicions were unfounded?'

Mr Hollingberry took out the bill. 'You're not cheap,' he said.

'I told you my terms when you engaged me. You accepted them then, and they haven't changed.' He stood up to bring the meeting to its close. 'If I were you, I'd give that matter some consideration.'

'What matter?'

'The fact that your wife needs friends.'

'What about her being… you know, not keen on… the other thing?'

'There could be many reasons for that,' said Joe, 'and chances are, none of them are her fault, but it's something you could discuss with her.'

'It most certainly is not.' Mr Hollingberry picked up his mackintosh. 'Good day to you. I'll send a cheque in the post.' He left as indignant as when he'd arrived.

Joe tapped on Maggie's door.

'Come in.'

'I thought you'd like to know,' he said, closing the door behind him, 'that Mrs H is innocent. She was only visiting a female friend. Mr H doesn't appear to be relieved by the news and doesn't see why his wife needs friends when she has him to talk to.'

'How ridiculous. Doesn't he know anything?'

'Nothing whatsoever, and he doesn't believe he has anything to learn. He must be very confident, because I know a great deal more than he does, and I still have lots to learn.'

'That's what sets you apart from men such as him, Joe.'

'Mm. One thing I'd be interested to know, is how Rainsley's coping with the Allard case.'

—— ►◄ ——

His curiosity was satisfied within the next few days, when he received a phone call from Jonathan Allard.

'Mr Pelier, we want you to take the case on again.'

'Do you, now? I'm afraid it's not as simple as that.'

'D' you mean you don't want it?' He sounded incredulous.

'I don't know yet.'

'What's the difficulty, then?'

'When you relieved me of the case, you criticised my handling of it. If you were so unimpressed then, why do you suddenly want me to accept it again?'

'That Rainsley chap's incompetent. He can't even speak French.'

'I know.'

'You might have told me that at the time.' His tone implied that the fault was clearly on Joe's side.

'If you remember, you were doing all the talking, the insulting

73

and throwing your weight about. You'd made your decision, and no comment on my part was going to change your mind.'

'I never insulted you.'

'You told me that Rainsley would do a better job, and that was the greatest insult you could have levelled at me.'

'Look, Mr Pelier, will you take the case or not?'

'That depends. If I do, you must understand that I'll do it my way.'

'Fair enough.'

'And another thing is that the last time I spoke to Fred Maçon, he made the point, somewhat unnecessarily, that those who suffered under Nazi rule find the memory painful. He said that some might respond slowly, and some not at all. That means you will have to be a damned sight more patient than you've been in the past.'

'All right, that's understood.'

'Finally, what did Rainsley find out?'

'Nothing at all. That's why we want you back on the job.'

'Well, if you'll keep your part of the agreement, I'll do my best for you. Before I can do that, though, I'd like my photographs returned to me.'

'Very well. Good day to you, Mr Pelier.'

'Good day, Mr Allard.'

After he'd put the phone down, Joe tapped on Maggie's door.

'What's happened, Joe?' Maggie had put the call through to him.

'I'm back on the Allard case.'

Her expression brightened. 'Quicker than you thought.'

'Yes, but this time it's on my terms.'

12

September

Joe had only just arrived the next morning, when Guy came to his office.

'Good morning, Guy,' said Joe, 'you're up and about early this morning.' It was Guy's habit to arrive almost on the stroke of nine, and the hour still lacked ten minutes.

'Very funny, Joe. Good morning. Will you find an alibi for me?'

'Why? What have you done?'

'Nothing. My client's alibi is no longer at her address. I'd like you to look into it, if you will.'

'Consider it looked into. Business is less than brisk, so just give me the details and I'll be on her trail.'

'Thank you. I have the file in my office.'

Joe followed him, greeting Maggie on the way as she arrived.

'I really don't know what to expect,' said Guy. 'The client is a known offender with a history of larceny, but he's told his counsel that he's innocent of the charge, so he's going to enter a plea of "not guilty".'

'Is it beyond the bounds of possibility that he might be innocent?'

'It's always possible. These are the details,' he said, handing Joe a typed sheet. 'Miss Susie Helliwell has been missing from her home since the fifteenth of August. The phone number you have there, by the way, is a coin-box phone inside the building. We've tried it, and no one can tell us a thing about her.'

'A little more than two weeks. It's not unusual for people to go away in the summer months.'

'From what I can gather, Miss Helliwell is unlikely to have taken a break. She is, let's say, a working girl and keen to maintain her income.'

Joe looked at her address and nodded. 'I shan't go immediately,' he said. 'Even if she's at home, she's not bound to be an early riser.'

'Even if she's at home,' echoed Guy with little enthusiasm.

The address was a flat in a run-down part of the harbour. Beside the front door, a row of bell pushes devoid of names maintained the tenants' anonymity. Presuming that the second bell from the bottom was connected to Miss Helliwell's first-floor flat, Joe gave it a push and waited. Another push and a wait of thirty seconds or so later, he gave up on the doorbell and tried the door, which turned out to be locked. He walked round the building and was surprised to find that the rear entrance door was slightly ajar, so he pushed it open and stepped inside. The passage to the front was deserted, and the old newspapers and other detritus that lay on the floor gave the impression that the place was uncared-for. The building seemed deserted, even though Joe knew that Miss Helliwell had lived there until fairly recently. Also, the mail on the inside of the front door was largely of a personal kind.

It wasn't the kind of case on which he could spend much time. There was a limit to Legal Aid funding, so he needed a result very soon. He made his way past the coinbox telephone that Guy had mentioned, and took the stairs to the first floor. The door to the flat was just off the landing, and he knocked on it.

At first, there was no response, but when he knocked again, a woman's voice said loudly, 'If that's Hargreaves, you'll get your money on Friday.'

Opening the letter flap, Joe said, 'I'm not Mr Hargreaves. I need to ask you about something.'

She said something else that he didn't catch, and then there were padding footsteps on what he suspected was linoleum. The key turned in the lock, and the door opened to reveal a woman of maybe forty in a nightdress and a faded rayon dressing gown. Her feet were bare, and her face bore traces of yesterday's make-up. Her hair, which had been bleached, showed dark roots.

'You are Miss Susie Helliwell, aren't you?'

'That, or anybody else you want me to be. You're a bit early, aren't you, love? I'm not dressed for callers, as you can see, but if you're just after a quickie, I shan't turn you away.'

'No,' he said, 'that's not what I came for.'

'Isn't it? Well, what did you come for, then? Listen, if you're one o' them fellas who like to sit an' talk about it, it'll cost you just the same, Time's money, when all's said and done.'

'No, it's not that. My name is Joe Pelier and I'm a private detective.'

'You can be anything you like while you're with me, love. Believe it or not, I've one fella who likes to dress up as an airman. Just the jacket and the moustache, not the trousers. Well, he doesn't need them, does her? Now I think of it, an' for all I know, he could be a pilot in real life.' As if re-living a recent experience, she said fondly, 'Just before the main event, he says, "Chocks away!" Just like that. Mind you, I've never had a private detective before. How do you want to play that?'

Joe shook his head firmly and said, 'I haven't come for sex. I really am a private detective, and I'm here just to make sure you're still around and that you'll be around when you're called to give evidence.'

'Give evidence? That's a bleedin' laugh after the number of times I've been up before the beak.'

'Sam Geraghty says he was with you on the night of the fifteenth of June.'

'Oh, that.' It was as if the matter were of little consequence.

'You agreed to give him an alibi,' he reminded her.

'Yes, he was with me all night. He's one of my regulars, Sam is.'

'Good. The problem is, his solicitor has been trying to contact you, and you weren't at home.'

'Oh.' Realisation dawned. 'That's why you're here.'

'Yes, I had to make sure you were available to give evidence.'

'When will it be?'

'I don't know yet. It probably won't go to court, but in any case, they'll want you to make a statement before anything can happen. You'll just need to go to the police station, and they'll take your statement there. You know where it is, don't you?' As the words left his mouth, he realised how stupid they must have sounded.

She laughed. 'If I don't know me way to the local nick by this time,

I need me eyes tested.' Suddenly, her expression changed. 'Ere, will I be all right, telling 'em he was with me?'

'You don't have to say what you were doing, just that you were together in a romantic tryst.'

'I've never heard it called that before, but if you're sure, I'll go along with it.' It seemed that she thought she should offer an explanation for her earlier absence, because she said, 'One of my clients has a boat and he took me out in it. We went all the way to Boulogne.' She considered that briefly and said, 'Now, I can say I offer an international service, can't I?'

'Yes, you can. Anyway, thank you, Miss Helliwell. I'll be on my way.' He walked to the door.

'Are you sure you don't want a quickie before you go?'

'Quite sure, thanks. I'm going to mow the lawn later, and I'll need all my strength for that.'

———▶◀———

Having reported to Guy, he told Maggie about his visit.

'She's cock-a-hoop now,' he told her, 'because she can offer an international service. Clients can choose their location – Folkestone or Boulogne. French currency and travellers' cheques accepted. Tipping is officially at the client's discretion but is nonetheless welcome.'

'Did she really offer to take you on as a client?'

'Oh, yes, but I was suitably polite in declining her offer.'

Maggie opened her mouth to say something and then decided against it.

'What's on your mind, Maggie?'

'It's just that I can't imagine why men do it.'

'Go with prostitutes? Thinking of her, neither can I, unless it's what we were talking about the other day. You know, something that doesn't happen at home. Just as an example, Miss Helliwell helps some clients act out their fantasies. One chap dresses as a pilot in the RAF.'

Maggie stared uncomprehendingly.

'Oh, he doesn't wear the trousers. Just the jacket and flying boots, I think she said. Maybe the flying helmet and parachute harness as well.'

She laughed silently. 'That's ridiculous.'

Joe looked hurt. 'I'm sorry you feel like that, Maggie.'

'Why?'

'No reason, except… I just feel misunderstood. It happens from time to time, although I should be used to it by now.' He looked away, hurt.

'Have I offended you?'

'No, not at all. It was silly of me. I mean, I can't expect you to feel the same way as I do about my Mountie's uniform.' He explained hurriedly, 'I don't wear the spurs, of course, but the riding boots, belt and holster are essential. I have a record that I play, too, of Nelson Eddy singing "Rosemarie." '

For a moment, she stared, and then incredulity gave way to realisation. 'Go and get on with your work, Joe,' she said, 'and let me get on with mine.'

'Are we going to have a cup of tea on the way home? Strictly office clothes, I assure you.'

She smiled. 'All right. Off you go.'

Joe spent the next half-hour in his darkroom, reprinting the photographs of the spurious Thomas Allard. Enquiries by Mr Allard had revealed that Rainsley had mislaid the original prints. It came as no surprise to Joe, and he printed extra copies for Fred Maçon.

Having replaced the missing prints, he looked again at the film to make sure there were no frames he'd overlooked, and he came to the conclusion that there was only the shot of the mystery man lathered up for shaving, and his head was partly obscured by the paper boy. If only for the sake of thoroughness, he decided to print it. He clamped the film into the film carriage of the enlarger and took out a sheet of paper, performing the process as meticulously as ever.

As he watched the image take form in the developing bath, he noticed something that would have been almost invisible on the film, and it had nothing to do with the man's face. His left arm was extended to take the newspaper from the delivery boy, and clearly, on the inside of his upper arm was a small mark that had to be a tattoo, and one of a kind that Joe found grotesquely familiar. Carefully, he passed the print through the stop bath and fixer, and then hung it to dry with the others while he went for his magnifying glass.

Back in the darkroom, he switched on the main light and examined the print with the aid of the magnifying glass.

Maggie must have noticed that the darkroom door was open, because she joined him and, after looking at the prints that were drying, asked, 'What have you been up to without telling your darkroom assistant?'

'Sorry, I thought you were busy.'

'I am, but I could have spared a few minutes.'

'In that case, come and look at this, Watson.' He gave her the magnifying glass and pointed to the mark on the man's arm.

'Just a minute.' She moved the glass back and forth to get the image in focus. 'I'm not an expert,' she said, 'but I think it's a tattoo. Either that or a birthmark.'

'But birthmarks don't usually come perfectly shaped, at least, not in my experience.'

'That's true.' She peered harder. Eventually, she said, 'It looks like an arrowhead or maybe a letter "A".'

'I'm inclined towards the latter. I can just make out the horizontal stroke.'

'What does it mean?'

'I think I can safely say that the Thomas Allard case has just assumed a new and particularly unpleasant dimension. It seems that a part of my past that I regard as worse than distasteful has returned as a reminder. '

'As usual, Holmes,' she said, handing back the magnifying glass, 'you've lost me completely. What's the significance of this discovery?'

'The significance, my dear Watson, is that, unless I'm strongly mistaken, that letter "A" is, in fact a tattoo, and that it served a sinister purpose. It is, I'm afraid, the man's SS blood group.'

13

They left the prints to dry and returned to Maggie's office, but she was still mystified. 'Please explain, Joe. I really don't understand.'

'Okay. Members of the Waffen SS had their blood group tattooed on their upper arm in case they ever needed an emergency transfusion.' He perched on the edge of her desk to explain. 'In the chaos of battle, paybooks sometimes went astray, and the man who needed the transfusion might be unconscious and unable to give the information.'

'Presumably, the SS was some German organisation?'

'Yes.' It was time to curb his excitement for the moment, and remember that Maggie had no knowledge of the world he was describing. 'The Schutzstaffel, or SS, was Hitler's political army. The Waffen, or "Fighting" SS, was the elite army, whilst the Allgemeine SS, which comprised the rest of the unholy outfit, was responsible for carrying out Nazi racial policy, the programme of mass extermination.'

'So they were the monsters I've read about in the paper. I never read any of the details of the Nurembourg Trials, of course. The general picture was sickening enough.'

'Exactly, but the Allgemeine SS weren't the only offenders. The Waffen SS were equally guilty in their own way.'

'It doesn't bear thinking about.'

'You're probably right. They were horrible people, and I do speak with some authority.' He eased himself off Maggie's desk and stood up again. 'I'm now more than ever determined to get to the bottom of Thomas Allard's disappearance,' he said. 'That is the first Waffen SS tattoo I've seen since I left Italy, and it's just evoked a few memories, none of which is particularly pleasant.'

———◆◄◆———

Jonathan Allard would need to be told, but Joe's priority was a letter to Fred Maçon. He set about it immediately.

Dear Fred,

I hope you're both well and that Nicholas Rainsley's visit wasn't too much of a nuisance. You will be interested to hear that he failed to impress the Allard family and that they have hired me again. I'm told these things can happen to the best inquiry agents. More interesting still, however, is the next piece of news I have for you.

Take a look at the upper arm in the first of the enclosed photographs. It appears to be a letter 'A', and it's in the exact same place where soldiers of the Waffen SS had their blood group tattooed. The indication, I'm sure you'll agree, is that our mysterious impostor is even worthier of investigation than we thought. I've taken the liberty of sending you copies of the other photos, in case someone you know is able to recognise the man.

I'll keep in touch.

Yours, with very best wishes,

Joe Pelier.

It seemed to Joe that the development might prove to be the motivation Fred's contacts needed. In the meantime, however, matters nearer home required his attention, and he was alerted to the fact when he found Maggie alone in the office on Friday morning, Guy having arranged to visit a client. Curiously, when he called in to see her, she returned his greeting without looking up from the filing cabinet she appeared to be searching, and it also struck him as odd that she was wearing sunglasses.

'Maggie,' he said, 'it's really none of my business, but wouldn't it be easier for you to find what you're looking for without those specs?'

'These sunglasses? Oh, I'm just getting over a migraine.'

'I didn't know you suffered from them. That's bad luck.' Strangely, she still had her back to him. 'Migraine apart, did you have a good weekend?'

'Yes, thank you. Did you?'

'Excellent, thank you.' It was time to clear up the mystery. 'Maggie, will you please turn and look at me? I feel as if I've done something to offend you.'

'Don't be silly. You haven't offended me.' There was an element of forced lightness in her tone. 'I'm just busy, that's all.'

As he approached her, he saw the bruising around her left eye. 'Maggie,' he said gently, 'let me see that eye.'

'I keep bumping into things,' she told him hurriedly.

'Fists, presumably. Don't forget, I have some experience of eye injury.'

Her expression told him that she knew she was found out. She nodded minutely.

'I'll get some ice.'

'Where?'

'The fishmonger's in Sandgate Road. I shan't be long.' He hurried downstairs. The fishmonger's was only a short distance away, but to save time, he took the car.

Five minutes later, he returned with a quantity of crushed ice in a brown paper carrier bag, which he emptied into the sink before its bottom could disintegrate. He then transferred some to a clean linen towel.

'Take off your sunglasses and brace yourself,' he advised her. 'I'll try not to hurt.' He held the ice pack against the bruise, holding her head with his free hand.

'There was no need for you to go to so much trouble,' she said, laying her sunglasses on the desk.

'There's every need, and it's no trouble.' He hesitated. 'Does that make sense?'

'I know what you mean.'

Holding the ice pack gently against her bruise, he asked, 'Has this happened before?'

'Only once. He has an awful temper, but he usually contents himself with shouting at me and slamming doors.' She added, 'He's at his worst when he's drunk.'

'I must say, he's not at all how I'd imagined your husband to be. Didn't you say you met him in the RAF?'

'I was in the WAAF, but he was in the Army. They came to guard our air station. It was before the RAF Regiment was formed.' She said uncomfortably, 'I feel quite disloyal, telling you these things.'

'I shouldn't be inclined to worry about that, considering the loyalty he demonstrated when he gave you this shiner.' To lighten the conversation, he said, 'I have a treat for you in my fridge. He doesn't deserve it, but you do.'

'I'm glad you think so. What is it?'

'Hare. Have you ever tried it?'

'No, what's it like?'

'More like game than rabbit. I think you'll like it. It's skinned and prepared,' he assured her.

For the first time that morning, she attempted a smile. 'You spoil me, Joe,' she said.

'I believe we had this conversation earlier. In any case,' he said, 'it'll do you no harm.' He juggled the contents of the ice pack to give her the benefit of the unthawed ice. 'And Heaven forbid that I should ever be responsible for something like this.'

She made no response, but asked instead, 'What happened to your eye?'

'It was a splinter from a fifty-millimetre shell.'

'Was that a big one? I'm not very familiar with metres and things.'

'Two inches,' he translated. 'Thankfully, it was before Jerry started arming his tanks with enormous artillery pieces, or I might not have been so lucky.'

'I'm glad you were lucky, even though you were wounded.'

'So am I, and thank you.' He looked at the ice pack and shook his head.

'What's the matter?'

'They don't make ice the way they used to.' He went to the sink to replenish the pack with fresh ice.

'I feel guilty, Joe.'

'Don't. One villain in your household is quite enough.'

'I mean, because you're doing all this.'

'I haven't finished yet. There's another aid to recovery that, to my everlasting shame, I'd quite forgotten.'

'What's that?'

He leaned towards her and kissed her bruised cheek. 'There,' he said, now you're bound to make a complete recovery.'

His action brought forth a smile. 'Who taught you to kiss-better? Your mother?'

'No, my sergeant-major. He had healing powers. At least, that was the defence I offered at his court-martial.'

She smiled again painfully. 'If you're not in a desperate hurry to start work,' she said, 'I have a favour to ask.'

'Ask away.'

'I'd like you to tell me one of your jokes. Will you do that?'

'All right.' It seemed a curious request in the circumstances, but he was pleased to oblige her. 'Let me think.' He struck a thoughtful pose and asked, 'Are you Roman Catholic?'

'No, C of E.'

'Okay. Two nuns allowed themselves to be seduced by a pair of unscrupulous monks. Then, after much soul-searching, they decided to come clean about it and make their confession. Well, as you can imagine, the Mother Superior was furious, and when she'd calmed down a little, she sent them both to the priest, who was equally livid. He said, "Such wanton wickedness must be punished. You will both say fifty Our Fathers and fifty Hail Marys. Then, you must each suck a fresh lemon." One of the nuns asked, "Why the lemon, Father? Is it to cleanse our souls?" He said, "No, it's to take the satisfied grin off your faces." ' Through his hands, he felt, rather than saw, her smile.

'Thank you. I feel better now.'

The office door opened, and Guy came in. Seeing that Joe was administering first aid, he asked, 'What happened?'

'I walked into a cupboard door,' Maggie told him. 'I'm all right. Joe just told me one of his jokes and it made me feel better.'

'I see.' Guy looked uncomfortable and said, 'Look, Maggie, if there's anything you want to discuss, you know you can speak to me at any time.'

'Thank you, Mr Wilcox. I know that.'

'I'll leave you in Joe's capable hands. I have a letter to dictate, but there's no hurry.' He left them.

Maggie said, 'I don't think he believed me.'

'Simple Simon wouldn't believe your story about the cupboard door, Maggie.'

'I must think of a better story.'

'Certainly, something needs to improve.' He took the ice pack from her face and winced at the sight.

'We'll be going shopping in the morning, as usual. I don't fancy wearing a headscarf in this hot weather, but I'll have to.'

'Where do you do your shopping?'

'In Hythe. Why?'

'I may see you around.'

———•┃•———

Joe did most of his shopping in Sandgate; the only shop in Hythe where he was registered was the bakery, and he left that until last.

In fact, having collected his bread, he spent some time in Hythe, looking idly in shop windows, until he saw Maggie. Even then, she was hard to recognise with her face covered by a headscarf and sunglasses. She and presumably her husband were just entering Woolworth's, and Joe crossed the road to join them.

He found them by the stationery counter. 'Hello, Maggie,' he said.

'Joe.' Maggie seemed flustered. 'Derek, this is Joe, a work colleague. Joe, this is my husband Derek.'

'How d' you do?' Joe took his hand and gripped it. A rewarding hint of pain crossed Derek's features, and Joe maintained the pressure while he assessed his new acquaintance, who was slightly built, and who seemed to wear a permanent frown, although that might have been the result of Joe's grasp.

Derek rubbed his right hand and asked, 'What do you do at the solicitor's, then?'

'Oh, I'm not one of the staff. He only calls on me when a client needs a bodyguard, someone who can deliver maximum pain without leaving too many bruises.' Maggie's sunglasses concealed any expression that might have crossed her face, but he knew she would be wondering why he'd chosen to tell her husband an outright lie. Her attention was distracted, however, by a wail of distress from a tiny child close by.

Crouching to speak to him, Maggie asked, 'What's the matter?'

In his tearful state, the child struggled to speak at first. Eventually, he said, 'I've lost my mummy!'

'Oh dear. Don't worry, we'll find her.' She took the child's hand and proceeded to search the store for the missing parent.

'That's quite a shiner that Maggie's got,' commented Joe.

'Yes, she walked into a cupboard door.'

'Oh yes? I know something about bruises and black eyes, having inflicted a few in my time, and I know she didn't get hers from a cupboard door. I also know where you live, and I'm going to tell you something now for your own good as well as Maggie's, so you'd better listen. If I ever hear that you've been knocking her about, I'll come and find you.' He was gratified to see abject fear occupy Derek's features. 'I can promise you, you won't like it, because when I hit, I hit hard, and I always do a thorough job.' He added, smiling, 'But then, I'm a professional, you see.'

'Some people aren't fit to have children,' said Maggie, having returned the tearful scrap to his mother. 'And she wasn't a bit relieved to see him. She just snapped at him for wandering off.'

'Yes,' said Joe, happy to agree with her, 'some people need to remember their responsibilities.' He gave Derek a final, meaningful look and said, 'I've enjoyed meeting you. Goodbye.'

———◦│◦———

A reply from Fred Maçon arrived on Monday. As Joe had anticipated, Fred was pleased to know he was back on the case.

Dear Joe,

Thank you for your letter. So we've seen the last of Nicholas Rainsley, thank goodness, and not before time. He hadn't a clue what he was looking for, and he was too arrogant for words.

Regarding the impostor, I agree that the mark looks very much like an SS blood group. I've put the word out that we're probably dealing with a war criminal, so I could hear something before long. I'll let you know immediately if I do.

Yours, with all good wishes,

Fred.

Joe made a routine report to Jonathan Allard by phone. Allard was typically impatient.

'Perhaps you should go to St Malo, Mr Pelier. You might be able to unearth some of these people.'

'Victims of the SS and the Gestapo are naturally reticent, Mr Allard. They endured horrors that we can barely imagine, and they need to be handled gently. Fred Maçon is more likely to draw them out than I am. He knows the people he's dealing with.'

'Oh, well, if you think so. Anyway, why haven't you got the war crimes people involved yet?'

'There's no evidence, as yet, that this man has committed a war crime. As soon as I have something for them to go on, I'll be in touch with the agencies.'

'All right, but this thing's taking forever.'

'These things do, Mr Allard. I'll be in touch as soon as I know anything.'

Joe put the phone down, thankful to have ended the conversation. His next task would be equally sensitive. He knocked on Maggie's door and entered at her invitation.

'Joe,' she said in a way that suggested she'd been waiting to speak to him, 'what on earth did you say to Derek on Saturday?' She was no longer wearing sunglasses, and her bruise had changed to a gentler hue, mainly yellow.

'Not much. It was, to coin a phrase, a brief encounter. What has he said?'

'He hasn't said anything, but he was very quiet after you left us in Woolworths, and he keeps looking out of the window at odd times, as if he's expecting someone to arrive. It's odd, because no one ever comes to the house.'

'How strange.'

Her expression of bafflement increased, and she asked, 'Also, why did you tell him that nonsense about being a bodyguard?'

'Ah, well, I'm sure you don't want him to think that we spend a lot of time together, so I let him know that Guy only calls on me from time to time, which is basically true. I had to think quickly about my role, and the bodyguard thing sprang immediately to mind.' As if the question had only just occurred to him, he asked, 'D' you think I might have scared him?'

'If you haven't, Joe, someone has.'

'Odd. You didn't tell him what I really do, did you?'

'I haven't spoken to him about you.'

'Good, because I don't want to look a complete fool.' Deliberately changing the subject, he asked, 'Did you have the hare?'

'Yes, it was lovely, thank you. Where did you get it?'

'One of my huntin', fishin' and shootin' acquaintances provided it. I find it pays to know the right people.'

'I'm inclined to agree.'

Peering at her bruised eye, he said, 'It's healing nicely. I knew it would.'

'It had to,' she agreed, 'after you kissed it better.'

'Good old SSM Tompkins. He knew a thing or two about first aid.'

'What is an SSM?'

'Officially, he's the squadron sergeant-major, but we always thought of Tompkins as the man to go to with a grazed knee or when we had something in our eye. He was the man who—'

'He taught you to kiss-better. I remember. Now, be off with you or I'll never get any work done.'

He had to agree. '*Au revoir*, Maggie.' He threw her a kiss.

14

J oe was surprised to receive another letter from Fred within the next
three weeks.

Dear Joe,

*I have just returned from St Malo, where I managed to find the
contact I mentioned. Unfortunately, she has asked me not to reveal her
identity. You'd be surprised at the fear that's still around. However,
I showed her the photos, and she identified the impostor. Apparently,
he's Hauptsturmführer Bernhardt Neuhaus of the Waffen SS. He was a*
Partisanjäger, *sometimes called a* Kopfjäger, *or 'head hunter'. I believe
that was the title they gave to those involved in pursuing resistance
fighters and saboteurs.*

*It is unfortunate that my contact insists on remaining anonymous,
but maybe the police will now show more interest in the case.*

Yours, with all good wishes,
Fred.

To hear of a witness who could identify Neuhaus but who refused
to be identified herself was too frustrating for words. Joe needed to
speak to Arthur Newcombe, which he did when the pair went fishing
that Sunday.

'Surely,' said Joe, 'the fact that this chap was in the SS and that he's living
under a stolen identity should be enough to start a police investigation.'

'I wouldn't put money on it.'

'Why not, Arthur? He's committed at least one crime, and being a
member of the SS must raise their suspicions. I've dealt with numerous
Waffen SS personnel, and none of them was innocent, believe me.'

Arthur seemed more interested in Joe's involvement in Italy than in his current case, at least for the moment, because he asked, 'How many convictions did you get?'

'Eleven officers and a dozen or so NCOs or other ranks. They weren't all involved in the Ardeatine affair, but they were all guilty of war crimes.'

Arthur whistled. 'That was quite a haul,' he said.

'I had plenty to go at.'

'If anyone in this country is going to be interested,' said Arthur, 'it's Scotland Yard Special Branch, but I wouldn't bank on it, as I said.'

'Why not?'

'Basically, I suppose, because they're too busy watching the new enemy.'

'Russia?'

'The Soviet Union, yes. If this had come up five or six years ago, you might have been in with a chance, but Nazi war crimes are old news, at least as far as this country's concerned.'

'And the matter of stolen identity comes under the jurisdiction of the Jersey police, who've already washed their hands of it.'

'The Paid Police, they call them.'

'Don't tell me they use unpaid volunteers, Arthur.'

'Why not? We do.'

———◆◀———

After another unsuccessful attempt to interest the Jersey police in a crime perpetrated under their noses, Joe turned to another source of advice, which involved a call to a different kind of agency.

'Will you connect me, please, with Major Francis Collingham?'

'Major Collingham. Who is calling?'

'Joseph Pelier.'

'Is that Mr or Monsieur Pelier?'

'Either. I'm not easily offended.'

'Please wait a moment, sir, and I'll try to connect you.'

Joe waited for maybe half a minute, and then a familiar voice came on the line.

'Joe, Francis here. How are you?'

'I'm well, thank you, Francis. And you?'

'Very busy, what with one thing and another.'

'Okay, I shan't keep you. Maybe we could meet for lunch. I need some advice.'

'Advice, eh? Not today or tomorrow, I'm afraid.' There was the sound of pages being turned. 'Thursday looks promising. How's it for you?'

'Perfect. Shall we meet at Raphael's at, say, one o' clock?'

'Thirteen hundred it is. I'll look forward to it, Joe.'

He joined Maggie at lunchtime, having made another dish of smoked mackerel pâté.

'How are things, Maggie?'

'At home? Quiet.'

'Good.' He unpacked bread, pâté and real butter.

'There must be half a pound of butter there,' said Maggie. 'Where did you find so much?'

'As I told you earlier, I never reveal my sources. Just enjoy it.'

'I shall,' she promised, 'but before I do, I have a question to ask.'

'The mackerel met their end bravely and without suffering,' he assured her.

She gave him a stern look. 'Never mind that, Joe,' she said. 'Did you threaten Derek?'

'You're asking me?'

'There's no one else here.'

'You know I'm the embodiment of gentleness. Take some more, by the way. Mackerel are plentiful.'

The stern look persisted. 'Don't change the subject. You threatened him, didn't you?'

'What makes you think that, for goodness' sake?'

Clearly impatient, she said, 'He described you as the "thug" who works for my boss.'

'That was naughty. What else has he said about me?'

'Nothing, really. He commented that I was keeping the company of some strange people, that's all.'

Joe leaned forward to ask quietly, 'Just how strange are these people you've been seeing?'

'Be serious, Joe.'

'All right. He thinks I'm a thick ear merchant, and I confess, I did rather give him that impression. Now, if he believes, for any reason, that retribution will fall on him from a great height if he ever hits you again, it simply means that you can sleep more soundly than before. In other words, it's his turn to lie awake and do the worrying.'

She gave a shrug of grudging acceptance.

'Anyway, it wasn't quite what you think.'

'What was it, then?'

He recalled the conversation and said truthfully, 'He told me you'd walked into a cupboard door. Now, think about it. As far as he's concerned, I'm a paid roughneck, who must have seen more black eyes than he's seen pints of old and mild – although that would be difficult – and he expected me to believe you'd got yours by walking into a cupboard door. It must have been obvious to him that I didn't believe him. All I did was warn him in the most helpful way that if he did it again he'd most likely find there was a price to pay.'

Maggie's expression remained implacable. 'You threatened him,' she concluded.

'But it seems to be working.'

With a hopeless look, she said, 'I just don't want any trouble.'

'Of course you don't.'

'I mean trouble with the police.'

'Why drag them into it? If I ever have to keep my promise, there'll be no witnesses and I certainly shan't leave any marks or bruises. It'll be his word against mine, and I don't think he'll want his unsavoury habit made public.' Joe hated argument, and it was time to end the current disagreement. 'Let's just forget that morning in Woolworth's and enjoy your newly-established immunity from assault and battery.' He looked at her through narrowed eyes. 'You're still cross with me, aren't you?'

'I am, really, even though you did it for my benefit.'

'There are Dover sole in my refrigerator. If I find, by five-thirty, that you've forgiven me, I'll give you a pair of them.'

She smiled in spite of herself. 'You're impossible, Joe.' Changing the subject, she said, 'I've been thinking about the man whose tattoo you discovered.'

'Neuhaus, yes?'

'What is a man like that doing here, in England?'

'As it's the last place you'd expect to find a captain in the SS, I imagine he feels safe here. Many of them escaped after the war. They organised escape lines, "rat runs" – although they didn't call them that – that took them to Argentina, Paraguay, Egypt and other places that welcomed Nazis, but not all of them escaped. It seems that Bernhardt Neuhaus was one of those who missed the boat.'

———•◄———

Even out of uniform, Francis Collingham would have been immediately recognisable by his military bearing and immaculately-trimmed chevron moustache. His undiminished passion for seafood was evident, also, by the enthusiasm with which he tucked into the Portuguese sardines.

'Let's see if I've got this right,' he said. 'This chap from Jersey was arrested in nineteen forty-four and sent to prison in St Malo. At some time, his identity and property were misappropriated by a man identified as having served as an officer in the Waffen SS, and you want this man to face justice.'

'More correctly, the victim's family are out for revenge. In this case, "justice" is no more than a convenient euphemism. The principal is a man of action rather than words.'

'The two words are often and readily confused,' commented Francis. 'What's your stance? Are you the disinterested professional, or are you also keen to see this chap in the dock?'

Joe thought before answering. 'You know how I feel about the SS,' he said. 'Also, he was a *Partisanjäger*, which means it's pretty well certain that he's guilty of war crimes.'

Francis held up a cautionary finger. 'You don't know that, although I'll agree it's likely. What you do know, however, is that he stole the missing man's identity and property, and that comes under the jurisdiction of Jersey police.'

'With no witnesses to the crime, they're not interested, Francis.'

'Without witnesses, no police force would be interested, especially the Jersey police. They're a force in the making, and the process is gradual and, at times, faltering. Fortunately, crime is so infrequent that the island's population feels no sense of urgency.'

'But surely, someone must be interested in Neuhaus's record as a *Hauptsturmführer* in the SS.'

Francis shook his head. 'You are, Joe, but I doubt if anyone else is. The Nuremberg Trials have passed into the pages of history, and they left such an unpleasant after-taste that most people, including the British public, are happy to see the book closed. The only agency that's still hunting war criminals with unflagging zeal is the *Mossad*, as Israeli Intelligence now calls itself, and they'll only be interested if the man's victims were Jewish. In any case, relations between Britain and Israel still have some way to go before the word "cordial" finds its way into the Hebrew-English dictionary.'

'At this stage, we've no way of knowing that there were any Jewish victims.'

Their conversation had to wait until the waitress had removed their dishes.

'As he was a *Kopfjäger*,' said Joe when she'd gone, 'the likelihood is that his victims were predominantly French.'

'That's if he was based in France.'

'He was identified by a woman who'd been held by the Nazis in St Malo prison.'

Francis raised an eyebrow. 'Would she give evidence in court?'

'I'm afraid not. She doesn't want to be identified.'

'Bugger. But that's so often the case. The Reich is no more, but the fear remains, and as long as ardent Nazis are free to roam, it's likely to go on remaining.'

They paused as the main course arrived, and then thanked the waitress.

'Ah, turbot.' Francis was a happy man.

'Would the French be interested in his SS past?'

'In a sense, yes.'

Joe suspected another blind alley, and he asked heavily, 'What sense is that?'

Francis helped himself to vegetables before replying. 'For some time now,' he said, 'the French have been operating an unofficial and highly secret escape route for Waffen SS soldiers.'

'What?'

'It seems incredible, doesn't it, but I assure you it's true. As you know, the French are great pragmatists. If the end justifies the means, *tout est bien.*'

'And what end could possibly justify helping war criminals evade justice?'

As Francis tried the turbot, his ecstatic expression told Joe that he would have to wait for an answer to his question.

'In eighteen forty-eight,' said Francis when his taste buds allowed him to speak again, 'King Louis Philippe founded the Foreign Legion, partly to contain the large number of dissidents entering his country after a series of failed rebellions elsewhere in Europe, but also to create a force of expendable manpower. After all, why risk the lives of honest Frenchmen in policing an expanding empire, he reasoned, when foreigners could be made to do the work and face the dangers instead? Also, if they were killed, who would miss them?'

'Oddly enough, I knew that,' said Joe, controlling his impatience. 'My father was a whale on French history, and it's all quite fascinating, but where is this leading?'

'France is in almost the same predicament as she was then,' explained Francis. In this case, the government knows where the dissidents are. Quite conveniently, they're contained within the Chamber of Deputies and they're all members of the Communist Party. However, the problem of the colonies remains. In particular, the French are currently struggling to contain the Viet Minh, the communist terrorist organisation in Indo China, where casualties are more plentiful than manpower.'

Joe could now see where his friend's argument was leading. 'So they're feeding ex-Nazis into the Foreign Legion to fight the Viet Minh?'

'Exactly. How much more convenient could it be? In one foul scoop, they're ridding the country of undesirables and they're bolstering up their colonial forces with – and this is important – some of the best-trained soldiers in history. You have to admit that.'

'I've never denied it, Francis. The Waffen SS were superbly trained as soldiers. It's their moral code and ideology that trouble me.'

'I think we're agreed on that. You'll see now, though, why the French won't be in a hurry to put your man in the dock. If you could magic him into France and they were to bundle him off to Indo China, chances are, the Viet Minh might do the job for you, but don't expect any other kind of help from the French government.'

'And that leaves me....'

'Up the Mekong Delta without a paddle,' confirmed Francis. 'I'm afraid that unless you can find a witness to this man's civilian crimes, your case ends here.'

15

OCTOBER

Joe was not completely surprised when his written application to the Préfet d'Arrondissement de Bretagne in St Malo prompted the familiar response that such an investigation would require evidence, of which there appeared to be none. A door had been closed firmly in his face.

At home, however, he was heartened by the signs that Maggie had forgiven him for his intervention in her domestic affairs. He was relieved, also, that there had been no repetition of the violence, although relations at the Earnshaw household appeared to be no easier than before.

The following Friday, at one of their lunchtime meetings, Maggie seemed distracted, and when Joe asked her if all was well, she shrugged the matter off by saying, 'It could be worse.' Then, after some thought, she asked unexpectedly, 'Will you tell me one of your jokes?'

'Even though they don't make you laugh?'

'I told you before, Joe, they make me feel better.'

'All right.' He searched his memory. 'Here's one.'

Maggie sat back in her chair, smiling in anticipation.

'Imagine a rural setting, a village, where its inhabitants enjoy a simple way of life.'

'All your jokes take place deep in the countryside,' she observed.

'Almost, but not all of them.'

'I'm sorry. Carry on.'

'Very well. The villagers had been celebrating a marriage. The feast was over, the last of the strong cider had been consumed, the last embarrassingly salacious reference to the happy couple had been made, and the bride and groom had gone to their cottage together.

Imagine, then, the reaction of the bridegroom's father when his son came knocking at his door. I should add that it was about one o' clock in the morning.'

'I'm glad you cleared that one up, Joe.'

'It's important, because the knocking at the door came as a surprise to his father, who'd gone to bed and was fast asleep by that time. Anyway, stumbling down to the door with half-opened eyes, he asked, "Who is it?" The young man answered, "It's me, Father. Let me in." His father was mystified. He asked, "What are you doing back here, son? Away with you to your bride." His son entreated urgently, "Don't send me back to her, Father. Let me in." "Nonsense," said his father. "Your bride and the marital bed await you. Go back and perform your duty as a bridegroom should, and remember everything I've told you." His son answered, "I can't, Father. It's too awful for words." His father said, "Nonsense. You'll enjoy it once you get the hang of it." "Father," pleaded his son, "you don't understand. She's just told me she's a virgin." "A *virgin*?" The older man uttered the word in horror. "Yes, Father," confirmed his son, scarcely able to repeat himself, "a virgin." His father opened the door and said, "You should have told me earlier. Come inside, son. If she's not good enough for the other village lads, she's certainly not good enough for you." '

Maggie smiled appreciatively. 'That was so silly,' she said, 'it was just what I needed.'

'Lunch is what you need,' he said, unpacking his case.

'What are you going to spoil me with now?' Joe had told her the previous day not to bring lunch, and now, he opened a greaseproof parcel to reveal a water-crust pie. 'Game pie,' he announced.

'What kind of game?'

'Hare and pigeon. They're always in season.' He cut into the pie and deposited a generous piece on to a plate, which he handed to her.

'It smells wonderful. Thank you, Joe.' She shook her head in mock-disapproval. 'You really shouldn't.'

'Good food is best enjoyed in pleasant company, and I have the pleasure of yours, so why not?' He opened a jar of mixed pickles to complement the pie. Bread and real butter followed.

'Did you do the pickling yourself?'

'Of course. There's no one else to do it,' he reminded her.

'You keep springing surprises. Was it one of the things you learned in Italy?'

'*Certamente*. Pickling is important in Italian cooking. In fact, with their climate, it's essential.'

'I'm as impressed as ever, and this pie is lovely, Joe, but I can't imagine that my company is as pleasant as all that.'

'If it weren't, would I spend as much time with you as I do?'

'Maybe not, but I'm not carried away with my own company.'

'Possibly that's because you're so haunted by your problem that it leaves you no peace.'

'Possibly,' she agreed, smiling as a new idea came to her. 'Have you much planned for the weekend?'

'Only the usual household drudgery.'

'Will you be at home tomorrow afternoon?'

'I'm always at home to you, Maggie,' he assured her, twitching his eyebrows like a villain in a melodrama. 'What have you in mind? A weekend of shameless abandon?'

'No, I thought I'd bring you a cake.'

'That's even better. I'll look forward to it.'

———◗◖———

On Saturday lunchtime, Joe received a phone call.

'Joe, it's Maggie.' She sounded disappointed.

'What's the matter, Maggie?'

'I can't come this afternoon. I'll explain later, but I've made the cake. If I can't get it to you tomorrow, I'll bring it to the office on Monday.'

'Don't worry. There's no hurry, and it'll be something to look forward to.'

His suspicion that the cake was less important than the visit was confirmed when she said, 'I wanted to get away for an hour or so, but it's unlikely. I must get back. I said I was going out to post a letter. If I'm any longer, he'll want to know why.'

'Are you all right?'

'Yes, I'm fine. I must go. Goodbye.' She hung up the phone, in most respects a prisoner in her own home.

———————

He arrived at the office early on Monday morning. He had some pictures to process, and he wanted them to be dry and ready for an appointment that afternoon. He was hanging up the prints when Maggie arrived. The darkroom door was open, and she came in.

She asked, 'What are you doing?'

'I've just finished printing some pictures of male infidelity,' he told her. 'I'd prefer not to, but circumstances dictate.'

'This may sweeten the atmosphere,' she said. 'I've brought the cake.'

'Thank you, Maggie. As priceless gems go, you sparkle brighter than the rest.' Leaving the prints to give her his full attention, he said, 'Something's troubling you. Is it the usual?'

'Oh, it's nothing awful. He sprained his ankle at work on Friday, and he couldn't go to the pub, which made him bad tempered until I went shopping for him. I felt like a child who's been confined to the house for being naughty, and just when I wanted to call on you.'

'Any particular reason?'

'Just the usual. Do I sound terribly self-centred?'

'I'm not aware of it.' He opened his arms as a gesture, and she allowed him to hold her, looking up after a while to say, 'This isn't why I came in here.'

'Let's call it a nice afterthought. We could even make it a regular habit and have a daily cuddle. I'm game if you are, and it might do us both some good.'

With her face buried in his smock, she said, 'I could so easily. Don't tempt me.'

He placed a tiny but deliberate kiss on her cheek. 'That's for the cake,' he said, 'even though this kind of thing's not really what I had in mind when I came in this morning either.'

She nodded self-consciously and then said, 'I must go and deal with the post.'

'I'd be inclined to check your make-up first. If you'll forgive the observation, your lipstick's a little smudged.'

'Oh, yes.' She hurried off to the washroom to make the necessary repair while he tidied the darkroom.

———◆◄———

At 5:25, he looked in on Maggie, who was still hard at work. He asked, 'Would you like a lift?'

'Oh, please. I'll only be five minutes or so, and we do need to talk.'

'Okay, you know where I'll be.' He gathered his things together, said a quick 'Cheerio' to Guy, and went down to his car. The words '… we need to talk' had a portentous sound that he found unsettling, but all would be made clear. He was sure of that, Maggie being the direct and honest person she was.

He hadn't long to wait, because she arrived only a few minutes later, pushed the post into the pillar box and joined him, apologetic for the delay.

'I was in no hurry,' he assured her, starting the car.

'You put up with an awful lot, Joe.'

'Do I? I really hadn't noticed. Maybe you're confusing tolerance with basic good nature.'

'Maybe I am,' she agreed somewhat absently.

'Are you concerned about what happened in the darkroom this morning?' It seemed the likeliest possibility.

'You have the uncanny ability of putting your finger on the very thing that's troubling me.'

'It's not difficult,' he said, pulling into the line of traffic.

'The trouble is, my feelings are very confused, because they go rather deeper than the cosy moment we had this morning.'

He turned into Sandgate Road before speaking. 'I'm getting the impression,' he said, 'that you find it hard to explain.'

'To put into words, yes.'

'Does it help if I tell you that I'm taking absolutely nothing for granted, that I don't see our "cosy moment" – a good name for it, I have to say – as the precursor of a steamy love affair?'

'It does help,' she said quietly.

'Will you be all right if I drop you in Red Lion Square?'

'Don't go out of your way, Joe.'

'It's no great distance.' He drove past the turning for his cottage and continued through Sandgate and on to the coast road to Hythe. 'I shan't be at the office for a while,' he said, 'maybe not for a few days, anyway.'

'Where are you going?'

'To Lancashire, to begin with. I have to find a missing person last seen in Salford.'

'I hope it goes well.' She still sounded preoccupied.

Respecting her state of mind, he drove on in silence. Then, as they entered Hythe, he said, 'I'll tell you a quick one before I drop you.'

'It'll have to be very quick.'

'Okay. It's actually a riddle rather than a joke. What's the difference between a randy, four-foot Eskimo in the Arctic Circle, and a eunuch in a sultan's harem?'

'Go on, tell me.'

'One's a frigid midget with a rigid digit, and the other is a massive vassal with a passive tassel.' He pulled into the side of the road to let her out.

'Thank you,' she said, smiling for the first time that afternoon. 'I'll try to remember that one. Good luck with the missing person.'

'Thanks. Take care, and don't give the other matter a moment's thought.'

She made no reply, but smiled and got out.

It seemed to Joe that she would explain things when she was ready. In any case, it was evident that she was in some emotional turmoil, married to a man she feared and resented, but mindful of the responsibility that came with marriage. It was a horrible situation to be in, and his best plan was to leave her some space.

16

All the usual elements were there: the slamming of the front door, the footsteps on the stairs, the noisy cascade in the bathroom as he relieved himself, and then his menacing presence in the doorway. Even with her back to him, Maggie knew he was there, but she lay still, feigning sleep and bracing herself for the next stage in the sickening ritual.

With a sigh, he sat on the side of the bed to remove his shoes, a process that might have been carried out quietly, but that seemed beyond his powers, because each shoe hit the floor with a careless thud. The removal of his shirt, trousers and underclothes, too, was accompanied by a series of assorted grunts that culminated in the heaviest of sighs as he sank into bed. A beery belch followed, rather like a full stop.

Maggie lay still, breathing regularly, but hoping strenuously that he would simply fall asleep.

After a short time, he moved closer to her and turned on to his side. At this stage she knew her hopes had been futile, a realisation that was confirmed when he grasped her arm, most likely to wake her up. She'd heard of foreplay; some girls in the WAAF had often spoken about such things freely, but she was unable to recall any mention of arm-grasping, any more than she could call to mind the kneading of breasts. She found the latter painful, and it was almost a relief when he moved on to the hem of her nightdress. There was some variation at this stage; he would either burrow beneath the fabric to inflict further mammary discomfort, or he would take the shortcut and invade her most intimate place. He carried out both options with equal clumsiness, and neither gave her any pleasure.

His next move was to make room for himself by the expedient of thrusting one knee between hers, like a human crowbar, at the same time reaching into the bedside drawer for a contraceptive.

The next minute or so was crucial, as fate decided whether or not he would gain an erection, although the level of alcohol in his bloodstream was more likely the deciding factor.

On this occasion, as on many others, he was denied that facility, and he threw the contraceptive on to the bedside table in disgust before flinging himself down petulantly beside her.

'I'm sick of it,' he said, making it sound like an accusation.

'Don't shout at me, Derek. It's not my fault.'

'It *is* your fault I can't get a bloody hard-on! If you'd just make yourself a bit sexier, it would make all the difference. Instead, you behave as if it's just another bloody chore.'

Without realising it, he could be remarkably perceptive, but she kept that observation to herself as long as there was still a chance he might settle down and go to sleep. Once more, however, her hopes were not to be realised.

'I don't know what I ever saw in you,' he said. 'You're no fun and you certainly don't get me excited anymore.'

'It couldn't possibly have anything to do with the gallons of beer you put away.'

'Are you trying to say it's my fault?' He made it sound like the most ridiculous suggestion ever.

'All I'm saying is that you're a heavy drinker, and the two go together.'

He sat up to continue the argument. 'So you're saying I can't get a hard-on because I like an occasional drink?'

'No,' she said angrily, 'I'm not saying that you like an occasional drink, because it's not true. I'm saying that you prop up the bar every night from opening to closing. It's not surprising you can't manage it.'

'You bitch!'

The blow landed on her left cheek, leaving her temporarily stunned. For the moment, she could make no sense of what he was saying. All she wanted was to get away from him, and she wrenched the bedclothes back to make her escape.

'I'm sorry, Maggie,' he was saying urgently. 'I didn't mean to do that. Come back to bed and we'll talk things over.'

'Leave me alone, Derek. I don't want to talk, I need to sleep.'

'I'm sorry,' he kept saying. 'I didn't want to hurt you. It just happened before I knew what I was doing.'

'Talk to yourself,' she told him, 'You're more likely than I am to believe your lies.' She left him still protesting his regret while the neighbours banged on the party wall, because they, too, needed their sleep.

Downstairs, she lay on the sofa, hoping miserably that the bruise wouldn't be too obvious in the morning. Joe was away, but Mr Wilcox would be there. On top of everything else, the embarrassment would be too much to bear.

It was the first time Derek had ever said he was sorry for hitting her. That and the sudden change in mood made his remorse less than credible. It was much more likely that he was reminded of Joe's threat, and that was another worry. She couldn't face the possibility of Joe getting into trouble because of her. With those worries, it was some time before she eventually drifted into sleep.

———◆◄———

When Derek came down, she had been up for some time and was making his breakfast. She'd already looked in the mirror and seen to her dismay the monumental bruise on her cheek.

Derek also saw it, and it prompted another spate of remorse and self-recrimination.

'I can't think what made me do that to you,' he said.

'You should have worked it out by this time. You've done it often enough.'

'Never again, I promise.'

'For what that's worth,' she said, putting scrambled eggs and toast down for him.

He asked, 'Aren't you having any breakfast?'

'No, I'm not hungry.'

'Look,' he said, 'why don't you telephone your boss and tell him you're not well? Have some time off.'

'Because there's work waiting for me.' It occurred to her, quite inconsequentially, that it was possibly the longest conversation they'd had in years, and it was still meaningless.

'You're tired. You look jaded.'

'And you're afraid someone will see this bruise.'

'I'm just concerned about you, Maggie.'

'Since when? You weren't concerned about me last night when you told me you didn't know what you saw in me, that I didn't get you excited, and that it was my fault you couldn't function. You certainly didn't show any concern for me when you hit me.'

'I've told you, I don't know why I did that.'

'I think we've established that.'

'It'll never happen again, I promise.'

'Until next time. Take your promises to work, Derek. Maybe they'll be worth something there.'

'Just promise me you won't go into the office today. You really do need a rest.'

'I'll think about it.'

He picked up his flask and the Oxo tin that served as his lunchbox, seemingly surprised to find them waiting for him.

'I did that before you came down,' she told him.

'Thanks.' It was the first time he'd ever thanked her for doing it. 'Look after yourself, Maggie.'

'With you around, I have to.' She picked up his plate to take it to the sink.

'As I said, you need to take it easy.' He looked preoccupied as he let himself out, but Maggie knew his concern wasn't for her welfare.

At five minutes to nine, she walked along the road to the telephone kiosk by the light railway and called the office. Mr Wilcox answered promptly.

'Guy Wilcox, solicitor and commissioner for oaths.'

'Hello, Mr Wilcox. It's Maggie. I'm afraid I'm not at all well, and I can't come in this morning.'

'I'm sorry to hear that, Maggie. I hope it's nothing too serious.'

'I should be over it in a couple of days,' she assured him, thankful that he was sensitive enough never to enquire in any detail into a woman's frailties. It saved her having to compound the lie.

'Well, take care of yourself. I hope you'll soon feel better.'

'Thank you, Mr Wilcox.'

Her next job was to call at the fishmonger's. She would get something for dinner as well as ice for her bruise.

———————

She called the office again the next day.

'I'm sorry, Mr Wilcox,' she said, 'but I should be back tomorrow.' She imagined the bruising would be minimal by then.

'If you're absolutely sure, Maggie.'

'I'm sure, Mr Wilcox.'

'Well, you will be careful, won't you?'

'I shall.'

'By the way, Joe telephoned yesterday. I told him you were laid up with something, and he asked me to pass on his good wishes. He also hopes to be back tomorrow.'

'Thank you, Mr Wilcox.'

She ended the conversation, now uneasier than before. Joe knew as well as Mr Wilcox that she'd never had time off work due to illness. She just hoped he wouldn't be suspicious.

———————

Derek was late. It was almost eleven, and closing time was ten-thirty. Maggie was perturbed, simply because it had never happened before. Derek was a creature of habit and therefore, by definition, tediously predictable.

The clock was showing ten minutes past eleven when the outer door opened, followed by the inner, and Derek stumbled helplessly into the room. His clothes were dirty and dishevelled, and congealed blood from his nose and mouth told its own story. He fell into his armchair, gasping.

'Derek,' said Maggie, soaking a cloth in water from the sink, 'what happened?'

Cut and bruised lips made speech difficult, and he was incoherent at first. 'Bastard,' she thought he said, 'that… bastard.'

'Tell me what happened to you.'

He whimpered when she touched his damaged lip.

'I'm sorry. I'm just trying to clean you up.'

He regained the power of speech sufficiently to say, 'That... thug... works for... your boss. He's... what happened, and I'm... going to see... him behind bars.'

She continued to wash the blood from his face, all the time nursing the leaden weight in the pit of her stomach caused by her concern for Joe. He'd evidently kept his word, and now he would have to pay the penalty.

In the morning, Maggie went to work, leaving Derek to feel sorry for himself. She would telephone his employer from the office, saying simply that he'd suffered a misfortune that had rendered him unfit for work. It would be up to him to furnish the details. She had no intention of lying on his behalf.

She was opening the post when Mr Wilcox arrived. Typically, he was quick to check that she was fully recovered.

'Yes, thank you, Mr Wilcox. I'm sorry I had to let you down.'

'You didn't let me down at all, Maggie, but I'm glad you're back.' He looked at her as if he were trying not to look as if he'd seen the disappearing bruise. He was a hopeless actor, embarrassingly so, but that wasn't the end of it, because she still had to face Joe.

She had almost finished dealing with the mail, when Mr Wilcox put his head around the door to say, 'Joe won't be in until late this afternoon. I just thought I'd let you know.'

'Thank you, Mr Wilcox.' She wondered what on earth Joe was up to, that he couldn't come straight to the office. There was nothing in his diary after the Manchester case. Could it be, she wondered, that Derek had fought back, and that Joe was injured, however temporarily? She dismissed the thought as unlikely, Joe being a different proposition from a helpless woman.

Shortly after lunch, the telephone in Joe's office rang, and Maggie went through to answer it.

'Pelier Inquiry Agency. How can I help you?'

'Hello,' said the voice, 'is Mr Pelier there?'

'I'm afraid we're not expecting him until later this afternoon. Can I take a message?'

'Yes, please. When he comes in, will you ask him, please, to telephone Inspector Godden at Hythe Police Station?'

'Of course.' With the familiar, sickening feeling in the pit of her stomach, Maggie wrote down the number and made a note of the officer's name. 'I'll do that. Thank you for calling. Goodbye.'

The likelihood was that Mr Wilcox would be the first to see Joe, so she tapped on his door with the note in her hand.

'Come in.'

'I'm sorry to disturb you, Mr Wilcox, but I thought I'd better give you this in case you see Joe before I do.'

'What is it, Maggie? You look as if you've seen a ghost.'

'I'm all right, Mr Wilcox,' she said, handing him the note. 'Inspector Godden wants Joe to phone him when he comes in.'

'Oh, is that all? He and Joe are old acquaintances. I imagine it'll be about some procedural matter.'

'Thank you, Mr Wilcox.' Maggie had an idea of what procedure the police had in mind, and the thought continued to torment her.

'Maggie?'

'Yes, Mr Wilcox?'

'Has the teapot gone on strike?'

Maggie looked at her watch. It was well past their normal tea time. 'I'm sorry, Mr Wilcox. I'll see to it now.'

'That's all right. Look, are you sure you're fully recovered? You don't look at all well.'

'I'm absolutely fine, Mr Wilcox. I'll bring your tea in when it's made.'

She made tea and took it into her employer's office with two precious ginger biscuits on a plate.

'Oh, thank you, Maggie. You can relax now. I've finished bullying you.'

'I'd never accuse you of that, Mr Wilcox.' Mention of bullying made her almost tearful, but she controlled it and braced herself to carry on with her work.

It was after four-thirty when the outer door opened, and then Maggie heard voices in Mr Wilcox's office. One of them was Joe's, but she couldn't hear what they were saying. Ordinarily, she wouldn't have considered eavesdropping, but nothing about the past three days had been at all ordinary.

Presently, her door opened and Joe looked in.

'Hello, Maggie. How's tricks?'

She heard herself say, 'Fine. How was your case?'

'Very successful. I'll tell you about it later, but I must go. Apparently, the police want me to help them with their enquiries.'

17

Joe had still not returned by the time Maggie left the office, so she could only fear the worst.

The house was also empty when she arrived, but that wasn't unusual, except that Derek hadn't been to work. She began preparing dinner, expecting him to turn up sooner or later.

He arrived about half-an-hour later, and it was clear from his deliberate and forceful movements as he entered the house that he was in a foul temper.

'Hello,' said Maggie. 'Did you go to the police?' She already knew the answer, but it seemed only civil to ask him. One of them, at least, might as well be civilised.

'I've just come from there.' He sat down heavily at the table.

'Would you like a cup of tea before dinner?'

He made no reply, but simply nodded in his boorish way.

'All right, I'll get you one.' She couldn't help comparing his response with that of Mr Wilcox that afternoon. Even so, she had to ask, 'Were the police helpful?'

'No, they bloody-well weren't. They were as much use as a rubber tent peg.'

'Oh dear.' She poured tea, wondering if there might yet be hope for Joe. 'What happened?'

'I don't want to talk about it.'

Clearly, he was in one of his spoilt child moods, so she didn't pursue the subject.

Dinner was taken in brooding silence, after which he announced abruptly that he was going out.

'It's probably a good idea,' she said. 'You'll feel better for it. You usually do.'

Unable or disinclined to respond, he left the house, slamming the outer door behind him.

She read until ten o' clock, and then went up to bed. She was tired after the tension of the day and was genuinely asleep when Derek returned, stirring only briefly at the noises of his homecoming. Then, as he seemed settled, she relaxed again and allowed herself to drift off to sleep.

———▸◂———

The following morning, he made no mention of his business at the police station, but ate the breakfast she prepared for him, picked up his lunchbox and flask, and left for work with only a brief word in parting.

As usual, Maggie was the first to arrive at the office. She greeted Mr Wilcox when he appeared, and opened the mail, looking out all the time, and with mounting apprehension, for Joe.

She'd just made coffee when he arrived, and he came to her office. He was in his usual sunny mood.

''Morning, Maggie. Everything okay?'

'Joe,' she said, unable to contain her fear any longer, 'what's been happening?'

'Ah, you're referring, not doubt, to the appointment with my old acquaintance Inspector Godden at Hythe Police Station.' He looked around her office and asked, 'Does the occasion warrant a biscuit or two? I believe we have some hidden away somewhere.'

'Of course.' She put some ginger biscuits on a plate, illogically keeping the left side of her face and its bruise away from him. He obviously knew what had happened to her, but she had no wish to draw his attention to the evidence.

'I imagine your beloved will have told you the story, but I'll fill in what details I can.'

'All he told me when he came home after the incident was that you were responsible, and that he was determined to see that you were locked up for it.'

Joe chuckled good-naturedly. 'He was the one who came close to being locked up.'

'I don't understand.'

'Okay. He told the police I'd beaten him up as he left whichever pub he'd frequented, so they naturally asked me to account for my actions on Wednesday night. It wasn't difficult, and I was able to present them with a fifty carat alibi, because, at the time I was alleged to have given your husband his just deserts, I was with a certain chief inspector at Manchester Central Police Station, having assisted in the apprehension of a pimp.' He smiled at her confusion. 'It was so late that I decided to stay overnight again and catch the first morning train. That's why I didn't arrive here until yesterday afternoon.'

Relieved but puzzled, she pushed the plate of biscuits towards him and asked, 'If you didn't do it, who did?'

'That's what I'm waiting to find out.' Then, as another thought occurred to him, he said, 'By the way, did he tell you how he came close to being arrested?'

'No, you mentioned it earlier, but he refused to say what happened at the police station.'

'I'm not surprised. Having named me as "the thug who does Guy Wilcox's thick-ear work", a description that caused dear old Sam Godden some merriment, and identified me as his assailant, he had it pointed out to him that a false accusation, and particularly a malicious one, was a serious matter, whereupon he got quite shirty and had to be restrained. In the end, I persuaded them not to charge him as long as he apologised to me.' He smiled at the memory. 'The words almost stuck in his throat,' he said, 'but he apologised, and they let him off with a caution.'

It was Maggie's turn to smile, and for the first time in several days. 'I was worried to death for your sake,' she confided.

'You needn't have given it a thought. Whoever gave him that beating did a thorough job, I have to say, but I wouldn't have left a mark on him, as I believe I once told you.'

Now keen to change the subject, she asked, 'How did the case in Manchester go?'

'Very well indeed, but I warn you, it's not nice.'

'I'll be brave.'

'Okay. The missing person was a girl who'd left home after a row with her parents and gone to several addresses before ending up in Salford. There, she was offered lucrative work in Manchester, which she accepted, never realising what she was letting herself in for. So, for the past year and a bit, she's been working the back streets of the city, constantly in fear of the pimp who'd taken her there and who was never far away. When I found her, she was covered in bruises, not all of them inflicted by clients, I have to say.' He looked more closely at Maggie's left cheek and said, 'I see you've been given the treatment as well.'

'Don't do anything, Joe,' she pleaded. 'Not after all that's happened.'

He shrugged. 'There's no need for me to do anything. Someone else did it for me.'

'Yes, let's leave it at that.'

'Okay, I'll be generous.'

With that worry out of the way, she returned to the story and asked, 'What happened then?'

'I persuaded her that her troubles would soon be over and left her safely in a room at the hotel where I was staying. It went down on expenses, of course. Then, very conveniently, the wretched man came looking for her and we had a brief exchange of views before I escorted him to the police station and handed him over to the Manchester and Salford Constabulary.' He finished his coffee and smiled. 'I arranged the emotional reunion of daughter and parents for yesterday afternoon, shortly before I was summoned to Hythe Police Station.' He appeared to reflect on that, and said, 'You could say it's been a progression from one police station to the next.'

Confusion took over briefly from concern, causing Maggie to ask, 'Is a pimp someone who makes a business out of prostitution?'

'Living on their earnings, yes. Mankind doesn't stoop much lower than that. I'd even be inclined to put pimps on the same despicable level as drug dealers.'

'I agree, but how did you persuade him to go with you to the police station?'

'I bounced him off a wall a few times, just until he began to see things from my perspective. It's something the police are not allowed to do, so I did it for them.' He added, 'If that sounds harsh, I have to say that, compared with the treatment he'd been giving the girls under his control, it was no more than a slap on the wrist.'

'I see.' It was a distant response, because her thoughts had returned to the business with Derek. 'I still feel awful,' she said, 'when I think about Derek's false accusation, and the fact that it was all because of me in the first place.'

'You're a good cause, Maggie. Let it rest.'

'I'm glad you're all right.' It was a gross understatement, but she was afraid to say more.

He said, 'You still have something on your mind. I can tell.'

She thought quickly. 'Will you tell me one of your jokes?'

'Okay, you look as if you need one. Let me think. Oh, yes, there was the man who'd just got his new pair of bifocal glasses. Have you heard it?'

'I don't see how I can have heard it. The only jokes I ever hear are the ones you tell me.'

'Okay. He called at the optician's and collected his new bifocals. The optician advised him to proceed with care at first. "You'll see two images of everything," he told him, "a big one and a small one. Remember that and be careful." Well, the man looked at his watch as he came out of the optician's doorway, and he saw two watches, a big one and a small one. The small one said it was almost mid-day, and the big one said the same, but more convincingly, so he decided not to go straight back to the office, but to call at the golf club for lunch. Anyway, when he arrived, he saw that the only other person in the bar was the club professional, so they had a drink together. The professional said, "I don't think I've seen you in here at this time, have I?" The man explained that he'd just picked up his new glasses and that he was rather pleased with them. The professional suggested that he tried them out by playing a round of golf before lunch, so off they went. The member tee-ed off first, incredibly with a hole-in-one. Then the professional did it in three. The member tee-ed off again and achieved another hole-in-one.'

'Surely not.'

'It's only a story, Maggie. Bear with me.'

'I'm sorry.'

'Shaking his head in wonder, the professional could only do it in four shots. The member tee-ed off again, achieving a third, incredible hole-in-one, and – please don't interrupt me – the professional simply couldn't believe it. "It's these bifocal glasses," the member explained. "I see two of everything, a big one and a small one." "Okay," said the professional, "but how does that help you?" "When I look down," said the member, "I see a big club and a small one, a big ball and a small one. I look towards the hole and I see two flags—" "I know," said the professional wearily, "a big one and a small one." "That's right," said the member. "I hit the big ball with the big club, aiming at the big flag, and hey presto, in goes the ball." "Well," said the professional, "I'm conceding this round. Let's go back and have a drink." In fact, they had several, after which the professional said, "In all my years in the game, I've never known anything like it." They had a drink on that, and then another, and then the professional said, "Look here, do you mind if I try those bifocals?" "Not at all," said the member, handing over his glasses. He was rather proud of them, you see. Well, the professional tried them on. "They feel a bit strange," he said. "Anyway, I'm going to the little boys' room. I'll see you in a minute." Off he went, and a few minutes later, he returned, walking stiff-legged because his trousers were soaked through. The member asked, "What on earth happened to you?" The professional said, "It's these blooming bifocals of yours. You know how you see two of everything?" "Yes," said the member, "a big one and a small one." "That's right," said the professional. "I looked down at my thingy, and I saw two of them, a big one and a small one. Well, I knew the big one wasn't mine, so I put it back." '

For only the second time, Maggie laughed at one of Joe's jokes. 'It was just what I needed,' she said.

'Good,' he said, standing up and peering at her bruise. 'That thing is just crying out for a spot of the SSM Tompkins cure,' he said.

'What's... oh, the sergeant-major,' she said, remembering.

'It's the only chance of recovery it's got,' he assured her grimly, leaning forward to administer the vital therapy. 'There,' he said, 'it'll heal in no time at all now.'

———•◄•———

Joe closed his newspaper and laid it on his desk. The result of the nineteen fifty-one General Election was now known. Britain had, once again, a familiar Prime Minister and would soon have a new government with a huge task ahead of it. It was just a shame they couldn't call on Sergeant-Major Tompkins to kiss everything better.

———◦⊲◦———

Later that morning, there was a call for Joe from Hythe Police Station. Maggie saw him pick up the receiver, and he sounded amused from the start.

After a minute, he grinned and said cheerfully, 'Good for him! Thank you, Inspector. That's a fitting end to the story. I trust our Polish friend's moved on now, and he won't have to face charges? Good. Thanks again.'

When he put the phone down, Maggie asked, 'What was that about?'

'Apparently, your hubby got into conversation with one of the itinerant Polish workers who were passing through. It seems the subject of Italy came up, and he called the Pole a "D Day dodger". As things turned out, it wasn't such a good idea, because the Polish chap collared him outside the pub as he left, and struck a blow or several for the Polish Brigade, who, for what it's worth, never dodged anything. They even took Monte Cassino after the rest of us had tried and failed.'

'Well, I don't approve of all this violence, but it was no worse than he deserved.'

'Why did he hit you this time, Maggie?'

'The usual, just a difference of opinion.' She didn't want to recall the incident, let alone discuss it.

———◦⊲◦———

Joe's next call came from Jonathan Allard, and it was no surprise to Joe that his principal was in an impatient mood.

'Where have you been, Mr Pelier?'

'Good morning, Mr Allard. I recognise your voice, of course. How are you?'

'I'm waiting for results, of which there has been no sign for some considerable time. What have you got to say for yourself?'

'We've had this conversation before, Mr Allard. Fred Maçon is trying very hard to find anyone who was held in St Malo prison at the time Thomas was there, and it's extremely difficult for the reasons I explained earlier.'

'Mr Pelier, I'm paying you good money to act for me, and I don't think it's too much for me to expect a little action.'

Joe breathed a reticent sigh. 'You're only paying me when I'm actually working on the case, Mr Allard.'

'Exactly, but you're not working on it.'

'There's nothing I can do without witnesses. I could go to St Malo and ask lots of questions and be none the wiser, simply because so many former victims of the Nazis are still terrified of reprisal.'

'In that case, damn' well go to St Malo and find some that have a degree of backbone. Surely, it's not too much to ask.'

Joe contained his anger and said, 'If you would prefer to hand the case back to Nicholas Rainsley, that, of course, is your prerogative—'

'Of course I don't want to do that. The man's an imbecile.'

'Then let me do it my way.'

'All right, just as long as you're doing something.'

Such exchanges were generally unhelpful, although Joe came off the telephone with the germ of an idea. He'd been waiting for Fred to make contact with former prisoners, and that was sensible enough, but he'd never considered those who had been working in the prison at the time, the French prison staff. In the former unoccupied zone, they would have been of no help whatsoever, but St Malo was occupied by the Nazis, and there must have been some anti-Nazi feeling among the warders. It was certainly worth looking into.

———◆◆———

He called in on Maggie at the end of the day to ask, 'Can I offer you a lift and a cup of tea on your way home?'

'You know,' she said, 'I think that would be more than acceptable. In fact, I'm so relieved that you're no longer implicated in recent events, I think it would be lovely. Thank you.'

'You don't need a reason, Maggie, but I'm gratified by your concern. It's been quite some time since I enjoyed that luxury.'

'It shouldn't be a luxury,' she said, picking up the post and securing it with a large rubber band. 'Everyone should have someone to care about them.'

'In an ideal world, they would,' he agreed, 'and for what it's worth, I care about you.' He demonstrated the fact by giving her waist a gentle squeeze.

'I know.'

They left the office, Maggie dropped the post into the pillar box, and they got into the car.

'You always bring back the rubber band,' he observed.

'They're so difficult to find, I have to.'

'President Trumann has a lot to answer for.' He pulled out into Bouverie Road West, noting that traffic was heavier than usual. 'All those cars that were laid up during petrol rationing seem to have been recalled to life,' he said.

'That has a ring to it.'

' "Recalled to life"? It's from *A Tale of Two Cities*.'

'Do you like Dickens?'

'Yes, very much. Do you?'

'Yes, I do.'

'There must be lots of things we have in common.'

'I expect so.'

'We should explore that some time,' he said, turning into Sandgate Road.

'You're quite a tonic, Joe.'

'If you say so.' He drove down the hill and took the turning for his cottage.

'This is a beautiful situation,' said Maggie.

'Close to perfection,' he agreed, stopping the car and opening the door for her. 'You know, you could move in if you wanted to. I mean, cast Derek aside for the bullying wretch he is, and then come to live the idyllic life here with me.'

'You say the daftest things, Joe, and if it weren't such a daft idea, it would be tempting.'

'Okay, let's have a cup of tea instead.' He went through to the kitchen and lit the gas under the kettle.

'On the night he hit me,' she said, 'I came closer than I ever have to demanding a divorce.'

'Who could blame you?' He motioned towards the sofa and chair, and said, 'Take a seat. It won't be long.'

'I just couldn't do that to Mr Wilcox,' she said, sitting in the armchair. 'I'd have to take a job somewhere else before I could do so much as consider it.'

'That would be a shame. Have you thought of discussing it with Guy? He's a reasonable man.'

'Yes, he is. I suppose it may come to that in the end.'

'Okay, it's a decision for you and no one else. I shan't try to influence you, even though I hate to see you treated the way you are.'

Changing the subject to a safer one, Maggie looked round the room and said, 'I know we mentioned *A Tale of Two Cities* earlier. Have you a copy I could borrow? I haven't read it since I was at school.'

'Yes, I'll just wet the tea and then I'll get it for you.'

He emerged from the kitchen with a tray of tea things, which he set down on the dining table before going to the bookcase, where he found the copy she wanted. 'Here,' he said, 'there's no hurry, so take your time over reading it.'

'Thank you. That's very kind of you.' She opened the book and found the first page of the novel. ' "It was the best of times, it was the worst of times",' she read. 'How glaringly appropriate.'

'These age-old works of literature can still have surprising relevance today,' he said, 'basically, I suppose, because no human problem is new. They've all been experienced many times.' He gave her a cup of tea while she thought about it. 'I'll probably go to St Malo soon,' he said, sitting down with his tea.

'What for?'

'To see if I can find someone who remembers the last year of the war. In particular, I need to find someone who's not constantly looking over his or her shoulder for vengeful Nazis.'

'Are they still around?' She sounded surprised.

'Apparently. There are devotees of the Führer who've never given up on world domination, even now he's no longer around to inspire them.'

'Their loyalty and dedication are remarkable, even though the whole thing is too awful for words.'

'That's how they think of it, Maggie. They see it as loyalty and dedication.' He nodded grimly. 'That's what I'm up against.'

18

NOVEMBER

With the unflagging help of Fred Maçon, Joe was now in communication with a retired *gardien de prison*, who had served at St Malo throughout the war. He insisted on writing to Joe in English, even though Fred had explained to him that Joe spoke French.

Dear Mr Pelier,

I comprehend that you seek assistance from prison workers who have working at St Malo Prison. I am voluntary in your request, but I prefer not to state facts in writing at this time. Instead, I am content to speak with you. I may be possible to giving names of others who may help also.

Can you unite with me for a discussion at 2000 hours on Tuesday, 20 November? I suggest at Le Chat Souriant in the Rue des Corsaires. Please say if you agree.

Sincere regards,

Jean-Claud Pavard.

Joe had Maggie type his reply in French, adding accents himself where necessary and by hand.

'I'll suggest to him, when we meet, that we speak French. It'll make the job easier,' he said a few days later, before he left for St Malo.

'It must be wonderful to be able to converse in another language.'

'It's all I've ever known, so it feels quite normal to me.' Remembering an earlier conversation, he said, 'At the time of the Ardeatine investigation, I was told that the army could have made use of my languages much earlier if I'd not been so reticent about them. They seemed to think it was my fault.'

'Was it?'

'No, I wasn't. They never asked me, so I never told them.' As an afterthought, he confided, 'If I'd had a desk job, I'd have been bored mindless for most of the war.'

'And you'd never have met Sergeant-Major... what was his name?'

'Tompkins. That's true, and then I'd never have had a clue about kissing things better.'

'And you do it so expertly,' she said, layering up sheets of typing and carbon paper, 'but you must leave me to get on with my work before Mr Wilcox gets impatient.'

'Okay. I just thought I'd look in before I leave.'

'*Bon voyage*, Joe.'

'*Merci bien*, Maggie.' He came round her desk to place a chaste, farewell kiss on her cheek. '*À bientôt, ma chère amie.*'

He left her office with a final wave, stopped for a few words with Guy, and then went down to his car.

———▸◂———

The journey to Southampton was long but uneventful, and he was able to reach the docks in good time and claim his berth aboard the company's newest steamer *Falaise*. He'd reserved the cabin, determined not to suffer a repeat of his previous crossing, and he was prepared to argue the case with Allard when he presented his expenses.

When the steward roused him the next morning from a deep and satisfying sleep, he resolved always to take a cabin in future. His experience was heightened by an excellent breakfast, and he was reminded that British Railways, the owners of the *Falaise*, were able to procure food from France as well as from Britain. The French had suffered appalling shortages during and after the war, but food rationing had finally ceased in 1949, and the population were now enjoying a greatly-improved quality of life.

He stepped off the ship and made his way to the car hire terminus, having previously arranged the hire of a Renault 4CV. With the possibility of meeting additional contacts, he had bought a three-day return ticket for the ferry. Also, rather than reserve a room in one of St Malo's hotels, he had chosen one he remembered from before the war, the Hôtel des Bains in Paramé, a small, coastal town two or three miles away.

He made the short journey and checked in at the eighteenth century inn, where he found the reception desk manned by a middle-aged woman, who sat surrounded by picture postcards and souvenirs of various kinds.

'*Bon jour,* madame. *Je m'appelle* Joseph Pelier *d'*Angleterre, *et J'ai réservé une chambre individuelle.*'

The woman's eyes opened wide and, after more than a dozen years, she and Joe recognised each other.

'Monsieur Pelier!'

'Madame Gilbert!'

For the time being, checking in was forgotten. Joe and his family had been regular visitors to Paramé before the war, and much had happened to them both in the intervening years. Madame Gilbert was distressed to hear of the elder Monsieur Pelier's death, and Joe was similarly sympathetic about the demise of her parents. Not surprisingly, the war had been devastating for the Breton family; Nazi troops were billeted at the hotel, which they treated with loutish disdain, and the locals, who had witnessed the sacrilege, bore a vicarious grudge in addition to several of their own. The news that Joe was on the trail of a suspected war criminal won Madame Gilbert's enthusiastic approval.

Eventually, she showed him to his room and left him to unpack. His appointment with M. Pavard wasn't until that evening, and he wanted to spend some time in the town, simply enjoying his old haunt again and reliving some of his pre-war holidays. Before that, however, he chose a picture postcard to send to his sister Marianne, who would also have fond recollections of Brittany. Then, having done that, he wrote another, this time for Maggie, and addressed it to her at the office.

Le Chat Souriant was the kind of bar that tour operators had begun to describe as 'a place of character' It gave the impression that it dated from the eighteenth, or even seventeenth, century, when the Rue des Corsaires was frequented by the privateers from whom it took its name. The higgledy-piggledy arrangement of beams looked alarmingly unsafe; even the floor was uneven, but the place had nevertheless remained standing for more than two hundred years. In such a crazy environment, it was little wonder the cat was smiling.

Jean-Claud Pavard was not smiling; in fact, he gave the impression that he took life seriously. He was also extremely fond of the anise-flavoured spirit the French called *pastis*. Joe preferred wine, but settled, on this occasion, for bottled beer.

'All prisoners are scum,' opined M. Pavard in French, having agreed to Joe's suggestion that, in the circumstances, French made more sense than English. 'Scum,' he repeated. 'That is why they are under lock and key.' He paused, in case Joe found his reasoning difficult to follow. When Joe nodded, he continued. 'They, on the one hand, are scum,' he reiterated, earning an irritated glance from two men drinking at a nearby table, 'but the Boche were inhuman bastards, and that is why I am prepared to help you if I can.' He peered without expression between dense eyebrows and untrimmed whiskers.

'That's very obliging of you, Monsieur Pavard,' said Joe. 'My enquiry concerns a Jerseyman called Thomas Allard. He was held in St Malo Prison from June nineteen forty-four. You may remember him particularly because he had a club foot.'

Pavard looked down into his glass. 'Club foot,' he repeated, as if something in the bottom of his glass might prompt his memory.

'Let me get you another drink.' Joe held up his hand for the barman. '*Pastis, s'il vous plaît.*'

The barman nodded and pointed questioningly at Joe's glass.

'*Merci, non.*' He had to drive back to the hotel at some stage.

The second glass of *pastis* seemed to jog Pavard's memory. 'He was an idiot,' he said matter-of-factly.

'He wasn't very intelligent,' agreed Joe.

'The other prisoners protected him,' said Pavard, as if it were the most ridiculous thing he'd ever known.

'Do you know what happened to him?'

Pavard appeared to search his memory. 'The idiot with the club foot?'

'That's right. Do you know what happened to him? That's what I'm trying to find out.'

Pavard shook his head. 'No,' he said. 'I can't remember.'

Joe had feared as much. He tried another approach. 'Do you remember Hauptsturmführer Neuhaus of the Waffen SS?'

It was as if a light had suddenly been turned on. 'Neuhaus? The devil incarnate. That's what he was.'

'What happened to Neuhaus?'

'He escaped when the Americans came.'

'How did he escape?'

Pavard emptied his glass, and Joe summoned the barman again.

'Monsieur?'

'Pastis and a beer, please.'

'You ask me how he escaped. It was a long time ago.'

'Six years,' said Joe. 'That's all. Try to remember how Neuhaus managed to evade the Americans.'

The barman arrived with their drinks, causing a temporary distraction. Eventually, Pavard said, 'They found remnants of Neuhaus's uniform in the incinerator.'

'So he changed his clothes. What happened then?'

'It was a long time ago. Much has happened.'

Joe was wondering if Pavard had been a drunkard when he was a warder, and then the Frenchman spoke again.

'The idiot with the club foot,' he said.

'What about him?'

'They took him away.'

'Who did? The Americans?'

'No.' Pavard eyed him impatiently. 'The Boche took him away with the other cripples and the idiots.'

'Where did they take him?'

'To a camp somewhere. I don't know.' He stared into his pastis for a while, until Joe suspected he'd fallen asleep. Then he said, 'Have you paper and a pencil?'

Joe took his notebook and pencil from his pocket and handed them to him, wondering what drunken nonsense he had in mind. The man was writing something, though, and it seemed to be a name and an address.

'There,' said Pavard. 'You can find out his telephone number from that.'
'Who is he?'
'Henri Forgeron. He also worked at St Malo Prison.'
'Do you think he may be able to remember something?'
Pavard seemed about to fall asleep, and then he said, 'Try him. He may know something.'
'Thank you, Monsieur Pavard.' Joe wrote the number of the hotel on a page of his notebook and tore it off. 'This is my telephone number. I'm staying at the Hôtel des Bains in Paramé. Please call me if you remember anything else about either Thomas Allard or Hauptsturmführer Neuhaus.'
When he left the bar, Pavard was gazing at nothing in particular. The situation was far from promising.

———————

Joe left it until the next day before trying the phone number Pavard had given him. He was unsuccessful at first, but he tried an hour later and M. Forgeron answered.
'Monsieur Forgeron,' said Joe, 'my name is Joseph Pelier. I am a detective from England, and Jean-Claud Pavard said you might be able to help me with an enquiry about a man who was imprisoned in St Malo in nineteen forty-four.'
'It is possible. What is the name of the prisoner?'
'Thomas Allard. He was a Jerseyman. He had a club foot and was of limited mental capacity.'
There was a lengthy pause, and then M. Forgeron said, 'I believe I can recall the man you describe, Monsieur Pelier, but I think it would be better to discuss the matter face-to-face. Where are you staying?'
'At the Hôtel des Bains in Paramé.'
'Good, I live in Paramé.'
'Would you care to join me for a drink at the hotel?'
'Most certainly. I have things of importance to do today, but I could meet you this evening. Shall we say at twenty hours?'
'Excellent.' Eight o' clock seemed to be a popular time for meetings. 'I look forward to seeing you then, monsieur. *Au revoir.*'

'*Au revoir,* monsieur.'

The conversation was promising, if only because, unlike Pavard, Forgeron sounded sober and articulate. Joe had to return to England the next day, so he needed a positive result, and he knew that Pavard was unreliable. Any defence counsel worthy of the description would tear his drunken, rambling testimony to shreds.

———◆◄———

Henri Forgeron was different altogether from Pavard, both physically and in his manner, which was polite without being deferential. He wore a well-trimmed, natural moustache and a brown, double-breasted suit.

Joe asked him, 'What would you care to drink, Monsieur Forgeron?'

Forgeron eyed the half-full bottle on Joe's table and said, 'The rough red would be very welcome.'

'I'll get you a glass.' Joe held up his hand to attract the waitress.

'You're a Frenchman,' commented Forgeron, 'but you say you live in England.'

'I'm half-French.' He broke off to ask the waitress for another glass for his guest. 'I grew up in England and served with the British army during the war. England feels like my natural home, although I still love to visit France.'

'Your accent is of the Ardennes, I believe.'

'You're very perceptive, monsieur. My father was from Sedan.'

'Thank you.' Forgeron accepted the glass of wine that Joe poured for him. 'Monsieur Pelier,' he asked, 'what is your interest in the prisoner you mentioned?'

'The family of Thomas Allard, the Jerseyman in question, have engaged me to detect his whereabouts, although the likelihood is that he is no longer alive.'

'The likelihood is stronger than you may think, monsieur. I remember him, chiefly because of his mental slowness, but also because of his pronounced limp.' He allowed his features to relax into a half-smile and said, 'I imagine you found Pavard unsympathetic towards Allard and, in fact, prisoners in general.'

'That's an accurate assessment of his attitude.'

Forgeron laughed briefly. 'I was a senior guardian,' he said. 'It was the next rank above that of Pavard and one that he never attained, largely because of the drunkenness that made him too sour towards his fellow men for his own good.'

'He was very scathing about Allard,' said Joe, attempting to bring the conversation back to his quest.

'Yes, I can imagine that.' Forgeron finished the wine in his glass and asked, 'What did he tell you about Allard.'

'Simply that he and other prisoners were taken away because of their physical and mental problems.' He caught the waitress's eye and asked her for another bottle of wine.

'That is correct. The prison received a visit, the latest of many from an officer in the SS. His name was Hauptsturmführer Bernhardt Neuhaus.'

Joe nodded, prompting a response from Forgeron.

'You have heard of this man?'

'Not only that. I traced him to an address in Essex, and I have seen him there. I have also a photograph of him that shows the Waffen SS blood group tattooed on his arm.'

Forgeron looked impressed. 'You sound knowledgeable about the SS, Monsieur Pelier.'

'I should be. I spent a great deal of time after the war, investigating them. Please tell me about Neuhaus's visit, monsieur.'

'By all means. He was a *Partisanjäger*, as you probably know. He was responsible for the arrest and interrogation of Resistance workers and, on this occasion, he was questioning a prisoner, when the noise from a nearby cell distracted him. He demanded to know what was happening, and when I told him that the prisoners were mental defectives, he ordered their removal. I am happy, if that is the word, to say that such deportations were carried out by the SS and not by prison staff.' He drank slowly, remembering. Eventually, he said, 'This was in the summer of nineteen forty-four, you understand, and the Allied forces were approaching. It was important to the Nazis that no evidence of war crimes should fall into their hands, and so, from Neuhaus's point of view, it made sense to evacuate tell-tale prisoners, which included Resistance suspects and so-called "mercy-killing" cases, to the concentration camps.'

'Do you know where he sent Thomas Allard?'

'As far as I know, they were all taken to Sachsenhausen.'

Even in the welcoming ambience of the Hôtel des Bains, Joe experienced the familiar chill he'd first encountered in Italy after Ardeatine. With an effort, he asked, 'Do you know what happened to Neuhaus?'

'Only by hearsay, monsieur. The story that is told is that he burned his uniform and presented himself to the Americans as a prisoner. Prison clothing was not difficult to acquire, you understand.'

'What about papers, identification papers and so on? Would it be easy for him to steal a prisoner's papers?'

Forgeron smiled at the naivete of the question. 'Prisoners' papers were taken from them and held in the prison office. Nothing would be easier for the SS or Gestapo. Why do you ask this question, monsieur?'

'Because Bernhardt Neuhaus is living in England under Allard's name.' He topped up Forgeron's glass.

'Thank you, monsieur. That makes sense, you know. With a German accent, he could never pass himself off as a Frenchman, but the Americans who liberated St Malo would be unlikely ever to have heard a Jerseyman speak.'

'If they'd even heard of Jersey itself,' agreed Joe. 'Yes, it all fits together. Neuhaus sent Allard to Sachsenhausen, stole his identity and passed himself off to the Americans as a Jerseyman.'

'But when he reached England,' said Forgeron, 'how would he maintain the pretence?'

'Jersey is a favourite holiday destination for many British families,' said Joe, 'but they seldom have contact with the *Jèrriais*-speaking Jersey folk. I don't think it would be difficult for him to fool them that his accent wasn't German, but Jersey. At least, it would be less difficult than my next task.'

'What is that, monsieur?'

Joe sighed at the prospect of reporting back to Allard. 'His cousins have told me that, if Neuhaus was responsible for his death, they want him to face justice. My difficulty will be in persuading the Sûreté that there is sufficient evidence to convict him and, unless I can lay my hands on a document signed by Neuhaus, committing those prisoners to Sachsenhausen, I may as well forget it.'

'All incriminating documents were destroyed before the Americans arrived,' said Forgeron, but I should be happy to give evidence that Neuhaus gave the order. I can also bear witness that he murdered several Resistance workers.'

For the first time, Joe scented success. 'Do you think you could identify him after this time?'

'Yes, I believe so.'

Joe took one of the photographs of Neuhaus from his briefcase and showed it to Forgeron.

'That is Hauptsturmführer Neuhaus,' confirmed Forgeron.

'Monsieur Forgeron, I am indebted to you. I need at least one more witness, and then I can approach the Sûreté.'

19

Joe arrived at the office as Maggie was opening the post. She looked up and smiled when she saw him. 'Hello, Joe,' she said. 'Did you have a good trip?'

'Excellent, thanks.' He deposited a carrier bag on her desk and asked, 'Have you brought sandwiches for lunch?'

'Yes, but nothing inspiring.'

'Join me, and we'll have French cheeses, olives and real butter.'

'I set off to work this morning,' she said, 'but I think I must have missed my way and I found Heaven instead.'

'There's some for you to take home as well,' he said, putting the carrier bag down beside her desk. As he did, he noticed the picture postcard he'd sent her. It was propped up by her pencil rack.

'Joe, thank you. That's wonderful.'

'I didn't bring you anything exciting, like perfume, in case questions were asked....'

'Yes, even with his alcohol-dimmed senses, he might have noticed that, although I never expected anything, really.'

'So I brought you these.' He gave her a paper bag, from which she took a box of three lace-edged handkerchiefs.

'They're exquisite,' she said examining one closely. 'Thank you ever so much.'

'I also brought you these,' he said, producing moisturising cream and nail polish. 'They're a bit ordinary, but there's no scent to give rise to suspicion.'

'They're very scarce in the shops and greatly appreciated by me. Thank you, Joe.'

'One day, I'll bring you something really exciting.'

'I'm excited enough with what you've brought me. Thank you again.'

'You're always welcome.'

Putting everything carefully into her bag, she asked, 'How did you get on?'

'Quite successfully.' He told her about the two potential witnesses and the undertaking he'd received from Henri Forgeron. 'So,' he said, 'I need at least one more witness.'

'But you're halfway there,' she asserted. Then, in a more subdued tone, she said, 'I suppose being taken to the concentration camp would mean the end for Thomas Allard.'

'It's more than likely, although I'll make enquiries, now I know where he was taken.'

'But he'd only daubed paint on a wall. Why did they send him to a camp?'

'He and several others served as evidence of the crimes the Nazis had perpetrated. St Malo was liberated in August forty-four, so the Allies couldn't have been far away when Thomas and the others were taken away. Basically, the Nazis were covering their backs and destroying evidence before making their escape.'

'I still don't understand what people like Thomas had done to be sent to one of those horrible places.'

'It's not nice,' he warned her.

'As usual, I'll be brave.'

'All right. The Nazis had a project that they called *Aktion T Vier*, the euthanasia of the physically deformed and mentally defective. It was devised initially to rid the Master Race of its less than perfect specimens, but members of the occupied races who were similarly afflicted often received the same treatment. I suppose the *Herrenvolk* just couldn't bear to see those less superbly-formed than themselves.'

She closed her eyes tightly, as if to shut out the image. 'That's just despicable,' she said.

'I'm inclined to agree. When I took this case on, the Allards told me they wanted someone who was sympathetic to their cause, and I was very sympathetic, but the thought of those helpless victims has turned it into something much more than sympathy.'

———◦◦◦———

Jonathan Allard was initially pleased with the outcome of Joe's trip. 'It demonstrates my point,' he said, 'that you have to get out there and find witnesses.'

'But only if you know where to look for them,' said Joe. 'For what it's worth, Henri Forgeron is searching for ex-warders who were at St Malo Prison when the town was liberated. For my part, I intend to go through the list of Sachsenhausen's survivors as soon as I can get hold of it. If Thomas's name isn't among them, we'll know the worst.'

'What's stopping you?'

Joe held the receiver at arm's length and counted up to ten. He could hear Allard's voice quite clearly.

'Mr Pelier, are you there? I asked you a question. What's preventing you from seeing the list?'

'I heard you, Mr Allard. I do not have the list, because for one thing, I've only just returned from France, and secondly, because I have had to ask the Soviet Embassy for sight of it.'

'What have they got to do with it?'

'Everything. They liberated the camp and consequently compiled the list.'

'How should I be expected to know that?'

Joe took another deep breath. 'Mr Allard, when I was training with my regiment, one of the first things they told us was always to pick a target before opening fire, because to blast off at random achieved nothing and gave away our position.'

Allard snorted. 'What has that to do with anything?'

'I'm trying to get on with the job, but your random, uninformed criticisms are making the job harder than it needs to be. Now, will you let me get on with it?'

'Pelier, I don't think I like your tone.'

'In that case, maybe you can form a vague impression of just how frustrated I am.'

'Under the circumstances, I'll ring off, but I don't appreciate your ill-mannered behaviour, and I don't expect a repetition of it either.'

Fortunately, Allard replaced the receiver before Joe could offend him further.

———◄►———

'How sharper than a serpent's tooth is an ungrateful client.' Joe made the observation whilst unpacking the items for lunch. On this occasion, he and Maggie had elected to eat in his office. 'Shakespeare said that, and he was right about most things.'

'I think he was writing about an ungrateful child.'

'Well, I'm sure he said it about ungrateful clients as well.'

'Sit down and tell me all about it.'

Joe took his seat obediently. 'I phoned him, having just returned from a hectic two days in France, and he wanted to know why I didn't have the list of survivors of Sachsenhausen Concentration Camp in front of me at that moment.' He related the conversation to her. 'He'd actually fired off at me without knowing that the camp was liberated by the Russians.'

'I'm not side-tracking, Joe,' she said with closed eyes, 'but this cheese is sublime.'

'That's the Brillat-Savarin, from Normandy. Jean Brillat-Savarin once said that a meal without cheese was like a beautiful woman with only one eye. The French tend to compare their cheeses with... the ultimate human collaboration,' he told her as decorously as he could.

'This cheese deserves a better analogy than that.'

In the interest of good taste, Joe forbore to argue with her.

Returning to the main topic, Maggie said, 'I don't understand people like Mr Allard. He behaves as if he owns you.'

'He's paying me, and it amounts to the same thing in his view.'

'He has a strange outlook on the world and its inhabitants.'

Joe speared a green olive with his fork and said, 'Before I went to France, I explained to him the problem in persuading victims of Nazi brutality to give evidence. I told him that the fear had never quite left them, and his response to that was that I should find witnesses with some backbone.'

'Shameful.'

'Particularly so, considering his dash for safety when the Nazis loomed large. I don't blame anyone who left the Channel Islands at the time, but I question their right to pronounce judgement on those who suffered during the occupation.'

'Poor Joe.' She smiled in sympathy. 'If the roles were reversed, I'd ask you to tell me one of your jokes.'

'You never know,' he said. 'It might just work.'

'Go on, then.'

Joe thought and, having thought, said, 'The trouble is, I know how they end, so there's no surprise for me.'

'Give it a try, anyway.'

'All right.' He began. 'A couple had been celebrating their silver wedding anniversary at the cricket club where they'd held their engagement party twenty-six years earlier.'

'Don't you mean their wedding reception twenty-five years earlier?'

'Maggie, please.'

'I'm sorry. Carry on.'

'All right. As the last of the guests departed, the woman said to her husband, "Do you remember our engagement party, when we waited for everyone to leave, and then we went outside and... you know, *did it* against the back fence?" "Oh, yes," he said, a little embarrassed but excited by the reminder. She asked, "Shall we do it again, for old times' sake?" "Yes," he said, "let's." So they went outside to the back fence, they looked around them to make sure there was no one around, and then, in the most romantic way, they relived that special memory. When it was over, she tidied her clothing, patted her hair into place and said, "That was truly wonderful, darling. You were so dynamic. I don't recall your being half so animated twenty-six years ago." He said, "Maybe not, but they hadn't electrified the fence then." '

'Oh, lovely,' said Maggie. 'Did it work for you?'

'The electric fence? I've never tried it. Call me a softie if you will, but I leave that kind of thing to hardier souls.'

'Not that, silly. I mean, did the joke make you feel better?'

'Oddly enough, it did.'

'Your jokes always make me feel better.'

'I'm glad to hear it, but you're not in need of cheering up today, are you?'

'No,' she told him cheerfully. 'That's because I can see a way forward, now.'

'Don't keep me in suspense.'

'All right,' she said, 'I've decided to get a divorce.'

20

Joe learned that Maggie had made her decision during a chat with Guy, who assured her that it would be unlikely to affect the good name of the practice. He told her that she should have little difficulty in obtaining a divorce on the grounds of physical and mental cruelty, and that he would be happy to act for her.

'When will you set the ball rolling?'

'Just as soon as I've found somewhere to live.'

'So you're going to tell him and then move out?' It sounded like a risky move.

'I'm not as brave as that, Joe. I'll wait until he's gone to the pub, and then I'll leave him a note, telling him I've left him and that he can address any communications through Mr Wilcox.'

'You're confusing bravery with foolhardiness, Maggie. I was hoping you'd opt for the note on the mantlepiece.'

'So,' she said more brightly, 'all I have to do is find somewhere to live.'

'What sort of place?'

'Oh, a flat, or even a cottage.' In her desire to escape, she seemed quite *blasé* about her future home.

'It'll only be temporary, I suppose.'

'That depends on how much I like it. Just now, Joe, anywhere that's free from boorish behaviour and the threat of violence is likely to have instant and lasting appeal.'

'I can understand that.' He thought for a moment and said, 'the cottage two doors along from mine has been empty for a while, and it's available to let.'

'Furnished or unfurnished?'

'It's furnished. I don't know how well, but that would be for you to find out.'

'That's good news. I'm just trying to visualise it.'

'I'll tell you what,' he said. 'You could call at the agents in Folkestone tomorrow. They may send someone with you, or they may just let you have the key. Either way, you'll be able to have a shufti.'

'Have a what?'

'I'm sorry. That was a hangover from my desert past. I meant that you could have a look at it then, while Derek's sleeping off his lunchtime session.'

———●◄———

Maggie arrived that Saturday with a man whom Joe recognised as a partner in Ellis and Co. of Folkestone. She waved as she passed Joe's window, and then disappeared with the agent into number four.

They emerged about twenty minutes later, and Joe, who had just lit the gas under the kettle, offered his hospitality.

'That's very kind of you,' said the agent, looking at him with a kind of recognition. 'I believe we've met at some time.'

'We have,' confirmed Joe. 'I'm Joseph Pelier, and you sold me this cottage three years ago.'

'Of course.' The agent shook his hand and said, 'Unfortunately, I'm unable to take you up on your kind offer, as I have another appointment, but thank you all the same.'

'I'll take you up on it, Joe,' said Maggie with barely controlled excitement. 'I want to tell you about the cottage.'

'In that case, Mrs Earnshaw,' said the agent, 'I look forward to seeing you next week.' They shook hands, and the agent returned to his car.

'Come inside and tell all, Maggie,' said Joe. 'The kettle's on.'

'Everything's covered in dust,' she told him as they went into the cottage, 'but I can put that right.'

'I'll give you a hand.'

'You?'

'I'll have you know I'm a dab hand with a vacuum cleaner and a duster.'

'Oh dear.' Maggie put a hand to her mouth.

'What's the matter?'

'I suppose I'll have to leave the vacuum cleaner at the house. Derek won't know how to use it, but I don't want it to look as if I've taken everything.'

'Use mine. I've got a Goblin.'

'Lovely.'

'He took over from the fairy who used to do the cleaning until I worked her to death.'

'Thank you. I appreciate that.'

The kettle began to whistle, so Joe went to make the tea.

'I've been meaning to ask,' said Maggie. 'What is that glorious smell? It can't be bread, surely?'

'Oh, yes, it can. I decided to buy a book and learn how to bake bread, having brought proper flour from France. Be assured, I shan't forget you, naturally.'

'You're truly wonderful, Joe.' She waited for him to put the tea things on the table before sitting on the sofa.

'Apart from the fact that it's covered in dust,' he asked, 'what can you tell me about the cottage?'

'It's very much like this one. There's one bedroom, which is all I need. I think the boxroom was originally a child's bedroom, but that's by the by. The furniture seems sound enough, but it all needs cleaning, although the dustsheets have saved a lot.' She shrugged happily. 'Basically, it's wonderful because it represents the next stage in my life.'

'And because it offers the idyllic seascape that appealed to you so much the last time you were here,' he said, offering her a cup of tea.

'Thank you. That's true.'

'How are you fixed for suitcases?'

'Suitcases?'

'When you make the exodus,' he explained, 'you'll need to move out all your belongings in one go. If it helps, I've got two cases and a valise you can use.'

She looked thoughtful. 'Thank you, Joe. I hadn't thought about it in such detail.'

'You can put all your cases into my car and we'll do it in one journey.'

'Joe, where would I be without you?'

'Let's hope you never find out.'

'There's something I need to ask you about.'

'Better do it now, while I'm here and in a good mood.'

'Okay, I have to provide an employer's reference, as I haven't got a bank current account, and I imagine Mr Wilcox will agree to that, but I need a character reference as well.'

'Oh.' Joe narrowed his eyes in mock-consideration. Finally, he said, 'I'll give you a character reference. What kind of character would you like?'

'If I have a choice, I'd like the kind that's honest and responsible, the kind a trustworthy tenant would have.'

'They usually come at ten pounds each, although I'd normally charge you a fiver. As there's an "r" in the month, I'll waive the fee on this occasion.'

'You're all heart, Joe.'

'Yes, but look at the time.'

'I should be going.'

'I'm thinking about my first attempt at baking bread.' He got up and went to the kitchen. A few moments later, he said, 'Come and look at this, Maggie.'

'I can smell it.' She joined him in the kitchen, where two freshly-baked loaves lay in their tins. 'Oh, well done, Joe.'

'Let me wrap one of these, and you can take it home. If you're a little late, you can tell him you've been shopping and found some special bread. I don't know how good it is, but it's bound to be better than the National Loaf.'

'It smells wonderful, Joe. Thank you.'

———◆I◆———

On the following Tuesday, Joe received a letter from Fred Maçon.

Dear Joe,

I'd no idea Jean-Claud Pavard was such an old soak, but Henri Forgeron sounds like a better bet. We're saddened, by the way, to hear about Thomas's end, and I'm still looking for possible witnesses so that

we can get that monster Neuhaus put away or whatever they do with war criminals nowadays.
  Best regards,
  Fred.

There was hope yet. He had to remain positive. Meanwhile, he busied himself with the small, bread-and-butter cases that came in. Christmas was on its way, and with it, no doubt, renewed interest in missing family members. It was a regular source of income.

----•◄----

One week later, they moved Maggie's property from her home in Hythe. As soon as she opened the door, he sensed the fear and urgency she must have been feeling.

'Everything's packed,' she said, motioning towards the three suitcases and Joe's old army valise.

'Are you sure?'

She nodded. 'I've checked and double-checked.'

'Okay, I'll load up the car.' Joe had expected more luggage, but he was mindful that clothes rationing had only ended two years earlier, and there was also the likelihood that Derek's drinking habit had imposed a severe limit on what Maggie could buy.

'I'll help you.'

'No, Maggie, you'll hurt yourself. Let me do it.' He loaded the three cases into the boot and laid the valise on the back seat. 'There,' he said, 'you're all set to go.'

She locked the door, and was about to put the key through the letterbox, but Joe stopped her. 'You never know,' he said. 'There may be something you've overlooked. Don't give up the key until you're absolutely sure you won't need it again.'

She gave him an odd smile and said, 'You've done this before, haven't you? I can tell.'

'No, I'm just more detached from it all than you are.' He started the engine. 'Say goodbye to the place, Maggie. This is where life begins to improve.'

142

She said nothing as they drove through Hythe and Sandgate. In fact, it wasn't until she opened the door for Joe to move the cases in that she broke her silence to say, 'You told me not to lift these cases.'

'And I meant it. They're heavy. Tell me which of them you want taken upstairs, and I'll do it now.'

'I was only going to say that you cared. He never did.'

'But you knew that. Do these all need to go upstairs?'

'I'm afraid so.'

'It's no trouble.' He took two of the suitcases up and left them in the bedroom. When he returned, he asked, 'What's in the valise?'

'Underwear,' she said, 'some bits and pieces and my night things.'

'I thought as much. Look, Maggie, there's no fire in here, and it's getting colder all the time. Why don't you stay at my place overnight, and then you've got Sunday to sort things out here.'

'It's an awful nuisance for you.'

'Not a bit of it. I'll enjoy your company. What were you going to eat tonight?'

'Oh… I had something earlier.'

'How much earlier?'

'Lunchtime, I think.' She looked uncertain.

'That settles it. I was going to get fish and chips. Does the prospect strike a happy note with you?'

'Wonderful.' She smiled again.

He took the remaining suitcase upstairs and then carried the valise to his cottage while she locked her door.

'After your stressful day,' he said, 'I think it will be best if I change the bed upstairs for you, where you'll be comfortable, and I'll take the sofa.'

'No.' She held up her hand in protest. 'I won't hear of it, Joe. You're taller than this sofa is long, and I'm not. I'll sleep down here and I'll be quite comfortable.'

'If you insist.'

'I do.'

———◆❙◆———

'I've never had wine with fish and chips,' she said. 'It feels somehow decadent and self-indulgent.' The used plates were still on the table, but Joe and Maggie had decamped to the sofa. The wood fire added to the relaxed atmosphere.

'I can't eat fish and chips without a robust white wine. It's the Frenchman in me. I drink wine with bangers and mash, baked beans on toast.... Anything, really. SSM Tompkins used to despair of me.'

'He was an important influence in your life, wasn't he?'

'In all our lives, the whole squadron looked up to him.'

She frowned. 'Did you really have squadrons?'

'Oh yes, tanks are the new cavalry. The SSM was the squadron sergeant-major.'

'I think of a squadron as a unit of aircraft.'

'Oh well, as the junior service, you were newcomers to the term. It was applied to cavalry and warships at first. Then the Royal Flying Corps and the Royal Naval Air Service used it before they were snatched away in nineteen-eighteen by the impertinent, newly-born RAF.'

She shook her head minutely to clear it. 'The wine and the warmth are making me confused,' she said. 'Surely, you were in charge of the... squadron, not SSM Tompkins.'

'That's a common misconception, Maggie,' he told her seriously. 'An officer without a senior NCO is like a mouse without a cheese knife.'

'You'll tell me anything. Would you like me to wash up the plates and cutlery?'

'Certainly not. You're my guest.'

'All right, we'll share the job. One of us will wash, and the other will dry.'

He nodded unsurely. 'I can see you're one of those people,' he said.

'One of which people?'

'The organised kind.'

'That's right.' She stood up to gather the empty dishes. 'Let's get started.'

'You're as bad as SSM Tompkins.' He got up to help her.

When they'd washed up the plates and cutlery, Joe said, 'I'll find you some bedding. How many pillows do you prefer?'

'Just one, please.'

He went upstairs to find a sheet, a blanket, a pillow and a pillowcase, which he brought downstairs. He asked, 'Will you be all right with one blanket, or would you like two?'

'I'll be all right, thank you. It'll be folded double, anyway.'

'I'll put another log on the fire just to be on the safe side. Then, while you have first go with the bathroom, I'll make up your bed.'

'You're the perfect host, Joe.'

He made up a bed on the sofa as well as he could, tucking the fold of the sheet between the cushions. Then he plumped up the pillow and turned down the covers.

'How inviting,' said Maggie. 'Thank you for doing that.'

'Would you like a nightcap?'

'Only if you've got one in my size.'

'I meant a drink.'

'I know. What have you got?'

'Cognac.'

'That sounds good, but will you make it a small one, please.' She waited for him to pour the drinks and said, 'I'm glad you suggested that. It's usually about this time that Derek arrives home. A drink might take the chill off the thought.'

'He's been your problem far too long, Maggie. Now, the problem is his, and it's richly deserved.'

They sat together, silent but with their thoughts in complete accord. Eventually, he took her empty glass from her and asked, 'Are you okay now?'

'I'm fine. That was just what I needed.'

'In that case, I'll leave you to your rest.' He paused, as if recalling something. Then he said, 'At this stage, SSM Tompkins would insist on kissing everyone goodnight. However, as you're the only one here....' He bent and kissed her cheek. 'Goodnight, Maggie.'

'Goodnight, Joe, and thank you for everything.'

'*Je t'en prie, ma chère amie. Bonne nuit.*' He went upstairs to bed.

21

DECEMBER

When Joe looked into Maggie's office the following Monday morning he found her tight-lipped and preoccupied.

'I've just put Derek through to Mr Wilcox,' she said. 'He was in a foul temper.'

'Guy will deal with him. Don't worry.' He took her hand and squeezed it.

'I have to do my shopping,' she said hopelessly, 'and I'm registered with shops in Hythe. How can I avoid him?'

'You can register with shops in Sandgate or Folkestone,' he suggested, perching on the edge of her desk. 'Until you can get that sorted out, let me do your shopping.'

'But that's putting you to a lot of trouble.'

'Not really. It shouldn't take long to change your registration. After that, it might still be a good idea if I come with you when you do your shopping, just in case you bump into him.'

'This is awful.'

'It won't always be.'

The door opened, and Guy came in, prompting a discreet exit by Joe. As he left the office, he heard Guy said, 'He didn't think you were serious, so I've told him that divorce proceedings are going ahead and that I'll confirm that in writing. I've advised him to find a solicitor.'

Joe waited a while before returning. When he did, he found Maggie more settled but still preoccupied.

'I'll have to take you up briefly on your offer,' she said. 'I had to get Mr Wilcox to speak to the Food Officer, and it seems I'm allowed to register with Sandgate shopkeepers as I now live in the district.'

'We could do it together,' he suggested. 'I have to buy my bread in Hythe, but that's not difficult.'

'So do I, for some reason.'

'Well, there you are. We were destined to be a pair, at least, to go shopping together.'

———————————

They did their shopping on Wednesday lunchtime and Saturday morning, and once the visit to the bakery in Hythe was out of the way, Maggie began to relax.

On the way home that Saturday, Joe said, 'I'm going fishing tonight. With any luck I'll get some schooling bass.'

Incredulous, Maggie said, 'But it's mid-winter.'

'Almost,' he agreed, 'but fish are hardy souls.'

'I was thinking of you, not the fish.'

'Oh, I just enjoy the warmth all the more when I get home.'

Maggie was quiet until Joe turned into the close, and then she asked, 'Do you think I could come with you?'

'If you really want to, I'd appreciate the company. Of course, you'll have to wrap yourself up like Nanook of the North.'

'You could have thought of someone a little more fetching.'

'I could have said Eskimo Nell,' he said, opening the passenger door.

'I heard some of that once and I wasn't impressed.'

'It's not fit for a lady's ears,' he agreed.

'Some of the WAAFs didn't mind. They seemed to be used to that kind of thing.'

'And I thought the RAF were cultured souls.' He unlocked his cottage door. 'Will you join me for lunch?'

'Lunch with you is always a surprise,' she said, 'so I will. Yes, please.'

As he prepared lunch, she asked, 'Where will we go fishing?'

'Dungeness Beach. I've got an extra stool you can use, so you won't be sitting on wet shingle. It tends to leave an impression, you know.'

'You're very considerate, Joe.' Then, after a moment's thought, she said, 'The locals call it "beach". Did you know that?'

'What?'

147

'They call shingle "beach".'

'I know, but in my book, a proper beach is all sand.'

'You have to go down the coast for that.' Going to the kitchen door, she asked, 'Can I help at all?'

'No, it's all done.' He carried a dish of pâté in and put it on the table.

'You're unbelievable.'

'I know. You'll like this as well. I've got a capon coming for Christmas, and I can't possibly eat it all by myself, so how do you feel about joining me?'

'You keep making offers I can't possibly turn down.'

'You'd be a fool if you did.' He went into the kitchen and returned with bread and butter.

'Is the capon coming from the butcher?' Rationing had to be considered.

He put a cautionary finger to his lips but said nothing.

'I see. I appreciate your invitation, and thank you, I'd like that. I've been so busy settling in, I haven't done a thing about Christmas.' She looked down as she said, 'In any case, it's going to be rather odd this time.'

———◆◄———

'How much have we got, Joe?'

He peered into the bucket and said, 'There's enough for both of us tomorrow and later in the week, and I said I'd give Guy a couple of pounds.' He picked up a bass and weighed it with the spring balance. 'This one's two pounds three ounces.'

'He'll love that.'

'Are you feeling cold? We can go home if you like.'

'Can we stay a little longer?' She was gazing across the calm sea as if it gave her some special pleasure. 'I've never done anything like this,' she said, 'sitting on the seashore in winter, just looking across to France under a starry sky.'

'You know what the seasoned locals say about seeing Boulogne, don't you?'

'What do they say?'

'If you can see it, there's rain on its way.'

She gave him a look of mock-impatience. 'I thought you were going to say something poetic,' she said.

'I used to leave all that to Sergeant-Major Tompkins. He'd sit for hours, rhapsodising about oases, wadis and so on.'

'What's a wadi?'

'To you and me, it's a valley, but it was something much more to Tompkins.' He put his arm round her shoulders to set the scene. 'Tompkins would say to me, "That's not just a wadi, sir, it's a bookmark in history. It could have been created a thousand years ago, when rivers ran through the desert, and date palms flourished." '

'And what would you say to him?'

'I'd tell him to stop talking nonsense and organise the camouflage nets for the tanks.'

'I don't believe a word.' Nevertheless, she allowed her head to rest against his, still looking out to sea.

Eventually, she said, 'I am rather cold, now I think of it.'

'Okay, we'll make tracks.' He packed away his rod and tackle while she loaded the picnic things into the car.

As they drove home along an almost empty road, she said, 'Thank you for a completely new experience. I thoroughly enjoyed it.'

'Not too cold, then?'

'No, not enough to spoil the occasion.'

'You're welcome to join me anytime.'

'Thank you.'

They lapsed into silence for the remainder of the journey. When they reached the cottages, Maggie leaned towards him. 'Don't forget Sergeant-Major Tompkins' example,' she said, inclining her face for a goodnight kiss.

'Goodnight, Maggie.'

'Goodnight, Joe, and thanks again.'

———◆◄———

A few days later, Joe called on Maggie at home, having been occupied most of the day with a new case.

'Come in,' she said. 'I'll put the kettle on.'

'Thanks, but I'm about to start cooking. I just came to ask you something.'

'The thing you're about to cook, will it keep?'

'For another day, easily.'

'Let me feed you for a change,' she said, closing the door after him.

'If you're sure.'

'Fairly sure,' she said, 'in fact, quite decided. Come and talk to me while I prepare things and cut myself.'

'I'll be on hand, then, to render first aid.'

She gave him an odd look and said, 'You think I'm joking, don't you?'

'Don't worry, I'm ready for anything.' He followed her into the tiny kitchen.

'What did you want to ask me?'

'To begin with, have you got a passport?'

'Yes, I renewed it after the war, although I can't remember why, because it's been no use to me. Why do you ask?'

'What are you making?'

'A sort of stew with vegetables and potatoes. It'll take about an hour if you can wait that long.'

'It'll give us time for a drink.' He looked at the vegetables and said, 'You've got most of the ingredients for a Bolognese sauce there. I've got a tin of tomatoes, if you're interested, but don't let me take over.'

'I'll try not to. Would you like a Bolognese sauce?'

'It's just a suggestion.'

'Go on, then,' she decided. 'Get your tin of tomatoes. We'll just have to imagine the spaghetti.'

'Potatoes will be fine. I'll be back in a sec.' He slipped round to his own cottage and returned with the tomatoes and a bottle of Burgundy.

Maggie looked at the wine with alarm. 'You're not going to pour that wine into the sauce, are you?'

'*Cara mia*, I've committed some heinous acts during my chequered life, but never in all my born days have I ever wasted wine, and I'm not about to start.'

'Thank goodness for that.'

'Can I help?'

'Would you mind peeling the carrots?'

'It'll be a pleasure.' He took the knife from her and began peeling.

'It's most unusual to meet a man who cooks,' she said.

He shrugged. 'Most men don't need to. I'm just one of life's wallflowers.'

'You still haven't told me why I need a passport.'

'You're quite right, I haven't. How do you feel about going on a day-trip to Calais to do some shopping before Christmas? The trip is on me, by the way.'

She stared at him and said, 'Whatever next? Night fishing, shopping in Calais.... When?'

'This coming weekend.'

'I can't think of a single reason why I shouldn't join you.'

'Think of all the reasons why you should. We'll get lots of delectable things we can't get in Blighty, breakfast on the *Maid of Orleans*, and lunch in Calais. What's wrong with that?'

'Nothing at all.'

'Of course,' he said, somewhat shamefaced, 'you'll return with your arms two inches longer than they are now.'

'Why?'

'Because we have to do it all on foot, so we have to carry everything.'

'That's all right,' she assured him. 'I've always wanted a longer reach.' She put chopped onions into the saucepan and began softening them.

'It's a familiar story. High shelves can be an impediment.'

'Speaking of stories, it's been quite a while since I've heard one of yours.'

'Are you in need of one?'

'No, but I just thought it would be nice. Don't feel that you're under pressure.'

'I'm at my best under pressure, Maggie. Let me think.' He put his thinking face on and said, 'Right. A young woman was driving in the depths of the countryside, when she ran out of petrol—'

'You've told me that one already, about the girl wanting all the bed to herself.'

'No, this is a different story, a different young woman and a different farm.'

'I'm sorry. Please carry on.'

'She came upon a farmhouse, where she knocked on the door and had a similar conversation with the farmer's wife to the one you remember. On this occasion, however, she had to share a bed with two sons, both of meagre intellect. After a while, she turned to one and asked, "Are you asleep?" He said, "Oi don't think so. Are you?" "No," she said, "I'm not, and I've got a new game to show you. Do you want to play?" "Arr," he said, "Oi don't moind if Oi do." So, to cut out the embarrassing bits that all grown-ups know about, she explained it all to the boy. Finally, she reached into her handbag for a contraceptive and said, 'Before we play this game, you must wear this on your thingy so that I won't have a baby." "All right," he said, letting her perform the necessary precaution. Now,' he said, sensing that Maggie was about to interrupt again, 'this isn't a shaggy dog story, so I'll just say that, having had her way with one son, she propositioned the other, asking him, also, to wear a contraceptive so that she wouldn't have a baby. Now, morning came, and the young woman bade farewell to the family and went on her way.'

'Did she get some petrol?'

'I imagine so. Anyway, the sons laboured in the fields until nightfall, when one said to the other, "Do you remember that maid who slept in our bed last night?" His brother said, "Arr. What about her?" The first son said, "Do you remember her saying we had to wear that rubber stocking-thing so that she wouldn't have a baby?" His brother said, "Arr." '

Maggie said, 'They say that quite a lot, don't they?'

'Maggie, please, you mustn't interrupt when I'm so close to the end of the story.'

'I'm sorry.'

'You're forgiven. He said, "You remember that, don't you?" "Arr," said his brother. "Well," said the first son, "as far as I'm concerned, she can have a flippin' baby, 'cause this thing's coming off. I'm dying for a jimmy riddle." '

Maggie smiled. 'That was quite good,' she said.

'It would have been better if you hadn't interrupted me.'

'I'll try not to do that again.'

'Don't worry too much about it. It's a woman's prerogative.' He watched her put the vegetables into the saucepan, and said, 'Let's sit down and have a drink.'

22

Christmas at Joe's cottage was remarkably cheerful, considering Maggie's recent, unavoidable preoccupation. On the day, she made a staunch effort, appearing in what Joe was inclined to call a 'reddish-brown' creation that he'd not previously seen, but which gained his immediate approval.

With the capon roasting in the oven, they opened the wine and then their presents. In a conveniently discreet moment in Calais, Maggie had bought Joe a silk tie, which both surprised and delighted him. She was just as elated when she opened Joe's present and found a bottle of *Joy* by Jean Patou. She removed the cap and dabbed some on her wrists, having been unable to find perfume in Britain since before the war.

'It's wonderful, Joe. Thank you.'

'And this is a superb tie,' he said, kissing the inclined cheek. Secretly, he felt inhibited. He'd always found her appealing, but particularly so on that day, in the new dress and the makeup she'd bought in Calais. He felt as if he'd been holding his feelings in check far too long, and yet she was only recently separated from her husband. This was her first Christmas away from him since their marriage. It was a delicate situation and, difficult though he found it, he had to respect that.

Eventually, they sat down to eat. Joe carved and divided the capon, prompting Maggie to say, 'You're so complete, Joe. You cook and do just about everything a woman would normally do.'

' "Just about" is right, Maggie. There are jobs that require a woman's touch, jobs that leave me feeling totally inadequate.'

'I don't believe that, but I shan't argue with you.'

'No,' he agreed, 'let peace and goodwill flourish.' Picking up his glass, he said, 'Happy Christmas, Maggie. Help yourself to vegetables and potatoes.'

'Happy Christmas, Joe.'

'Unfortunately, we have no Christmas crackers,' he observed.

'Yes.' She looked puzzled. 'I don't remember seeing any in France.'

'You wouldn't. They never caught on over there, and they were seldom a feature of my childhood, except at school parties.'

'You poor little scrap.'

'One Christmas,' he told her in his storytelling way, 'my sister Marianne and I made some crackers. She was good at handicrafts and she designed them and put them together. I simply wrote the mottoes, limericks, conundra, jokes and so on.'

'Is there such a word as "conundra"?'

'There must be. I used to write them.'

Looking down at her plate, she said, 'This is truly excellent.' Then, as another thought occurred to her, she asked, 'You didn't put dirty jokes into Christmas crackers, did you?'

'Not *very* dirty ones.' On reflection, he added, 'But I did get a severe telling off from my mother about one of them.'

'Go on,' said Maggie, 'I'll buy it.'

'A man offered a girl a lift home on the crossbar of his bicycle, and when she climbed off, she realised it was a girls' bicycle.'

'That's just smutty.'

'I know. It was funny enough to make my father snigger behind his napkin, and naughty enough for my mother to suspect I was keeping doubtful company. My worst crime, though, was in letting my sister see the joke before I put it into the cracker.'

'Did you really let her see it?'

'It was Marianne who told me the joke in the first place.'

She gave him a speculative look, as if deciding whether or not he were telling the truth. Eventually, she asked, 'Were you older than your sister?'

'No, younger by one year. She was a bad influence on me.' He decided that they'd talked enough about him, so he asked, 'Have you any brothers or sisters?'

'No, my mother always said she'd suffered so much, giving birth to me, that no power on earth was going to make her repeat the experience.

I think my father had heard the same complaint so often, he shared her reluctance. It was either that, or he reckoned she'd be impossible after a second confinement.'

'More wine?' He picked up the bottle.

'Yes, please.'

He refilled her glass and said, 'It's my belief that, however unwittingly, parents can make their children feel guilty for being born.'

'That's true.'

'Marianne and I were fortunate in that we were able to operate together as a subversive team. It was great fun.'

'Do you keep in touch?'

'Yes, she'll phone me later, or I'll phone her. It's better if she does it, then I don't run the risk of having to make conversation with Geoffrey, her husband.'

'Is he so awful?'

'I think I told you earlier, he doesn't live in a normal world. If I were to say, "Hello, Geoffrey, how are you?" I'd get a grunt and an unintelligible word or two, but if I said, "By the way, Geoffrey, I've heard on the grapevine that x equals minus b plus or minus the square root of b squared minus four a c all over two a," he'd say, "It certainly does, but I think it could be improved upon." Then, he'd describe the improvement. That's what we're up against. Mind you, if I were to throw in a bit of differential calculus on top of the equation, he'd get completely over-excited, and Marianne would have to crush one of his powders.'

Maggie was smiling. 'I don't believe a word of it,' she said.

'You should, in case you ever meet him.' Looking at her empty plate, he asked, 'Would you like some more? There's more of everything.'

'No, thank you. It was lovely, but I don't want to overdo it.'

'You're probably wise. There's the pud to negotiate next.'

In a tone of disbelief, she asked, 'Christmas pudding?'

'What else?'

She shook her head slowly. 'I can't help wondering how many people are sitting down today to a meal like this.'

'Six,' he told her confidently.

'How do you know?'

'There's you and me, and then there's the chap who supplied the capon, his wife and their two children.'

'You have influential friends.'

'Yes, and I supply them with things as well.'

'I shan't ask.'

'It's better not to,' he agreed, 'although these things are all relative.'

'What did you mean,' asked Maggie as they sat on the sofa, 'when you said that these things are all relative?'

'When did I say that?'

'When we were eating. You were talking about the man who supplied the capon.'

'Oh, yes.' He thought for a moment. 'Yes, you see, he and I help each other out from time to time with small items, whereas some people are operating a black market for profit. There's a world of difference between the two.'

'There is,' she agreed, 'and you've helped me out lots of times.'

'Ah well, you see, you understand after all.'

For a while, neither of them spoke. The only sounds were the wind against the shuttered windows, and the soft ticking of the log in the grate. After a while, Joe put another log on the fire, creating a rush of sparks that died down as the flames took hold of the log.

Maggie stirred and said, 'This is the closest I can imagine to perfection, sitting here by the fireside and hearing the wind outside. If only we could preserve such moments.'

'That's what memory is for. "Roses in December" and all that.'

'Who said that?'

'J M Barrie.'

'He had a point.'

'He had, but enjoy it as well while it's here.'

'Oh, don't misunderstand me.' She leaned forward to make her point. 'I *am* enjoying it.'

'Good,' he said, slipping his arm round her shoulders.

She responded by resting her head against his. 'It's a wonderful feeling after all the unpleasantness of the last few years,' she said. 'You know, I'm surprised to find that I don't feel at all guilty about leaving him.'

'You've no reason to feel guilty.'

'Reason never had a look-in.'

Almost without thinking, he took her hand and stroked it with his thumb. 'What do you mean?'

'There was no room for logic or fairness in our marriage. Guilt was quite arbitrary.' She stopped herself. 'It's no subject for Christmas Day. I'm sorry.'

'If it makes you feel better to get it off your chest, don't hold back. It's as good a time as any, and you won't upset me.'

'You're very understanding.'

'I know you've been going through a desperate time, that's all.'

'You've said it. You know, he punished me for the most ridiculous things that weren't my fault.'

Joe gave her shoulder a squeeze, reluctant to say anything in case it interrupted the flow.

'Sometimes, he punished me because his drunkenness made him clumsy and unable to… do certain things.'

He nodded, realising now what she meant about the absence of logic and fairness. Sympathy made him hold back a lock of her hair and kiss her gently on her temple.

'You and he couldn't be more different, Joe,' she said, turning her head towards him.

'That's a relief.'

'You already knew that.'

'A touch of irony, that's all. If I were like him, I'd do the decent thing and jump over a cliff.'

'But he'd never do the decent thing. Decency is an alien concept in his world.'

'You've left his world behind,' he reminded her. 'Everything's going to be fine.' Their faces were inches apart. Almost unable to prevent himself, he bent, and touched her lips with his once, then twice, before hers parted in willing collusion, and they kissed deeply and with a sense of new-found freedom after months of self-denial.

Breaking off, he asked, 'Is it too soon?'

'No,' she said, 'and it's very welcome.'

'I didn't want to take advantage.'

'I know.'

They kissed again, slowly and at length, enjoying every tiny moment. After a while, Maggie said, 'Joe?'

'Mm?'

'This is going to sound awful, but have you got the necessary thing?'

'Things, plural,' he assured her.

'Oh, good.'

'First things first, though. If you'll excuse me, I'd best put a match to the fire upstairs and make it warm and welcoming.'

'Go on, then.'

Scarcely able to believe his good fortune, he took a box of matches from the mantlepiece and went upstairs to light the fire. With that done, he fastened the window tightly and closed the shutters. Flames were now leaping up from the grate, and the fire was drawing nicely. He replaced the fireguard and went downstairs.

'All done,' he reported, taking her in his arms again.

'I haven't done this for ages,' she said, meeting his enquiring glance with, 'this and just... being like this.'

They returned to the sofa to give the fire time to take off the chill upstairs.

'You may have been out of practice,' he said, 'but you've got the idea again. I knew it wouldn't take long.'

'So you're an expert in these matters, are you?'

'I've had my moments,' he said. 'They were so long ago, I struggle to remember them, but I've only to look at the notches in my bedpost to know that they really happened.'

After ten minutes or so, he inclined his head towards the stairs and asked, 'Would you like me to give you a few minutes start?'

'If you don't mind.' She smiled unsurely. 'I won't always be so shy.'

'Of course you won't.'

When he went upstairs a few minutes later, he found her beneath the covers.

'Are you cold?'

'Just a little.'

He put another log on the fire before removing his underclothes and joining her. 'Let me warm you,' he said, taking her in his arms. Surprisingly, her body was warm to his touch.

'I'm not really cold,' she confessed, 'just a little nervous.'

'It's the first time with someone new,' he said as they kissed. 'It's bound to be daunting.

'This is the first time I've done it with anyone other than... with anyone else.' It was as if she were reluctant to speak Derek's name in case it cast a shadow over the event.

'I didn't realise that.' He kissed her again slowly, reluctant to hurry something that that he'd anticipated for so long, but that was clearly causing her some disquiet, despite her initial enthusiasm.

She began to respond to his leisurely attentions, so he lingered for a while before moving gradually downward to her full breasts. As he did so, she gave a soft moan of pleasure that she repeated when he kissed them again, returning, little by little, to her lips, while his hand explored her body, delighting her with new and unexpected sensations.

———◦┼◦———

'I used to wonder what the excitement was about. I told you about the man I was engaged to before Derek, didn't I?'

'Yes.' He remembered that. 'The navigator in the RAF?'

'That's right. We were engaged, but we never did anything like this for fear of starting a baby. We were as innocent as each other.'

'There's nothing wrong with that.'

'No, but what I'm saying is that Derek's way, when he was able to do it, was the only way I knew, and it gave me no pleasure at all.'

'No?'

'Quite the reverse. When I could, I'd pretend to be asleep, in the hope that he'd not bother me.'

At a loss for an appropriate observation, he continued to listen.

'He said I wasn't sexy enough, and that was why he couldn't usually do what was necessary.'

'Do you mean he couldn't rise to the occasion?'

'Yes.' She smiled shyly, plainly unused to discussing such things.

'Maggie, there's absolutely nothing wrong with you. The likeliest culprit was alcohol. It's a well-known fact.'

'I know,' she said, closing her eyes at the memory, 'but when you're told something often and forcefully enough, you find yourself believing it.'

That was true enough. He'd seen evidence of it time and again. 'In that case, Maggie,' he said, 'start believing this, that you're a lovely, desirable woman, who's been raising my excitement level for some considerable time.'

'I'm also an adulteress,' she said without obvious shame.

'With an excellent excuse.'

With the shadow of past misery now dissipated, she smiled and asked, 'How long have I been raising your excitement level?'

'Since I moved into Bouverie Road West. It began in a modest way,' he explained, 'and it gradually gathered momentum. Of course, I'm a patient sort of chap, and not one to declare his interest openly, especially when the lady in question is prohibited by reason of marriage, but the flame continued to burn nonetheless.'

She laughed. 'You make it sound like something from a romantic novel.'

'It's funny you should say that. I've often thought of writing one.'

'I don't believe you.'

'That's your privilege, but I've felt for some time that the genre would benefit greatly from a fresh approach, not to mention the inclusion of a few dirty jokes.'

She laughed at the thought. 'I wonder if it would catch on,' she said.

'Of course it would. Think of it as humorous relief, something to provide contrast and respite between soulful, tear-jerking passages. I'm sure it would find an enthusiastic following.'

'You know,' she said, 'you're just like Rolls-Royce.'

'In what way?'

'You think of everything.'

23

On Thursday afternoon, the day after Boxing Day, Maggie was typing a letter when Mr Wilcox came to her office.

'Maggie,' he said in an unusually careful tone, 'there's a policeman to see you.' Standing aside, he beckoned the constable, a man of middle years, into the office. 'I'll leave you to talk,' he said, 'but if you need me, Maggie, you know where I am.'

'Thank you, Mr Wilcox.' Intrigued, she waited for the policeman to speak.

Consulting his notebook, he said, 'I'm afraid I have some bad news for you, Mrs Earnshaw. You are Mrs Margaret Earnshaw?'

'*Margherita* Earnshaw.'

'I beg your pardon,' he said, striking out the incorrect name in his notebook. 'How, exactly, is that spelt, Mrs Earnshaw?'

'M-A-R-G-H-E-R-I-T-A.'

'Thank you, Mrs Earnshaw, and you reside at number thirty-four—?'

'No longer. I moved out last month.'

'But you are married to Mr Derek Earnshaw of that address?' Curiously, he seemed to frame all his questions as statements.

'Yes, I am. What's happened?'

'Mr Earnshaw was found at his home earlier today…. I'm sorry, Mrs Earnshaw. He was found dead.'

'Dead?'

'I'm afraid so. I have to ask you to formally identify him. He's currently at a funeral parlour in Hythe.'

Stunned, she asked, 'How did it happen?'

'We don't yet know. All we know is that, when Mr Earnshaw failed to report for work this morning, someone called at his address to investigate his absence and, whilst unable to make contact with him, noticed that the bedroom curtains were still closed. He contacted us, and we called out the keyholder, the landlord to enable access. Your husband was found dead, I'm afraid, in his bed.'

'And you've no idea how he died?'

'Not at this stage, madam. The likelihood is that there will have to be a post mortem examination.'

'Oh, good grief. I must tell Mr Wilcox.' She hurried to her employer's office and knocked on the door.

'Come in.'

Maggie opened the door to find Mr Wilcox and Joe together, and felt a curious kind of instant comfort. 'Mr Wilcox,' she said, 'my husband has been found dead, and they want me to identify him.'

Joe stood up immediately. 'You mustn't go alone, Maggie,' he said. 'I'll come with you.' Seeing the policeman in the passage, he asked, 'Will it be all right for me to bring Mrs Earnshaw in my car?'

'Yes, sir.' The policeman looked again and said, 'It's Mr Pelier, isn't it?'

'That's right.'

'I think we can trust you, sir. Mr Earnshaw was taken, for the time being, to Browne and Sons in Hythe.' Then, turning to Maggie, he said, 'You naturally have the right to have him transferred to an undertaker of your choice, Mrs Earnshaw, once the formalities are out of the way.'

'All right,' said Joe, 'we'll see you at Browne and Sons.'

———— ▶◀ ————

After dinner, they sat together on Joe's sofa. 'The policeman was so formal and correct,' said Maggie.

'In the circumstances, I suppose it's only right.'

'Of course it is, but it's the strangest thing that, even in spite of those circumstances, I noticed that he split an infinitive. Isn't that odd?'

'Reprehensible.' He tutted for good measure.

'I meant, that I should notice a detail at such a time as that.'

He nodded sagely. 'Nothing escapes the finely-tuned ear of the secretary. What did he say?'

'He wanted me to formally identify the body.'

Joe screwed up his eyes in distaste. A grammatical error of the kind up with which one should not put.'

'Who said that?'

'I think Churchill said something similar. If I misquote him, I'm completely unrepentant, as he inflicted the same discourtesy so often on dear old Bill Shakespeare and assorted poets.'

As they watched the burning log, Maggie said, 'They found an almost-full bottle of sleeping pills on Derek's bedside table. The date on the label was the twenty-first of December. He'd kept saying he was going to ask the doctor for something to help him sleep. I just hope he didn't take an overdose. I couldn't bear to have that on my conscience.'

'If there were pills in the bottle, it's unlikely. If he'd wanted to take his own life, you'd think he'd have swallowed the lot.'

'Do you really think so?'

'Yes, I do. In any case, there's nothing to be gained by conjecturing. You'll know nothing until they've done the post mortem.'

She nodded in silent agreement.

'Meanwhile, I'm here when you need me. Otherwise, I'll let you breathe your own air. Whatever and whenever you decide.'

She snuggled closer. 'I don't want to sleep alone tonight,' she said.

'In that case, I expect you'll want a bedtime story.'

'Only if you have one handy.'

'All right.' He adopted thoughtful pose and began. 'A zebra noticed that the zoo keeper had left the bolt undone on the outside gate. "Ha," she said, "now I can find out more about the outside world." She crept out and tiptoed down the road.'

'Can zebras walk on tiptoe?'

'If they can't, you'll go to bed without a story.'

'Sorry.'

'Eventually, she came to a farm, and was surprised to see a chicken. The surprise, you understand, was because she'd never seen one in her life. "Hello," said the chicken, "what kind of animal are you?" '

'Did the chicken speak fluent zebra?'

'Doesn't everyone? Be quiet and listen.'

'Sorry.'

'The zebra said, "I'm a zebra." "Oh," said the chicken, but she made no comment, being well brought-up. The zebra asked, "What are you?" "I'm a chicken," said the chicken, a little surprised that the zebra didn't know that. "Oh," said the zebra. "What do you do?" "I lay eggs for people to eat," she said. It made perfect sense, so the zebra took her leave of the chicken and journeyed on until she met a cow, whereupon, a similar conversation took place, during which the zebra learned that cows give milk for people to drink and use for cooking and baking. "What a fascinating world this is turning out to be," said the zebra, walking on until she met a stallion. "Hello," said the zebra, "what are you?" I shan't tell you what the stallion said, because, if you've been paying attention, you've probably beaten him to his line. The important thing is that the zebra asked him, "What do you do?" "And the stallion said, "Take those fancy, striped pyjamas off and I'll show you." '

When Joe looked, he found that Maggie was fast asleep. It had been a tiring afternoon.

——▸◂——

The post mortem was performed fairly promptly, but more than a week passed before the coroner recorded his verdict as 'Death by Misadventure.' He had concluded that, whether by mistake or deliberately and with the intention of ensuring that he slept soundly, Derek had taken twice his normal nightly dose of chloral hydrate. The excess would not normally have proved fatal but for the level of alcohol in his bloodstream. In the event, the two formed a lethal cocktail.

'I've decided to ask Browne and Sons to take care of the funeral,' said Maggie when she and Joe were alone at his cottage. 'They have a good reputation in the town.'

'Look,' he said, 'it's a personal question, I know, but a funeral can be an expensive manoeuvre. Will you be all right?'

'Yes, thank you. I took out insurance on his life some time ago, so there's no problem there.'

'Had he any relations who need to be notified?'

'Only a cousin I telephoned this afternoon, and she fell out with him years ago. He made a career of upsetting people.'

' "Nothing in his life became him like the leaving it." '

'That sounds like a quotation.'

'It's from *Macbeth,*' he told her confidently.

After a moment's thought, she said, 'I wonder if Shakespeare told dirty jokes.'

'Only in the lowest of male company. He told his jokes in rhyming verse, you see, and that was frowned upon in Tudor circles.'

'Was it?' She sounded sceptical.

'I just said so. He wrote his plays in blank verse, as a gentleman should, but his jokes were in rhyming couplets. They were kept very short to lessen the risk of interruption by the fair sex. It was a good idea, and one I've considered on occasions.'

'I'm learning not to interrupt.'

He looked at her in mock disbelief.

'Do you know why women interrupt?'

'I'm not brave enough even to offer a guess.'

'When a woman is relating – let's say – an experience to other women, they will join in, teasing out little gems of detail that help build up a proper picture. In this way, they are helping her tell her story.'

'Even though they weren't there at the time?'

She nodded. 'As I said, they tease out details that are so important in a description. They encourage the storyteller to embellish her picture.'

It made no sense to Joe. 'But a chap can tell a story all by himself.'

'Ah, men call that telling a story.' Clearly, she wasn't impressed. 'A man was walking down the street when he saw another man carrying a grandfather clock on his shoulder. That's a man's description, but a woman would describe the street, the season, the time of day, the weather, the clock and the men themselves. She'd paint a proper picture.'

'Incredibly, you still ask me to tell you jokes, even though I'm a humble male and, as such, unequal to the task.' In truth, he was feeling somewhat nettled.

'But you do it properly. You *can* tell a story.'

'In that case,' he said, partly placated, 'why do you keep interrupting me?'

'For the same reason as a woman interrupts another woman. I'm helping you. Don't you see?'

He tried to make sense of what he'd heard. 'So, when you interrupt me just when I'm working up to the conclusion of a joke, I have to keep reminding myself that you're only being helpful.'

As if he'd finally grasped an elusive concept, she said, 'Yes, that's right.'

'This is why the word "comedienne" is yet to find its way into the dictionary. A joke needs timing, Maggie. If the end is rushed or, even worse, if it's delayed, it's no longer funny.'

'Well, maybe not to a man,' she conceded.

'It's like visiting a foreign country. All this time, I've been telling you jokes, and you say they make you feel better—'

'They do, Joe. They've helped me through some awful times.'

He sighed heavily. 'Okay, as composite species, we were born to disagree. In future, however, when I'm telling you a joke and you try to interrupt me just as I'm going for the vital line, I'll hold up my hand like a policeman stopping traffic—'

'And I'll know to keep quiet.'

'We'll both find it inhibiting at first, but they say that practice is everything.'

—————◗◖—————

As Maggie dealt with preparations for Derek's funeral and the clearance of the house with more expertise and clear-headedness than Joe could ever have mustered, work went on as usual, and he was encouraged to receive a letter from Fred Maçon.

Dear Joe,

I have been in communication again with the Resistance member I told you about. She has information not only about Tom, but about other prisoners who were put to death on Neuhaus's orders, or who died during torture at the hands of his men. She has also mentioned other possible witnesses. Everyone is hesitant about giving evidence in court, but some are prepared to make sworn depositions before a juge de paix *(I don't know what the English equivalent is, but I imagine you will know). Even so, I'm still hoping to persuade them to give evidence in court.'*

Yours with all good wishes,
Fred Maçon.

Hopefully, it was a step forward, but he needed to take advice about procedure in French criminal law. In particular, he was curious about the value of a deposition, even when it was sworn before a justice of the peace.

24

Derek's funeral was a muted affair, attended only by Maggie and two of his nursery colleagues. For the sake of propriety, Joe stayed away, but he was on hand at his cottage when Maggie returned.

'It was the strangest experience,' she said, accepting a cup of tea. 'I heard everything the vicar said, but it was as if he were talking about someone else.'

'I imagine the vicar didn't know him all that well.'

'He didn't know him at all, and that was perhaps as well in the circumstances.'

'Perhaps,' agreed Joe, whose thoughts were finding their own direction.

'What's on your mind, Joe?'

'I was wondering if you'd be all right on your own.'

Maggie looked as if she'd missed something. 'When?'

'Of course, you don't know. I'm going to France again tomorrow, but I'll be back on Friday morning.'

'Of course I'll be all right.' She seemed more interested in Joe's trip to France. 'Who are you going to see this time?'

'The woman who refused to give evidence at first, and I hope I'm going to see another possible witness.'

'Has the woman had a change of heart?'

'Apparently, although Fred says she'll still take some persuading. You see, whilst these people are prepared to make sworn statements, French criminal law requires more than that. They really will need to give evidence in court and allow themselves to be cross-examined by a defence counsel.'

'Just as they would in England, I suppose.'

'Much the same,' he agreed. 'Only the hats, the gowns and the language will be different.'

———◆|◆———

Now that Joe appeared to be making progress with the case, Allard was happy to pay for another overnight berth, and the crossing to St Malo was as comfortable as before despite the strong breeze that had materialised. A member of the crew found Joe's reaction to the forecast amusing. Force six was apparently small beer to experienced sailors, but Joe was inclined to take the line that anything livelier than a flat calm sea and motionless clouds was to be viewed with caution.

Falaise docked at seven forty-five, local time, and Joe collected his hire car, a Peugeot 203, which pleased him so much on the short journey to Paramé that he felt momentarily unfaithful to his beloved Rover. A second blissful reunion with Mme Gilbert at the Hotel des Bains, however, served as a distraction, and any guilt was promptly dispelled.

After unpacking, he set about telephoning his contacts, one of whom was frustratingly unobtainable. The other, Mme Julie Durand, answered her phone immediately.

' *'Allo?*'

'Madame Durand? This is Joseph Pelier. I believe you were expecting a call from me.'

'Of course, Monsieur Pelier.' A hesitation in her voice seemed to contradict her words.

'Rather than speak on the telephone, would you prefer that we meet somewhere?'

'Yes, monsieur, but not at my home.'

The fear was still there. He could sense it. 'Perhaps you would care to join me at my hotel for dinner this evening. I'm staying at the Hotel des Bains in Paramé. My invitation includes Monsieur Durand, naturally.'

'I am a widow, monsieur.'

'I'm so sorry, madame.'

'You are kind, monsieur, and yes, I should like to dine with you. At what time?'

'Shall we say, at nineteen hours?'

'At nineteen hours, monsieur.'

'Madame Durand, are you acquainted with Mademoiselle Estelle Torrent?'

Her reply was guarded. 'Yes, monsieur.'

'I ask because I have been trying to contact her also and for the same reason, but she does not answer her telephone.'

'That does not surprise me, monsieur. She is a teacher in the kindergarten, but she may be contacted at her home after approximately seventeen hours.'

'I am indebted to you, madame. We shall see each other this evening, then?'

'Of course, monsieur.'

She ended the call sounding a little less troubled than before, but he knew he had a task ahead in persuading her to give evidence.

He spent the remainder of the day enjoying, as before, the ambience of pre-war holidays, his memories and nostalgia unaffected by the winter scene.

At around five, he tried Mlle Torrent's number again and was rewarded with an answer. If anything, she sounded more wary than Mme Durand had been, but he was pleased when she agreed to join them for dinner at seven. It was a stroke of good fortune, being able to see them together; with luck, they might possibly recall more than they would have individually.

———◂▸◂———

Neither Mme Durand nor Mlle Torrent could be much older than thirty, but they were both completely grey. Mme Durand, particularly, had a haunted look that affected Joe deeply as he listened to their story.

'Hauptsturmführer Neuhaus had no feelings other than his malevolent beliefs,' said Mlle Torrent. 'He was a machine rather than a man. His actions were those of a psychopath.'

'And you say, monsieur, that he is hiding in England?' It was as if Mme Durand was still afraid of him.

' "Masquerading" would be a better word,' said Joe. 'He stole the identity of a Jerseyman, a cripple of low intellect, and is now living in Essex.' He reached into his briefcase and took out the photographs he'd taken outside Neuhaus's home.

Both women recoiled with shock as they recognised their tormentor more than six years after their imprisonment. Mlle Torrent was the first to speak.

'That is Neuhaus,' she confirmed. 'You mentioned the Jerseyman, monsieur. Had he a club foot?'

'Yes, and his name was Thomas Allard. His family have asked me to investigate his disappearance.'

'Oh, that poor, wretched man.' Mlle Torrent covered her face for a moment, prompting Joe to offer her his handkerchief.

'Thank you, monsieur, but we shed the last of our tears a long time ago.'

Mme Durand nodded in silent agreement.

'This is all very upsetting for you, ladies,' said Joe, 'but I am determined to make Neuhaus face charges.'

Mme Durand said, 'You ask a great deal, monsieur. There are vengeful Nazis still at large.'

'I know.'

Mlle Torrent shook her head impatiently. 'You do not know the Nazis, monsieur. They are capable of unimagined evil.'

'I've never suffered at their hands,' he admitted, 'but I fought them for five years and I spent the early post-war years investigating a war crime. If it helps my argument, I sent two dozen of them to face trial.'

Mlle Torrent looked at him in surprise and said, 'You are a hero, monsieur.'

Joe was quick to disagree. 'I was an ordinary soldier doing his job,' he said. 'If anyone was heroic, you ladies have earned the description many times over.'

'You are kind, monsieur.'

'As for vengeful Nazis, they are active because they believe the authorities have stopped hunting them. If I can persuade the *Sub-Préfet* to have Neuhaus charged with his crimes, they will go again into hiding, but to do that I must have witnesses.'

Mme Durand asked, 'What witnesses have you, monsieur?'

'So far, only Monsieur Henri Forgeron, a senior guardian at the prison.'

Mme Durand nodded. 'We know M. Forgeron. He was one of the better guardians at St Malo. He had no sympathy for the Nazis.'

Joe refilled their glasses. 'What can you tell me about the way Thomas Allard died?'

'I saw it happen,' said Mlle Torrent. 'From the women's cells we could see the prisoners being removed, and we could hear the Nazis quite clearly. They shouted most of their orders.'

Joe nodded, anxious not to stop the flow.

'They were sending prisoners to a camp. I think it was Sachsenhausen, although I may be wrong.' She hesitated.

'Don't worry. Go on.'

'One of them pulled the crippled man out of his cell – he could never move quickly enough for them – and Hauptsturmführer Neuhaus stopped them. He said, "I have a better use for him, but I must be sure he is dead." It seemed a strange remark, but then he took out his pistol and shot him in the head.' She stopped, clearly distressed by the memory.

'I'm sorry to put you through this ordeal, mademoiselle, but I must know the facts. Are you sure the prisoner was Thomas Allard?'

She nodded mutely. Eventually, she said, 'He was an imbecile, he had a club foot, and the other prisoners called him "Tom".'

'Thank you, mademoiselle. I'm very grateful.'

It seemed that Mlle Torrent was not yet finished, because she said, 'When the Americans came, we saw Hauptsturmführer Neuhaus with them. He was in civilian clothes and he was thanking them loudly for liberating France.' She grimaced at the memory. 'Some of us tried to tell them who he was, but none of them understood French, and they were not inclined even to try to understand what we were telling them. They thought we wanted food, so they gave us some of their rations, also cigarettes and... chewing gum.'

'They would,' said Joe. 'Thank you again, mademoiselle. You have been most helpful.'

Mme Durand had been listening quietly to Mlle Torrent's account, occasionally closing her eyes as some aspect of it returned to haunt her, but now, she said, 'I will give you a list of French prisoners whom Neuhaus killed or sent to the concentration camps.'

'I will help you,' said Mlle Torrent.

'That will be of the greatest value,' said Joe, 'but I have to ask you both to do something of even greater importance. Are you prepared to give evidence in court against Neuhaus?' As Joe waited for their answer, he was conscious of the fear their former tormentors were still able to wield. Eventually, Mlle Torrent answered.

'Yes,' she said quietly, 'I will give evidence.'

'So will I,' said Mme Durand.

———◆◆———

'As members of the Resistance, they faced torture and violent death, and then I had to ask them to do something else that clearly terrified them. It was most unpleasant.'

'You must have given them some reassurance,' said Maggie, 'when you told them that bringing Neuhaus to face trial would send the others scurrying for cover.'

'Some reassurance, yes, but the Nazis made a thorough job of terrifying them for life.'

'And now they've made you feel bad.'

'If you'd been there, Maggie, you'd have felt the threat, just as I did. It was tangible, there, in that restaurant.'

'It must have been awful.' She stroked his hand and asked, 'Would you like me to stay tonight?'

'When you stroke me like that, how can I resist?'

'Well then, I'll just have to make the effort and keep you company all night.'

'I'm sure I'll find that very... soothing.'

'I imagine Sergeant-Major Tompkins drew the line at that.'

'He knew how far to go,' confirmed Joe.

———◆◆———

'Do you feel better now?'

'Yes, thank you.'

She kissed him softly and said, 'It's better than a joke for making you feel better, isn't it?'

'It always was, but a joke was the most I could offer you in the early days.'

'True.' She lay still for a while before asking, 'Will you tell me one now, before I go to sleep, like a bedtime story?'

'All right.' He searched his memory for gentle, bedtime jokes and remembered one. 'A man was driving his lorry along the A-something-or-other, when he saw a girl looking for a lift, so he pulled into the side of the road. "I'm trying to get to Winchester," she said. "Okay," he said, "hop in."'

'Probably the A twenty-seven. It seems to ring a bell.'

'What?'

'The road to Winchester, the A twenty-seven. I remember it from somewhere.'

'But you don't know where he was coming from.'

'That's true.'

'All right, it was the A twenty-seven.'

'It doesn't have to be.'

'It was, Maggie. All right?'

'Sorry.'

'Okay. Well, they'd been on the road for a while, and the girl said, "It's ever so good of you to give me a lift. I'd like to pay you." He said, "There's no need." She said, "Oh, but I'd like to. The only thing is, I've no money." He said, "In that case, how are you going to pay me?" In a very seductive, sexy voice, she said, "I've got something very special that lorry drivers really enjoy." Suddenly alarmed, he asked, "How did you find my bacon sandwich?"'

'That was lovely, Joe.' Maggie's voice seemed to come from far away, but Joe didn't mind. It wasn't one of his best jokes, anyway.

25

Over the next two weeks, Joe received copies of sworn statements by Mme Durand, Mlle Torrent and M. Forgeron as well as a long and sickening list of Neuhaus's victims. It was a damning catalogue of his period of responsibility for Reich security in Brittany.

Very carefully, Joe prepared his presentation to the *Préfet*, giving Neuhaus's current location and basically, as he described it to Maggie, 'handing him to the French authorities on a plate.' This time, he was confident of a result. Meanwhile, he had other cases; none of them as big as the Allard case, but that was how he made his living, with lots of small cases. It was a fruitful period, as well, because, by the end of January, he'd located two missing persons and one missing beneficiary, who turned out to have predeceased the testator. It was no doubt good news for the surviving beneficiaries, but Joe had no way of knowing that. Neither was he interested, as his thoughts became centred on his application to the *Préfet* in Brittany.

At last, the bulky letter arrived, and Maggie handed it to him with a letter opener. She watched him slit open the envelope and take out a single sheet, and it must have been plain to her after the first few seconds that the news was less than encouraging.

'It's from the assistant to the *Préfet*,' he said. Apparently, the *Préfet* has been absent on compassionate leave. Wherever he's been, though, he certainly hasn't seen my application. His assistant, however, has seen it and he reckons there's insufficient evidence for a case to be brought against Neuhaus.'

'That's nonsense. He's got three eye witnesses. What more evidence could he want?'

'There's something fishy about this business, Maggie, and I mean to find out what it is. If I make a call to France, will you ask the GPO to advise the cost, and I'll pay Guy for it?'

'Of course I will.'

Joe picked up the letter again and the telephone. When the operator answered, he asked for the telephone number on the letter. It took a while for the connection to be made, but the *Préfet*'s office answered. It was a surprisingly good line.

'I should like to speak, please, with the secretary to the *Préfet de Police*,' he said. 'My name is Joseph Pelier and I am calling from England.'

The next voice he heard said, 'This is the Secretary to the *Préfet*. How may I help you?'

'Good morning, madame. My name is Joseph Pelier. Are you able to tell me, please, when the *Préfet* is likely to return from leave?'

'*Le Préfet* returned to the office today, Monsieur Pelier. May I ask what your business is with him?'

'I wish to make an appointment with him.'

'He is very busy after his period of absence, monsieur. It would be easier for you to see his assistant.'

'I don't doubt that, madame, but I don't wish to see his assistant. I wish to see the *Préfet* himself on a matter of legal importance.'

'The telephonist said you were calling from England, monsieur. Do you have the right to see the *Préfet*?'

'I am a French citizen, madame, and that gives me the perfect right.'

'Very well, monsieur. *Le Préfet* will be able to see you on Friday, the eighth of February at eleven hours.'

'That is excellent. Thank you, madame.'

'You are most welcome, monsieur.'

Maggie, who had been trying, with some difficulty, to follow the conversation, waited for him to replace the receiver, before saying, 'I heard you asking for an appointment, but that's as far as my French goes. Were you successful?'

'Yes, I was. She tried palming me off with the assistant to the Prefect, but I insisted on seeing the man himself. I had to tell a white lie, but all's fair, as I see it.'

'What did you say?'

'I told her I was a French citizen.'

Maggie pursed her lips. 'Naughty, naughty, but this means another trip to France, doesn't it?'

'It does, and I'll bring you something nice this time.'

'Bring yourself back, Joe. That's all I ask.'

———•◄———

Back in his own office, Joe telephoned Allard with the news. Its reception was much as Joe had anticipated.

'That's ridiculous, Mr Pelier. Anyway, who is this assistant, and why didn't you speak to the Prefect himself?'

'Because he was absent from his office by virtue of compassionate leave.'

Allard snorted. 'So, what is your next move?'

'I've made an appointment to speak with the Prefect of Police himself on Friday, the eighth. I'll leave on the seventh and return on the ninth.'

'I'll have you know this is costing a fortune, but I suppose it's the only way. Now that we know how Tom met his death, I'm determined to see that monster in court.'

———•◄———

The shock news of the King's death on the sixth seemed to bring everything to a halt, but normal life soon followed, and Joe was able to make the journey to France.

He located the *Bureau de la Préfecture de Police* without difficulty and registered his arrival. The receptionist spoke to someone and said, 'Unfortunately, the *Préfet* has been delayed by an urgent matter. If you wish, you could speak to his assistant.'

'Thank you, no, I shall remain here until the *Préfet* is available.'

'As you wish, monsieur.'

Joe waited almost an hour, during which he read *Le Figaro* from the front page to the back, including the advertisements. Eventually, a smartly-dressed woman, possibly in her forties, came to speak to him.

'Monsieur Pelier?'

'The same.'

'*Le Préfet* will see you now, monsieur.'

'Thank you.' He followed her down a passage lined with dark oak panels. 'You keep him well hidden,' he observed.

The woman made no reply, but tapped on a large oak door and opened it. 'Monsieur Pelier is here,' she announced.

Joe entered the huge office, which contained the mixed aromas of furniture polish and cigar smoke. The Prefect sat behind a correspondingly large desk, and Joe imagined that the dimensions of offices and desks mirrored the importance of their occupants. Presumably, the quality of their cigars also varied accordingly.

'Monsieur Pelier,' said the Prefect when they had shaken hands, 'what is this matter that is so important that it could not be dealt with by my assistant?'

'A matter of great importance, Monsieur le Préfet. The SS *Hauptsturmführer* responsible for the deaths and deportation of a large number of French citizens in St Malo lives currently in Essex under the stolen identity of a Jerseyman whom he murdered here in nineteen forty-five. I have three witnesses who are prepared to give evidence in court and I have a list of this man's French victims. They were murdered in St Malo prison. Others were sent to concentration camps.' He passed his presentation across the desk.

The Prefect gave the documents a cursory inspection. Finally, he asked, 'What is your interest in this man Neuhaus, Monsieur Pelier?'

'I am, as my introductory letter states, a private inquiry agent engaged to ascertain the facts relating to the disappearance of the Jerseyman Thomas Allard.'

'I see.' The Prefect looked as if he were about to deliver some bad news, and when he spoke, he confirmed it. 'This is most unfortunate,' he said. 'Clearly, you have worked extremely hard on this case, and over an extensive period of time, but now I have to tell you that this office can take it no further.'

'But why, Monsieur Préfet, when it is clear that this man is a multiple murderer?'

The Prefect folded his hands on his desk and leaned forward, as if he were about to explain something very complex. 'For several years after the war, Monsieur Pelier, we hunted down Nazi war criminals, bringing many to justice. We pursued that policy, in fact, until the people of France were tired of hearing about such cases. I understand that the same weariness is prevalent in England.'

Joe refused to be drawn on that. Instead, he said, 'Unfashionable and unpopular it may be to prosecute Nazi war criminals, monsieur, but this case could prove highly beneficial to you, your office and the French Government.'

'Oh?'

'Whilst I was waiting to be taken to you, I read a copy of *Le Figaro*, and I learned, among other things, that the Communists in the Chamber of Deputies are accusing the French Government of channelling ex-Waffen SS soldiers into the Foreign Legion to combat the Viet Minh in Indo China.'

The Prefect looked uncomfortable. 'Really,' he said, 'you should not believe everything you read in the newspapers.'

'In normal circumstances, I would not, but I have heard the same story elsewhere.'

'Where?'

'I spent the early post-war years investigating Nazi war crimes. During that time, I made a number of contacts in military intelligence.'

Clearly unsettled, the Prefect said, 'This is dangerous, irresponsible gossip, monsieur. It should go no further.'

'But wouldn't it do you and the Government some good if its critics learned that you were prosecuting, rather than recruiting, a Nazi murderer with the blood of countless local victims on his hands?'

The Prefect pushed the bundle of documents back to Joe. 'I must bring this interview to a close, Monsieur Pelier,' he said. 'You have abused the hospitality of the *Préfecture*.'

'Have I really? Look at those names, Monsieur Préfet, the names of patriotic Frenchmen and Frenchwomen who risked torture and death for their country, and who finally succumbed to those fates.' Joe opened the list and jabbed at it with his finger. 'Just look at the horrifying number of victims and tell me again that it is unfashionable to pursue war criminals. Go on, read the names of those who gave their lives for occupied France, and then turn your back, not only on their memory, but on justice itself!' Uncharacteristically, Joe was angry, and his voice had risen during the last sentence, but the Prefect's attitude left him completely unrepentant.

Angrier than ever, the Prefect tried again to push the list back to Joe. As he did so, however, something caught his notice, and he stopped quite suddenly and stared, as if mesmerised by his discovery, his anger now suddenly quelled. 'On reflection, Monsieur Pelier,' he said in a more sober tone, 'I should like you to leave these documents in my possession. It is just possible that criminal charges might be brought against this man Neuhaus after all, and a high-profile extradition might, I agree, be advantageous at this time.'

'I hope the extradition will only be reported retrospectively. We don't want Neuhaus to take fright, do we?'

'Of course not, Monsieur Pelier. That goes without saying.' After a moment's thought, he said, 'If such a prosecution is possible, you may expect to hear from the British police.'

———◆◆———

Joe gave his report to Allard, who was more conciliatory than usual, and re-joined Maggie in her office.

'Thank you for the perfume, Joe,' she said. 'I hope it wasn't too expensive.'

'It's nothing like as expensive in France as it is in this country,' he assured her. 'They don't have the burden of sixty percent luxury purchase tax.'

'And not everyone knows a lovely man who goes to France and brings perfume for them. I'm very lucky.'

'I suppose you are,' agreed Joe, 'but then, so am I.'

'You're very clever too, persuading that prefect-chap to prosecute Neuhaus. How did you do it?'

'It was all down to passion.' Joe adopted a theatrical no-nonsense look. 'I took him by the lapels and held him against the wall, eyeball to eyeball, and told him that, not only was he a disgrace to his calling, but that his mother would be ashamed to call him her son. He soon backed down.'

'I don't believe a word of it.'

'All right. It was the strangest thing, because he was sweeping away the list of victims and telling me to clear off, when he suddenly stopped.

He was staring at the list as if it had suddenly assumed new meaning, and then, as calmly as anything, he told me to leave the dossier with him, and that, yes, there was the possibility that Neuhaus might be made to face charges.'

'Maybe he'd found a long-lost relative in the list.'

'I've had a good look at it and I couldn't find anyone with his surname.'

'It could have been someone on his mother's side,' she suggested.

'Possibly, or it may have been simply an acquaintance. At all events, I'm eternally grateful to whoever it was, because he or she caused him to make the most spectacular about-turn I've ever seen.'

'I suppose we'll never know, but thank goodness it did the trick. She looked at the clock and said, 'Tell me a quick joke and then let me get on with this letter.'

'All right.' He searched his repertoire and found one. 'A man was driving his Rolls-Royce along the road, when he saw a girl needing a lift.'

'This isn't about a bacon sandwich, is it?'

'No it isn't. Be quiet and listen.'

'Sorry.'

'Good. He stopped to offer her a lift, and she climbed in. After a while, she said, "This is a nice car." He said, "Yes, it's a Rolls-Royce Phantom Three." She was very impressed, as you can imagine, because it wasn't just any old Rolls-Royce, and not just a Phantom One or a Phantom Two, but a Phantom Three, so he asked her, "Are you comfortable, or would you like the seat further back?" She asked, "Can you do that?" "Of course," he said, and he touched a button on the dashboard to adjust the back of the seat. "Gosh," she said, "that's clever." "Well," he said, "you'd expect Rolls-Royce to think of everything, wouldn't you?" Then he asked her, "Can you see out, or would you like the seat a little higher?" I think he was showing off, but she said, "Go on, then. Let's have it a bit higher." Between you and me, I think she was high enough, but she was curious to see what else the car had to offer. Anyway, he touched another button, and the seat rose by about two inches.'

'Will a Rolls-Royce really do that?'

'Yes, Maggie. Please try not to interrupt.'

'Sorry.'

' "That's wonderful," said the girl. "I told you," he said, "Rolls-Royce think of everything." After a while, the girl said, "I'm hungry. Have you anything to eat?" "Look in the glove compartment," he told her. "You'll find a sandwich in there." She opened the glove compartment and felt inside, but as well as the sandwich, she found two golf tees. She asked, "What are these?" He said, "They're to rest my balls on when I'm driving off." "Gosh," she said, "Rolls-Royce really *do* think of everything!"

———◄►———

Later that evening, Maggie asked, 'What's involved in extraditing that Neuhaus man?'

'It's actually a complex business. As I understand it, under the terms of the extradition treaty in force, the prosecuting authority in France has to contact the British Foreign Office, who then contact the Home Office. If they're satisfied that Neuhaus should stand trial in France, they'll order his arrest. The whole thing will then go before a High Court judge, who will examine the evidence and decide whether or not Neuhaus is to be extradited. When everything is settled, they'll hand him over to the French authorities, and the rest will be up to them.'

'It does sound involved,' she said, pouring him another drink. 'I suppose the fact that he helped himself to Thomas Allard's cottage is insignificant beside all the crimes he committed in France.'

'It may be, but I'm still going to send the evidence I've got to the Jersey Police. I hate leaving a job half-done.'

'I'd say you've done a very thorough job.'

'Well yes, but you see, you're just a shade biased.'

She shook her head. 'No, you're wrong.'

'Am I?'

'Yes,' she said, punctuating her argument with repeated kisses, 'you see, I'm very, very, *very* biased.'

———◄►———

A little later, Joe received a letter from Fred Maçon, reacting to the news about the proposed extradition.

Dear Joe,
Let me offer my congratulations on an excellent piece of work.
I have spoken with Mme Durand and Mlle Torrent, who also send their thanks and salutations. For some reason, it had slipped Mlle Torrent's mind that one of the victims on her list was, let us say, not unknown to the Préfet de Police, although he would naturally prefer the fact to remain a secret, certainly from his wife and immediate family.
Meanwhile, you have succeeded in this huge task. Congratulations again! Should you find yourself on Jersey at any time, please call on us. You will always be welcome.
Yours with all good wishes,
Fred Maçon.

When he showed the letter to Maggie, she was less cryptic than Fred.

'A discretion, do you suppose?'

'It's not unknown. They tell me the French are noted for it, although I really couldn't comment. One thing I will say, however, is that, after all the hitches and disappointments, this case finally looks as if it's heading towards a successful conclusion.'

'It has to be a good sign.'

'Yes,' he agreed, 'although I shan't relax completely until I hear from Essex Police.'

26

Joe returned from a wearisome marital case to learn that an officer had telephoned from the Essex and Southend Combined Constabulary, asking him to return the call when convenient. If he guessed correctly, it was the first intimation that the French were going ahead with the prosecution and, as Joe's final bonus from Allard depended on Neuhaus's arrest, he decided that no time was more convenient than the present.

Taking Maggie's note into his office, he telephoned the number on it and was connected with the Essex force.

'Good morning,' he said. 'My name is Pelier. I'm returning a call from Chief Inspector Luckhurst.'

'Please hold the line, sir. I'll try to find him for you.'

Joe waited patiently until the line reopened, and a voice said, 'Luckhurst speaking.'

Chief Inspector Luckhurst, this is Joseph Pelier. I believe you telephoned me earlier this morning. I'm just returning your call.'

'Mr Pelier, yes, this is quite a case you've turned up, isn't it? Not your usual kind of thing, I imagine?'

'It's quite unusual for a private detective, I'll admit, but I've been searching for evidence since last May, in the hope of being able to interest the authorities in the case.'

'Have you really? Well, the French Sûreté have put together what looks like a strong case against this chap, and the word from on high is that he must be extradited if at all possible. Of course, the matter will have to go before a judge.'

'So I understand. When do you propose to make the arrest, Chief Inspector?'

'Next week. I mean, there's no hurry, is there? He's not going anywhere. Naturally, we'll need you to come with us for identification purposes. When everyone's ready, we'll move in and make the arrest.'

* * *

'Now that we've eaten,' said Joe, 'are you going to stay overnight and let me make endless love to you?'

'Are you likely to get cramp in your calf muscle again?'

'I hope not. That was very embarrassing as well as agonising.'

'And,' she said in mock-censure, 'it happened just as… things were coming to a dramatic conclusion.'

He gave her a sideways look. 'Now you know what it's like to be interrupted just as you're getting to the best bit.'

She gave that some thought and said, 'It's a new experience for me, Joe, as you know, and I'm still encountering new sensations, but I can't say it felt like a joke.'

'Good. Stay the night, and I'll try not to get cramp.'

'Let's not make a joke of it, either.'

'As if I would.'

'I wouldn't put it past you. All right, seeing as it's Friday.' As she watched him put a fresh log on the fire, she said, 'You know, I could never have joked with Derek the way I do with you.'

'Considering the nature of his problem, it might have been a touch on the foolhardy side,' he agreed.

'I don't just mean,' she said, lowering her voice, 'about… *hanky-panky*. We couldn't joke about anything at all.'

'Hanky-panky?'

Faintly embarrassed, she said, 'I've never needed to call it anything until now. Can you wonder that I struggle to find a name for it?'

'Why struggle? It's much more fun to do it than it is to talk about it.'

'I agree.'

He stared into the fire, letting his mind follow its course.

'What are you thinking about, Joe?'

'Bernhardt Neuhaus and, more particularly, when the Essex lot are going to arrest him. I'll be happier when this business is settled and the French, or at least, our people, have him in custody.'

'It's completely beyond your control, isn't it?'

'Frustratingly so. I think a drink is in order. Will you join me?'

'Just a small one, please.'

Joe poured two glasses of cognac and gave one to Maggie.

'Thank you. Look, Joe, I've been wondering if the Neuhaus man might still be dangerous.'

'I doubt it. He's put so much effort into posing as an innocent Jerseyman, now settled in England, that I doubt if he has so much as a pistol in his possession.'

'I hope not.' The possibility seemed to worry her until, after a while, she said, 'One of your dirty jokes might help at this stage.'

'You never know.'

'Go ahead, then.'

Joe inhaled the vapour from his cognac and thought. Eventually, he said, 'I know. You'll be familiar, I imagine, with Ruby Coxcomb's page in the *Daily News*?'

'I've seen it, but I wouldn't say I'm exactly familiar with it. I've never paid much attention to agony aunts.'

'Most of the letters they get are quite boring,' he said, 'but I do remember her being interviewed by a journalist on her fiftieth birthday. He asked her about the highs and lows of her career and, naturally enough, she mentioned certain memorable letters that she'd received from her followers. I remember one in particular. It read:

'Dear Ruby,

I hope you can help me, because I'm at my wits' end. The fact is, my husband is a sex addict. He will not leave me alone. All the time, he insists on having intimate relations with me. It happens at all hours of the day and night, and it's not always in the bedroom. I've had to submit to his demands on the refrigerator, the wash boiler, and even the cooker. Needless to say, we've been banned from the electricity and gas showrooms. Where will it end? The ordeal goes on, and on, and on. He surprises me at the most inconvenient moments. What can I do?

Yours,

Frantic of Finsbury Park.

P.S. Please excuse the shaky handwriting.'

'They get sillier,' said Maggie.
'But you almost laughed at that one.'
'I often laugh at your jokes, but later, when I'm alone. I need time to think about them.'
'I never think of them as having a delayed-action fuse. I must make allowance for that in future.'
'Maybe I'm the one with the delayed action fuse.'
'Oh, I don't know,' he said, looking at her out of the corner of his eye.
'You're naughty.'

———◆◄———

On Monday morning, Joe dropped Maggie at the end of the road to buy her newspaper. He went on to park in his usual place and took the stairs to his office. Guy hadn't yet arrived, so he picked up the mail, taking out any that were addressed to him, and left the rest on Maggie's desk. He went through to his own office, completely unprepared for her breathless arrival.

'Joe, look at this,' she demanded, placing a copy of the *Daily News* on his desk.

His eyes went to the headline, which was about the forthcoming trial of the mathematician Alan Turing, who was charged with gross indecency with another man. I just feel sorry for the poor man,' he said, wondering why Maggie was so excited about the trial. 'It's no fault of his. He's only what nature made him.'

'Not that,' she said impatiently pointing to the next story down.

Joe followed her finger and read:

Essex Man Named as Nazi War Criminal
(From our Paris correspondent).

Essex Police are poised to extradite a man living in Romford, Essex, who, they claim, is Bernhardt Neuhaus, at one time an officer in the feared and hated SS.

A Deserving Case

He is accused of the murder of a number of French Resistance fighters and the deportation of many more to various concentration camps.

He is believed to be living as Thomas Allard, and claims to be a citizen of Jersey.

'Hell's bells!' Joe picked up the telephone and asked for the Essex and Southend Constabulary. 'Someone in the *Préfecture de Police* must have tipped off the French press, and they passed the story on to this rag,' he said.

A voice said, 'Chelmsford Police. How can we help you?'

'Good morning. My name is Joseph Pelier. I should like to speak urgently with Chief Inspector Luckhurst, please.'

'Please hold the line, sir. I'll see if he's in his office.'

After half-a-minute or so, Joe heard a welcome voice. 'Hello, Mr Pelier. Luckhurst here.'

'Good. Have you seen the *Daily News* this morning?'

'Someone's just shown it to me.'

'How bloody irresponsible can some people be?'

'You're talking about the press, Mr Pelier, so it's a good question. I've informed the London airports, so they're on the lookout for someone using the name Thomas Allard. If he turns up, airport security will hold him until we arrive. Unfortunately, I have an urgent case calling for my attention, so I must cut this conversation short.'

'Do you have someone who can call at the travel agencies in Romford? There can't be all that many.'

'I'm sorry, Mr Pelier. I must go.' The receiver went down.

Joe swore. 'I'm going to Romford,' he told Maggie.

'I heard.'

'I'll probably be back tonight. Will you cancel my ten o' clock appointment? Tell them something credible.'

'All right. Is there anything else I can do?'

'Yes, will you get Thomas Cook's number in Romford, ask them for their address and the addresses of any other travel agencies in Romford?'

'Okay.' She set to work immediately while Joe spoke to Guy. When he returned, she had all the information he needed. There were just three travel agencies in Romford, and he now had all the details.

'Thanks, Maggie.'

'You're welcome. Be careful.'

'I will.' He kissed her and left the office.

———◆◆◆———

Romford was a long and frustrating drive. The last time, he'd set off long before the rush-hour, but now he had to contend with day-time traffic and the usual London congestion. After what seemed an interminable journey, he reached Romford and found his way to the office of Thomas Cook and Son.

A smiling young man greeted him. 'Good morning, sir. Can I help you?'

'I hope so.' He showed his business card and asked, 'May I see the manager?'

'I'll get him for you, sir.' He disappeared into a back room and returned after a short time with a smart, middle-aged man who seemed curious. He asked, 'Is there a problem, sir?'

'Yes, but it's none of your making, I assure you. I'm a private inquiry agent,' he explained, showing his card again. 'The police are involved in this case, but I got here before them. We're looking for a known criminal living in Romford and using the name Thomas Allard. Can you tell me, please, if anyone by that name has recently booked a flight through this agency?'

The manager seemed unsure. 'This is unusual and irregular,' he said. 'As far as I know, private detectives don't get involved in criminal matters.'

'If you telephone Chelmsford Police and ask for Chief Inspector Luckhurst, he'll vouch for me.' He would be lucky to find him there, but Joe saw no point in complicating matters.

'Oh well, I suppose it'll be all right.' With no clients in the office, he called in a loud voice, 'Has someone called Thomas Allard booked a flight recently?'

His enquiry brought forth a series of responses, all of which were negative.

'Thank you, everyone,' said Joe, giving a card to the manager. 'If he shows up, I'd be grateful if you'd let me know.'

The manager assured him that he would.

His next call was at Altham's, one of the small, family-owned agencies. The manager was off the premises, but Joe spoke to each member of the booking staff and ascertained that no one called Thomas Allard had booked a flight through them.

The third travel agency was Bennetts, a firm that had started between the wars, offering excursions to Belgium and France, to those still sufficiently curious about the Western Front to take the trouble to visit it. Since the Second World War, they had branched out into mainstream travel, and were therefore worth a visit. They were also situated quite close to Neuhaus's place of employment.

When Joe arrived, the manager was nowhere to be found, so he spoke directly to the booking staff, who assured him that Thomas Allard had not so far contacted them. He was thanking them all for their assistance and asking them to call him as soon as the spurious Allard put in an appearance, when the branch manager returned, demanding to know who was dealing with 'this man.'

'They all are,' Joe told him, 'and they've been very helpful indeed.'

The manager bristled. 'What's this about?'

'I asked for their assistance in a police matter, and they gave me their wholehearted co-operation. I must say that they were a damned sight friendlier than you.' He left the agency and went in search of somewhere where he could relieve himself and then eat.

——◂▸——

'What a day,' he told Maggie, when he returned to the office at a little after three-thirty.

Her answer was to give him a cup of tea and her full attention.

'I hope I don't have to go to Romford again. It was a foul journey both ways.'

Maggie was about to offer her sympathy, when Joe's telephone rang. Wearily, he picked it up.

'Joseph Pelier,' he said.

'Mr Pelier,' said a male voice, 'I'm one of the booking clerks at Bennett's Travel. I was here when you came in this morning. I haven't been able to call you until now, because the manager's been here all the time and he's been in an awful temper, but the man you're looking for booked a flight this morning to Cairo with BOAC from London Airport. It's Flight E143, leaving at seven-thirty tonight.'

'Thank you very much indeed. You've been immensely helpful.'

'You're welcome, Mr Pelier.'

Joe pressed the switch on the cradle and asked for Chelmsford Police Station. When he was connected, he asked for Chief Inspector Luckhurst and was told, after a search, that the chief inspector was out on a case.

'Will someone take a message for him? It really is very urgent.'

The telephonist put him through to Luckhurst's office, where a detective constable agreed to take the message.

'Tell him, please, that Bernhardt Neuhaus, N-E-U-H-A-U-S, has booked a flight to Cairo, leaving London Airport at seven-thirty tonight.' He gave the details of the flight.

'And who shall I say called, sir?'

'Joseph Pelier.' He spelt his surname. 'Chief Inspector Luckhurst needs that information urgently. Oh, and tell him that I'm leaving now for London Airport. I'll see him at Airport Security.'

27

For the third time that day, Joe undertook a long journey through dense traffic, the only new feature being the level of adrenaline involved. Neuhaus would naturally arrive before him, but the flight would not depart until seven-thirty. He could depend on that, if little else. He just hoped there would be no major delay between Folkestone and the airport.

He was making better progress than he'd dared expect, and was beginning to relax a little, having joined the South Circular, when traffic began to slow down ahead, and he was obliged to do the same.

The line of traffic crept by instalments for more than forty-five minutes, until a police diversion sign directed it off the South Circular, where an incident of some magnitude had clearly occurred.

For what seemed an age, he and the others followed the diversion, eventually re-joining the South Circular at Brixton. According to the clock on the Rover's dashboard, it was now past six o'clock. He pressed on, driving as fast as traffic would allow, realising at the same time that Luckhurst and his party would also be making their way through the heavy London traffic. All the time, his stomach felt as if it were tied in a huge knot.

Another slow queue had Joe almost reconciled to losing Neuhaus for good, but the obstruction appeared to be only temporary, and he was able to pick up speed.

Cautiously relieved, he reached London Airport at six minutes past seven, parking the Rover and hurrying into the newly-constructed airport building.

Once in the Departure Lounge, he looked around for Neuhaus. A great many faces were obscured by newspapers and magazines, and he was frustrated also by the multitude of grey heads until he reminded himself that Neuhaus's hair was closer to white. His best option was to look more closely, and he did so, glancing surreptitiously at a number of innocent passengers, none of whom was Neuhaus. He was beginning to worry, when a man in a dark suit, reading the *Daily Telegraph,* caught his attention. A brief sighting as the man turned a page prompted Joe to reach for the photograph he'd taken as Neuhaus was leaving his home. One look told him his search was over. Elated by the culmination of months of toil and setbacks, he stopped in front of his quarry and asked, 'Are you Mr Thomas Allard?'

Neuhaus looked up in surprise. 'Yes?'

Looking at Neuhaus for the first time in the flesh, he noticed the eyes particularly, because they were cold, grey and predictably, at least from Joe's point of view, quite soulless. 'Will you come with me to Airport Security? There's a query about your booking.'

Neuhaus was rattled, but he didn't ask Joe who he was, which was surprising for someone who had lived for so long under a regime that demanded identification as a way of life. It was possible that the ubiquitous trilby and trench coat made Joe look anonymously official. At all events, Neuhaus simply asked, 'What is the problem?'

'Come with me, Mr Allard. It won't take long, and I'll explain everything.'

'But I'm waiting for my flight to be called.' He spoke with a slight German accent, even after seven years, and Joe wondered at the insularity of the British people that they could believe that his was the speech of a Jerseyman.

'It won't take a minute, I assure you.' Joe intended holding him for much longer than that.

'I really don't see…. Oh, all right, but this is very annoying.' He stood up, and Joe guided him to the security office, where he bundled him inside, startling the plain-clothes official behind the desk.

'We'll be joined shortly by police officers from Essex,' he told the official. 'They're going to arrest this man.' As he spoke, shock registered on Neuhaus's features. 'I believe you were asked to look out for him.'

The public address system chimed and a voice said, 'BOAC Flight E One Four Three to Cairo is now boarding. Will passengers for the flight please proceed to Gate Four?'

'We know nothing about that,' said the official. 'Anyway, who are you? If you're a police officer, at least let me see your identification.'

'No, I'm not with the police. I'm just giving them a helping hand.' He saw Neuhaus's eyes darting here and there, obviously looking for an escape route. 'I'd better explain,' he said, 'that this man is an ex-officer of the SS. He was Hauptsturmführer Bernhardt Neuhaus of the Waffen SS, but he's been masquerading these past seven years as a Jerseyman called Thomas Allard, a man he murdered in nineteen forty-five.'

'This is ridiculous,' said Neuhaus, sounding increasingly German in his anxiety. 'I've never heard of Bernhardt whatever you called him, and I've no idea what this ridiculous man's game is, but I have an aeroplane to catch. Tell him to release me at once.'

In spite of the circumstances, Joe couldn't help noticing that Neuhaus had never lost the Teutonic insistence on smartness and grooming. His hair and moustache were immaculately trimmed, and despite the urgency of his attempted abscondment, he had shaved meticulously.

Passengers for the Cairo flight had now passed the security office and were heading for the gate.

The airport official was dithering. 'Look,' he said, 'we know absolutely nothing about this. I've got no power to detain anyone without express orders.'

Joe said, 'If you allow him to escape, you'll be in serious trouble with the police, I promise you.' As he spoke, he felt Neuhaus struggling to free himself.

'All right,' said the official. 'You'd better keep him here until the police arrive.'

Neuhaus was panicking. 'Let me go,' he said. 'This whole business is a complete nonsense.'

The PA system chimed again. 'BOAC Flight B One Three Eight to Nairobi is now boarding. Will passengers for the flight please proceed to Gate Five?'

'You must let me go,' insisted Neuhaus. 'This man is a lunatic. Don't listen to him. I shall miss my flight if you don't make him release me at once.'

The door opened, and a youthful, uniformed policeman joined them. 'I'm PC Crossland from the Middlesex Constabulary,' he announced. 'I've been sent to keep an eye out for a man called Thomas Allard.'

'And not before time,' said Joe. 'This is your man.'

'Gate Four is now closed,' the PA system informed anyone unfortunate enough to have arrived late for the Cairo flight.

The PC had left the door slightly ajar, and Neuhaus saw his chance. Tearing himself away from Joe's grasp and hurling the constable to one side, he launched himself with surprising agility through the doorway, stumbling for the moment, almost falling, recovering and then running towards the queue of passengers currently making their way to Gate Five.

Joe and the constable reached the door at the same time. 'I'm sorry,' said Joe, also shoving the unfortunate PC aside, 'but this is my prisoner.' He sprinted after Neuhaus, who was pushing his way into the queue in front of a woman with a capacious handbag, which sprang open, scattering its contents over a wide area.

'I'm sorry, madam,' said Joe, also pushing her aside.

'What *are* you playing at?'

'I'm sorry,' Joe repeated.

There was pandemonium ahead, where Neuhaus was forcing his way through the rest of the queue, and Joe was obliged to do the same, albeit apologetically. A large, angry-looking man, possibly a Kenyan, actually confronted him, barring his way.

'I'm sorry,' said Joe. 'That man is a criminal.'

Sourly, the man said nothing, but stepped aside to allow Joe through. A woman behind Joe shouted, 'Someone call security or the police! This is disgraceful!'

The queue for the Nairobi flight was almost at the gate. Passengers for the Cairo flight had reached the aircraft and were boarding. Neuhaus was still shoving his way past the passengers for Nairobi, scattering them as he went.

Beyond the crowd, Joe could see that the last of the passengers for Cairo were on the staircase, and the hostesses were about to follow them. The tractor was in position, ready to tow the staircase away.

Apologising hurriedly, Joe squeezed past the passengers at the gate. He'd lost sight of Neuhaus for the moment, but there was no mystery about his whereabouts, and he pressed on, determined to stop him before he reached the aircraft. Once he was on board with the door securely closed, even the police would be powerless to reach him, and he would be on his way to Cairo, a welcome guest of King Farouk.

A Deserving Case

As Joe broke through the gate, he saw that the two hostesses were still at the foot of the mobile staircase, both looking mystified at the sight of Neuhaus sprinting towards them.

The fugitive was almost up to the staircase now, and Joe emerged from the Nairobi queue, dispensing with good manners for the moment and ignoring the shouts and complaints of those he swept aside.

Breathless and in a state of panic, Neuhaus reached frantically for the handrail, knocking one hostess to the ground in his haste. Joe summoned his strength in a desperate flying tackle that brought Neuhaus and him to the ground. Neuhaus was struggling desperately until Joe punched him once in the region of his left kidney, causing him to scream and jack-knife, helpless in his agony.

'That was for the real Thomas Allard, you murdering bastard,' he told him, forcing him into an arm lock and hauling him to his feet. Now, with his prisoner under restraint, he waited for the constable from the Middlesex force to join him, although, in the event, he was relieved to find that the PC did not arrive alone.

'Thank you, Mr Pelier. I imagine you are Mr Pelier?'

Joe recognised Chief Inspector Luckhurst's voice.

'That's right, Chief Inspector.'

'Well done. We were delayed in traffic, but it seems you got here in the nick of time.'

The passengers for Nairobi were now pouring out on to the concrete approach to their aircraft, but the men from Chelmsford as well as the Middlesex PC had made it through the crowd, as uniformed police always would. The sergeant who stood beside Luckhurst produced a pair of handcuffs.

'Yes,' said Joe, regaining his breath, 'this man could have given Houdini a run for his money. He's already escaped twice. Put the bugger in handcuffs before he makes it a hat trick.'

Luckhurst formally arrested Neuhaus, informing him of his rights, and the party turned towards the gate.

Joe found that the hostess who had been unlucky enough to be in Neuhaus's path was close-by, possibly having witnessed the struggle. Noticing that one of her stockings had become laddered during her unfortunate tumble, and that she was also nursing an injured hand, he asked, 'Are you all right, my dear?'

'I'm quite all right, thank you, sir.' She smiled reassuringly, no doubt mindful that one of her duties, even at moments of personal inconvenience, was to be reassuring.

'He's a wanted criminal,' he explained unnecessarily, although it seemed to him that the public should be kept informed. 'I'm sorry you were caught up in the arrest. Will your hand be all right?'

'It's only grazed, but thank you for your concern, sir.'

As Joe re-joined the others at Gate Five, Luckhurst asked passengers to let them through. 'There's nothing to see,' he told them, but they seemed to believe otherwise, watching in fascination as a prisoner was led away in handcuffs after a dramatic pursuit.

Neuhaus was still catching his breath, the blow to the kidney having hindered his recovery. He looked drained as he walked beside the officer whose handcuffs he shared, and said to Joe, 'You are not, I believe, a... policeman?'

'No, I'm a private inquiry agent.'

Neuhaus made no comment about that, but asked breathlessly, 'How... did you... find me?'

'You were foolish enough to sell Allard's cottage,' Joe told him. 'Had you not done that, you might never have been suspected, let alone captured. I traced you from the details you left with the estate agent and the lawyer, and a photograph I took outside your home in Romford showed the Waffen SS blood group tattooed on your arm. You were positively identified by several of your surviving victims.'

Neuhaus looked puzzled. 'When have you seen me without a shirt?' It seemed to matter to him.

'A boy was delivering newspapers. You took yours from him on your doorstep. I believe you were shaving when he arrived.'

Neuhaus nodded. It had possibly been a normal occurrence, but something else was puzzling him. 'How did you know,' he asked, 'about... SS blood groups?'

'I spent a great deal of time after the war, investigating Nazi atrocities in Italy. I sent almost a dozen of your comrades to the gallows and a similar number to various prisons in Germany.'

'You speak of your deeds with pride, Mr....'

'Pelier.'

'You admit that, Mr Pelier, and yet you speak of German war crimes.'

Joe was unpleasantly reminded of the double standards he'd encountered in Italy. Nazi prisoners had always been quick to accuse the Allies of equal wrongdoing. The bombing of Dresden might have become a favourite topic had the opportunity ever been allowed. 'Not pride, Neuhaus,' he argued. 'At least, not the kind you understand, the kind that led you to inflict torture and murder on innocent men and women. I prefer to think of it as professional satisfaction. I had a job to do, and I'm satisfied that I did a thorough job.'

'I only did what was necessary,' said Neuhaus unashamedly. 'It was my duty to apprehend saboteurs and assassins, and that was what I did.'

Joe had heard the same story many times in Italy, and it still sickened him. 'Those people had suffered the invasion of their homeland, Neuhaus. What did you expect them to do? Greet the Nazi hordes with welcoming banners and portraits of Hitler?'

Neuhaus remained unmoved. 'It was my duty to rid the *arrondissement* of undesirables. That was what I did. No more and no less than that.'

'The only undesirables in Brittany were there on the orders of the bloodthirsty megalomaniac you called your *Führer*, Neuhaus, and I am pleased to have assisted in the capture of one of them.'

There was reaction in Neuhaus's eyes at Joe's description of Hitler, but he quickly abated. 'Of course,' he said as they reached the security office, 'they won't convict me. The public have lost their appetite for the apprehension of so-called war criminals.'

'I wouldn't place a bet on it, Neuhaus.'

'We shall see.'

'Oh, we shall,' said Joe.

Again, Neuhaus made no comment, but said, 'So this all this happened because of that crippled half-wit in St Malo Prison.'

'An unfortunate human being in need of kindness and compassion,' commented Joe, 'not the treatment you inflicted on him. He didn't deserve to be killed and robbed of his identity and his property so that his murderer could escape justice.'

'He was crippled and he was an imbecile.' Neuhaus's voice had risen in his bid to justify his actions. 'If he had survived, what kind of life would he have had?'

'I'm told that he led a life of contentment, doing a job he understood and enjoyed, right up to the arrival of Nazi troops on Jersey. In any case,

Neuhaus, what gives you the right to decide whether a person should live or die?' Joe knew the answer to that question, even if Neuhaus didn't, but their conversation was interrupted as Chief Inspector Luckhurst finished speaking with Airport Security and then turned to him. 'Thank you for all your help, Mr Pelier.'

'It was my pleasure, Chief Inspector. He had me worried for a moment out there, but it was no trouble.' As he spoke, he realised that his elbow and the knuckles of his right hand were raw and bleeding from his desperate rugby tackle.

'Good. He'll spend the night in Hayes Police Station, and we'll move him to Chelmsford tomorrow. I imagine some time will elapse before he makes the journey to France.'

Neuhaus looked up suddenly from his embittered thoughts.

'Yes, Neuhaus,' said Joe, 'you'll be tried in France, not in Britain. You're wanted for a great many acts of murder and torture that you committed in St Malo. Thomas Allard was only one of your victims.'

'But the French Government no longer persecutes National Socialists,' he protested.

'Yes, I understand that they've taken to recruiting them to serve with the Foreign Legion in Indo China, but don't worry. You'll be spared that ordeal, because they've agreed to make an exception in your case. They're not going to "persecute" you, either, to use your ridiculous euphemism. They're going to prosecute you. Goodbye, Hauptsturmführer Neuhaus. *Auf nimmer Wiedersehen*, because I'm delighted to say that we are unlikely to meet again.'

———▸◂———

At the end of a long and tiring drive, Joe saw that there was a light on inside his cottage, and he found the door unlocked, so he wasn't surprised when he found Maggie waiting for him. As he entered the room, she held out her arms for a hug.

'Thank you for phoning me,' she said. 'It set my mind at rest.'

'I imagined you'd be here,' he said.

'What actually happened? I know you caught him, but that's all you told me.'

'We got him in the nick of time, just as he was trying to board the aeroplane. He'll be held in custody until the extradition is approved, and then he'll go to France as a guest of the Sûreté.'

She hugged him again. 'My hero,' she said. 'Well done, Joe.'

'I'm no hero, Maggie, but I'm very, very….'

'Tired?'

'Hungry.' He reflected, and said, 'Tired as well, I suppose, although that's hardly surprising.'

'When did you last eat?'

He had to think before he could answer that question. 'I had a snack in Romford at lunchtime,' he recalled, 'and it's the most remarkable thing, but I can't remember, now, what I had.'

'I'll cook you something for supper. I expect you're ready for a drink as well?'

'Yes, please. I think you'll find a bottle of Bourgogne *rouge* in the kitchen.'

'A bottle of what?'

'Sorry, red Burgundy.'

She went to the kitchen and returned with the bottle, two glasses and a corkscrew. She asked, 'Will you open the bottle? You're better at it than I am.'

'It's the Frenchman in me,' he said, picking up the bottle and plying the corkscrew with exaggerated panache.

'What happened to your hand?' She stared with dismay at the dried blood on his knuckles.

'There was a bit of a struggle.'

'Oh, no.'

'It was no more than a minor scuffle. I brought him down just short of the goal line. He'd just knocked a perfectly innocent and charming air hostess flying, laddered one of her stockings and hurt her hand, so he had it coming to him.'

'You didn't tell me there'd been fighting.'

'It wasn't really fighting, not what I'd call fighting, anyway. I hit him and he stopped struggling.'

'I'm glad I didn't know about all that earlier.' She took a glass of wine and said, 'Let me clean those wounds and put something on them. Where do you keep your first-aid things?'

'In the kitchen, on the shelf above the refrigerator. I'll show you.'

He pointed out the first-aid box and submitted to treatment.

Maggie bathed his knuckles. 'You'll have to be brave,' she said, opening the bottle of iodine.

He screwed his eyes up tightly. 'I can take it,' he said.

She poured iodine on to the dressing and covered his wounds before examining his elbow. Close inspection revealed that three layers of clothing had provided a cushion, at least to some extent. The elbow was bruised, but the skin was intact. 'Hold up your arm,' she said.

'Why?'

'Would you have questioned Sergeant-Major Tompkins? Do as you're told.'

He held up his arm, and she kissed his bruise. 'Now it'll make a complete recovery,' she told him.

'I honestly believe,' he said, that Tompkins couldn't have done that better.'

'I'm glad you think so. I'm going to cook something for you. I brought some things from my cottage. They're fairly basic, but I don't imagine you'll mind that.'

'Not for one minute.'

'How does corned beef and bubble-and-squeak with a fried egg sound?'

'Like an angels' chorus.'

He took a seat gratefully in the sitting room, but it wasn't long before he joined her in the kitchen, unable to sit still for long after the events of the evening. It was like waiting for a merry-go-round to stop before he could get off.

'It won't be long,' she assured him, 'although there's probably time for a dirty joke.'

'Are you sure?'

'If it's not too long.'

'Very well. I shall be concise. It concerns two nurses, who were talking in a hospital. It was the night shift, and things were quiet. One said to the other, "Did you know that the man in bed four has 'WEAR' tattooed on his thingy?" "Surely not," said the other. "He has," insisted the first nurse. "I've just seen it." "I must see this," said the second nurse, a most attractive young woman with a voluptuous figure, and she went to bed four to inspect the evidence for herself. She returned, smiling, and said, "It doesn't say 'WEAR' at all. It says, 'ONE UP RARE'." "Surely not," said the first nurse. "I've just seen it," insisted the second. "It's a strange thing to have tattooed anywhere, and especially... there," said the first nurse. "I mean, it's not as if it means anything." "I agree," said the second, "but maybe it has a special meaning for him. Maybe it's his way of making sure he remembers something, like tying a knot in his hanky." Just then, a third nurse joined them. She was so absolutely gorgeous that all the male patients were in love with her. She asked, "What are you two whispering about?" The first nurse said, "I thought the patient in bed four had 'WEAR' tattooed on his, you know... his thingy." "And I went to have a peep," said the second nurse, "and it actually said, 'ONE UP RARE.' " "How odd," said the third nurse. "Are you sure?" "Go and see for yourself," they said. So the third nurse went for a look. She returned after a while, looking smug. "You're both wrong," she said. "It says 'WESTON-SUPER-MARE' "!'

'Wonderful.'

'I'm glad you think so.' He stood behind her, parting her hair while he kissed her neck softly.

'You'll ruin my concentration.'

'I don't care. I love you, Mrs Earnshaw.'

She turned, beaming. 'Do you mean that?'

'Have you ever known me say anything I didn't mean?'

'I don't think I have.' With that quibble out of the way, she said, 'I love you, Mr Pelier.'

They kissed to confirm it, and then Joe said, 'There's something I've been meaning to ask you.'

'Ask away. I'm very approachable.'

'All right. I'm going night fishing again at the weekend. Would you care to tag along?'

'Well yes, I suppose so.' Her tone betrayed her disappointment, so he quickly relented.

'Good, and there's one other thing.'

'What?'

'How do you fancy being the future Mrs Pelier? You'll be *Madame* Pelier, of course, when we travel in France.'

Her face brightened again. 'Only temporarily and just until you make me the actual Mrs and Madame Pelier.'

'*C'est garanti.* So, are you game?'

'It depends. Will I have to speak French?'

'Only at the very peak of coital ecstasy. It's not a great deal to ask, and it doesn't call for an extensive vocabulary. I think you'll soon get the hang of it.'

'I'll do my best.' She kissed him by way of celebration, and then, looking over her shoulder, she said, 'You'll have to put me down if you don't want your supper to burn.'

---◆---

Much later, as they lay together in the darkness, she asked, 'What was that Neuhaus man like?'

'You've seen his photos.'

'I know, but I mean as a man.'

'I'm not sure he qualifies for that description, Maggie. At least, not the kind of man anyone would want to know.' He described the cold, grey eyes and harsh, judgemental outlook. 'His was the worst kind of evil, because he felt no shame for what he'd done. He even hinted that I was no better than the Nazis, because I'd sent so many of his *Kameraden* to face trial.'

'Couldn't he see any difference at all?'

'Evidently not. He maintained that he was doing a necessary job.'

'You had quite a conversation with him, then?'

'Yes.' He turned on to his back, visualising again the steely look and set, unrepentant expression. 'He told me his job was to rid Brittany of undesirables, by which he meant Resistance fighters and saboteurs. We disagreed about that, but I can't imagine he was impressed by my point of view.'

'Did he mention Thomas Allard?' It seemed important to her.

'Yes, he did. He was unimpressed that his arrest had come about because of a man he called "that crippled half-wit", and he showed no remorse for Tom's murder.'

'You call him "Tom", as if you knew him.'

'I heard so much about him and I lived with his misfortune and his fate on my mind for so long that I feel I came to know him.' He saw that her eyes were wet. 'No one can hurt him now,' he reminded her.

'I know. It's just knowing that he was so simple and helpless. He deserved so much more, and Neuhaus killed him for his own, scheming purpose.'

'He tried to justify the killing, saying that a cripple and an imbecile would have no kind of future. As you can imagine, we disagreed about that as well.'

Maggie lay silent, no doubt turning the events over in her mind. After a while, she asked, 'How do you feel, now that you've brought the case to its conclusion?'

His mind returned to his conversation with Neuhaus. 'I feel a kind of long-awaited satisfaction,' he said. 'I derive no pleasure from the knowledge that Neuhaus will almost certainly suffer the death penalty; that's the law, and we have to accept it, but I'm glad for the sake of his victims that I've been able to hand him over to the authorities.'

'Mr Allard should be pleased, for once.'

'He should,' he agreed. 'He hasn't been an ideal client, and I shan't miss him at all.' He gave a little more thought to Maggie's question and said, 'More than anything, I suppose, I feel that I've discharged a special kind of trust.'

'What do you mean?'

'Just that I owed it to poor, innocent Tom to put his murderer in the dock. He really was a deserving case.'

The End

Lightning Source UK Ltd.
Milton Keynes UK
UKHW010627100821
388609UK00001B/15